# Breathing Walls

Victor Crowe

Published by Antillas Publishing House, 2026.

This is a work of fiction. Similarities to real people, places, or events are entirely coincidental.

BREATHING WALLS

**First edition. January 19, 2026.**



ISBN: 979-8232837785

Written by Victor Crowe.

# Table of Contents

# Chapter 1: The Unbelievable Bargain

The incessant thrum of the city had become a physical ache, a persistent vibrato in Alice's bones that sleep no longer soothed. Years of cramped apartment living, the suffocating embrace of exhaust fumes, and the gnawing anxiety of dwindling savings had worn them down, Alice and Tom, to a raw, exposed nerve. They craved space, silence, and the uncomplicated joy of breathing air that didn't carry the city's weary sighs. Their dream was a quiet rebellion against the relentless pressure, a yearning for a sanctuary where the loudest noise would be the rustle of leaves, and the most pressing concern would be the shade of paint for the living room walls.

Their search had been a protracted affair, a marathon of online listings and weekend drives through increasingly rural landscapes. Each open house, each carefully staged farmhouse, felt like a step further away from the life that had begun to suffocate them. They'd seen charming cottages that were too small, grand Victorian houses that were falling apart, and modern boxes that lacked any soul. Hope, a delicate bloom, had begun to wither under the harsh sun of reality. Then, one dreary Tuesday evening, amidst a pile of forgotten flyers and a half-hearted scroll through a real estate website, Alice found it.

The listing was an anomaly, a digital siren song that snagged their attention with the impossible. "Sprawling Country Estate – Unbeatable Value!" the headline screamed, accompanied by a few grainy, slightly faded photographs. The price was so ludicrously low, it felt like a typo, a cruel joke. Alice blinked, rubbed her eyes, and checked the digits again. It couldn't be real. Tom, drawn by her sudden stillness, peered over her shoulder. "What is it?" he asked, his voice tinged with the familiar weariness of another disappointing lead.

"This," Alice breathed, pointing to the screen. "Look at this. It has to be a mistake."

Tom's eyebrows shot up. He zoomed in on the photographs. A large, stately house, nestled amongst mature trees, with expansive grounds that seemed to stretch into the horizon. It looked a little dated, perhaps, a touch in need of a loving hand, but undeniably grand. There was a sense of history about it, a quiet dignity that spoke of generations past. It was the kind of house they'd only dared to whisper about in their most optimistic moments, a place that felt plucked from the pages of a novel, not from a real estate agent's desperate ploy.

"That price... it's... impossible," Tom stammered, his skepticism warring with a burgeoning excitement. "What's the catch? Is it condemned? Is there a haunted graveyard in the backyard?" He tried to inject levity into his voice, but the tremor of disbelief was evident.

"There's no mention of anything like that," Alice replied, her fingers flying across the keyboard, pulling up more details. "It's listed as 'needs some modernization,' and 'sold as seen.' But the square footage alone... it's more than triple what we'd get in the city for ten times this price." The sheer scale of the property was staggering. Acres of land, a substantial house with what looked like at least five bedrooms, multiple outbuildings, and a sense of complete seclusion.

They booked a viewing for the following Saturday, the intervening days a blur of anxious anticipation. Alice found herself rereading the listing countless times, scrutinizing every word, every pixelated image, searching for the hidden flaw, the disqualifying condition that would explain the unbelievable bargain. Tom, usually the more grounded of the two, seemed equally captivated, his usual pragmatism momentarily suspended by the sheer allure of the possibility. He'd caught Alice looking at him with a hopeful glint in her eye, a look that mirrored his own burgeoning dreams, and a shared, unspoken understanding passed between them. This was it. This was the chance they'd been waiting for.

The drive to the property was long, winding through increasingly picturesque countryside, the city's oppressive concrete yielding to rolling hills and emerald fields. The air grew cleaner, fresher, carrying the scent of damp earth and pine. As they turned onto a long, gravel driveway, bordered by ancient oak trees that formed a leafy canopy overhead, their breaths hitched. The house emerged from the trees like a forgotten queen, grand and imposing, bathed in the soft afternoon sun. It was even more impressive in person.

The real estate agent, a man named Mr. Abernathy, met them with a practiced, if slightly tired, smile. He was impeccably dressed, but his eyes seemed to hold a hint of weariness, as if he'd seen this magic trick play out one too many times. He spoke with a practiced ease, highlighting the house's "potential" and "unique character," but he was remarkably vague when Alice pressed him about the property's history or why it was priced so dramatically below market value.

"Previous owner was... reclusive," he'd offered, a carefully neutral explanation that offered no real insight. "Estate sale. Needs to be sold quickly."

As they walked through the cavernous rooms, dust motes dancing in the shafts of light that pierced the grimy windows, Alice and Tom's initial excitement began to solidify into something more profound. The house, though in need of work, possessed a warmth and grandeur that spoke of a life lived, of memories held within its walls. The spacious living room, with its imposing fireplace and bay window, felt like a perfect spot for cozy evenings. The kitchen, though dated, was large enough to host a feast, with a charming pantry that Alice immediately envisioned filled with preserves and freshly baked bread.

"Imagine," Tom said, his voice echoing in the high-ceilinged hall, "imagine this place with a fresh coat of paint, maybe some new carpets. We could finally have the space we've always dreamed of. A garden, Tom! We could finally have a proper garden." Alice's eyes sparkled, her mind already racing with renovation ideas, with possibilities. The sheer scale of the house, the sprawling grounds, the absolute privacy – it was a sanctuary, a haven, the embodiment of every aspiration they had nurtured during their years of city confinement.

They explored the grounds with a growing sense of awe. The vast expanse of lawn, the mature trees that offered shade and seclusion, the rambling rose bushes that hinted at past beauty – it was a paradise. Duke, their boisterous Rottweiler, seemed to revel in the freedom, his powerful frame a blur as he bounded across the grass, his happy barks echoing in the still air. He seemed to sense the promise of this place, his tail wagging with an infectious enthusiasm.

"This is it," Alice declared, a profound sense of certainty settling over her. "This is our fresh start."

Tom met her gaze, his eyes shining with a reflection of her own joy. "It's perfect," he agreed, pulling her into a tight embrace. "Absolutely perfect."

The house felt like a gift, an answered prayer, a miraculous confluence of circumstance that had landed them precisely where they longed to be. They could already envision their future unfolding within its walls: Christmas mornings by the grand fireplace, summer barbecues on the expansive lawn, lazy Sunday mornings with coffee in the sun-drenched kitchen. The sheer improbability of the price, the quiet seclusion, the undeniable charm – it all coalesced into a dream realized, a perfect facade of happiness and security. They were stepping into a new chapter, one filled with promise, peace, and the idyllic tranquility they had so desperately sought. The city, with its suffocating grip, felt like a distant, faded memory, replaced by the vibrant, hopeful reality of their dream home. This was more than just a house; it was the culmination of their shared aspirations, a testament to their resilience, and the beginning of a life they had only dared to imagine. The future, bathed in the golden light of their newfound paradise, seemed utterly, blissfully, secure.

The drive back to the city was a strange mix of exhilaration and a lingering, almost imperceptible disquiet. Alice replayed the afternoon's events in her mind, the joy of finding their perfect, impossibly priced home warring with a faint prickle of something she couldn't quite name. Mr. Abernathy's carefully chosen words, his almost too-smooth demeanor, replayed like a scratchy record. "Reclusive," he'd said. "Needs to be sold quickly." It was the speed, the sheer eagerness with which the sale seemed to be facilitated, that gnawed at her. In the competitive, often drawn-out world of real estate, such haste felt... unusual.

Tom, beside her, was humming a cheerful tune, his hand resting on her thigh. He radiated a contentment that was infectious, a stark contrast to the subtle tension that Alice felt coiling in her stomach. "Can you believe it, Al?" he said, squeezing her leg. "We actually did it. We bought a country estate for the price of a city shoebox. It's a miracle."

Alice offered a weak smile, forcing herself to push away the intrusive thoughts. "It is amazing, Tom. Truly." She tried to focus on his happiness, on the shared dream that had felt so tangible just hours before. But the image of Mr. Abernathy's subtly evasive eyes kept intruding. He hadn't offered a single shred of information about the previous owners, about the house's past. It was as if the property had materialized out of thin air, a pristine, unblemished offering dropped into their laps.

"Did you notice how little he said about the people who lived there before?" Alice ventured, her voice carefully casual.

Tom's humming faltered for a beat. "Well, he said they were reclusive, didn't he? Probably just wanted their privacy. And it's an estate sale, so maybe the family wants to move on quickly." He shrugged, his attention already drifting back to the prospect of garden plans and weekend projects. "Honestly, Al, does it matter? It's ours now. That's all that counts."

His easy dismissal, while reassuring, also solidified Alice's unease. Tom was a pragmatist, but he was also incredibly optimistic, especially when it came to their shared aspirations. He was quick to embrace the positive, to see the silver lining. Alice, on the other hand, had a more ingrained habit of looking for the storm cloud behind the silver lining, a tendency honed by years of navigating the precarious financial landscape of city life. She felt a responsibility, a need to ensure that their hard-won escape wasn't built on a foundation of overlooked risks.

"I suppose you're right," she conceded, though the words felt hollow. She glanced at their reflection in the rearview mirror, the city skyline looming in the distance, a stark reminder of the life they were leaving behind. It was a life of constant vigilance, of calculated risks and meticulously managed expectations. And now, it seemed, that vigilance was proving difficult to shake, even in the face of such overwhelming good fortune.

The following week was a whirlwind of packing, of dismantling their city existence piece by painstaking piece. The excitement was palpable, a fever that ran through their small apartment, fueling their efforts. Duke, sensing the shift in atmosphere, was a constant furry shadow, his tail a perpetual blur of anticipation. Yet, for Alice, the unease persisted, a low hum beneath the surface of her frantic activity.

On Wednesday, as they were clearing out a box of old newspapers, Alice found a local history pamphlet for the area where the estate was located. On a whim, she flipped through it, looking for any mention of the grand old house. There was no specific entry, but there were snippets about the founding families, the early industries, and the general character of the region. Then, her eye caught a small, almost insignificant paragraph describing the development of the surrounding land in the late 19th century. It mentioned a prominent family, the Abernathys – a different branch, she assumed, from the agent – who had owned a significant portion of the land, and who were known for their...

*eccentricities*. The pamphlet offered no further details, merely a cryptic allusion to "unusual social practices" and a swift decline in local prominence.

Alice reread the passage, a shiver tracing its way down her spine. "Eccentricities." It was such a mild word, so easily dismissed. But combined with Mr. Abernathy's evasiveness, it felt like a breadcrumb, a subtle hint dropped into the narrative. She tried to rationalize it, to tell herself it was simply the outdated language of a local history booklet, that every old family had its share of colorful anecdotes.

That evening, while Tom was out picking up takeout, Alice decided to do some discreet online research. She searched for "old Abernathy estate," "local legends [town name]," and variations thereof. Most of the results were mundane – property records, genealogical sites, faded newspaper clippings about town events from decades past. But then, buried deep within a forum dedicated to local folklore, she found a thread that made her breath catch. It was titled, "The House on Willow Creek Road."

The posts were sparse, dating back several years. One user, whose username was simply "Local

*Lore," wrote: "They say that house has... history. Not the good kind. Old Man Abernathy who owned it last... well, folks didn't see him much. And when they did..." The post trailed off, leaving a void filled with unspoken implications. Another user, "Whispers*from*the*Past," chimed in: "My grandmother used to say it was built on... something else. Something that didn't like being disturbed."

Alice's heart began to pound. This was more than just small-town gossip. The word "disturbed" echoed in her mind, a chilling counterpoint to the tranquility they had so eagerly embraced. She scrolled further, her fingers trembling.

"I wouldn't go near that place if I were you," wrote "Watcher

*on*the_Hill." "There are stories. Things that happened. Things that were... buried."

Buried. The word resonated with a terrifying weight. Alice closed her laptop, her mind a tempest of conflicting emotions. The bargain was too good to be true. Mr. Abernathy's evasiveness, the cryptic online whispers – they were all pointing towards something, a shadow lurking just beyond the bright promise of their new home. She looked at Tom, who was happily detailing his takeout choices, his face alight with anticipation for their final city dinner. How could she voice these nascent doubts, these tendrils of unease, without sounding like a killjoy, like someone determined to spoil their hard-won dream?

She decided to try a different approach. The next day, while packing the last of their kitchen items, she steered the conversation towards the neighbors. "I wonder if there are any friendly faces around the estate," she mused. "It would be nice to have someone to wave to, maybe borrow a cup of sugar from."

Tom chuckled. "I'm sure we'll find some lovely folks. You always do, Al. You have a knack for making connections."

"Maybe," Alice said, picking up a box of mismatched mugs. "I just hope they're not too... provincial. I don't want to be the city folk who don't understand the local ways."

The drive out to the estate for their final walkthrough before closing was tinged with a different kind of anticipation. It wasn't just the joy of their impending new life; it was a subtle, almost subconscious mission. As they approached the long, tree-lined driveway, Alice scanned the neighboring properties, searching for any sign of life, any indication of who might live nearby.

They saw a few houses, set back from the road, nestled amongst the trees. One, a charming, slightly dilapidated farmhouse, had a woman tending to her garden. Alice slowed the car, a plan forming in her mind. "I think I'll just pull over for a moment," she announced, her voice betraying none of the nervousness she felt. "I just want to stretch my legs."

Tom, preoccupied with checking his phone for last-minute emails, nodded absently. "Sure, Al. Don't be long, though. We need to get to the lawyer's office."

Alice got out of the car, taking a deep breath of the country air, trying to appear as relaxed as possible. She walked towards the farmhouse, Duke trotting happily beside her, his tail giving a friendly wag. As she approached the garden, the woman looked up, a weathered face framed by a wide-brimmed straw hat. She had kind eyes, but they held a flicker of caution as she saw Alice and Duke.

"Hello," Alice said, offering a bright smile. "Just admiring your lovely garden. We're the ones buying the old Abernathy place."

The woman's expression didn't change, but there was a subtle stiffening in her posture. "Oh," she said, her voice polite but reserved. "That's... quite a place."

"We're so excited," Alice continued, trying to draw her out. "It's such an incredible bargain, we almost can't believe it."

The woman gave a short, almost imperceptible nod. "Bargains can come with their own... price," she said, her gaze drifting towards the imposing silhouette of the Abernathy house through the trees. There was a finality in her tone, a quiet certainty that sent a fresh wave of apprehension through Alice.

"What do you mean by that?" Alice asked, her curiosity piqued, the unease deepening into a genuine concern.

The woman hesitated, then seemed to make a decision. She wiped her hands on her apron and walked a few steps closer to Alice, her voice dropping to a near whisper. "That house... it has a long memory. And some memories are best left undisturbed." She looked directly at Alice, her gaze steady and serious. "Mr. Abernathy, the agent, he's just doing his job. But he knows. Everyone around here knows. That house... it's seen things. And it holds them."

Alice's blood ran cold. "Seen things? What kind of things?"

The woman shook her head slowly. "Just... things. Unhappy things. The kind that linger. You're young, and you're looking for a fresh start. I hope you find it. But be careful. Some foundations are built on more than just earth and stone." She offered a small, sad smile. "Welcome to the neighborhood, I suppose. Just... be aware."

With that, she turned back to her garden, a clear signal that the conversation was over. Alice stood there for a moment, the woman's words echoing in her ears. "Unhappy things." "Some foundations are built on more than just earth and stone." She felt a chill that had nothing to do with the gentle breeze. Duke nudged her hand, sensing her distress, and she stroked his head, her mind racing.

Back in the car, Tom was impatiently tapping his foot. "Everything alright, Al? You were gone a while."

Alice forced a smile. "Yes, just chatting with the neighbor. She's... interesting." She didn't elaborate, didn't want to overload Tom with her growing apprehension just yet. She could see the way his eyes lit up when he spoke of the house, the sheer unadulterated joy of it. She didn't want to be the one to cast a shadow over that.

But as they drove away, Alice couldn't shake the feeling of being watched, of being observed by unseen eyes from the darkened windows of the grand old house. The whispers of doubt had begun, subtle at first, like the rustling of leaves in an autumn wind, but growing steadily louder, promising to be the first dissonant note in the symphony of their dream. The impossible bargain, once a beacon of hope, was slowly beginning to feel like a gilded trap, its splendor concealing a darkness she was only just beginning to glimpse.

The air inside the house on moving day was thick with a potent cocktail of dust motes dancing in the shafts of sunlight and the faint, almost medicinal scent of fresh paint. It clung to the back of Alice's throat, a tangible reminder of the transformation underway. Boxes, stacked precariously in the cavernous foyer, formed abstract sculptures that shifted and settled with each excited echo of their footsteps. Tom, his face flushed with a radiant, almost boyish glee, practically bounded through the rooms, his voice booming with plans and possibilities. "Imagine it, Al! This could be your reading nook!" he exclaimed, gesturing towards a deep-set window seat in what would become her study. "And the fireplace here... we'll have it restored. Picture us, curled up with a fire, a glass of wine..."

Alice followed him, a slower, more deliberate pace marking her exploration. Duke, their hulking Rottweiler, was a furry whirlwind of delighted investigation, his powerful paws thudding on the polished hardwood floors. He sniffed every corner with the intensity of a seasoned detective, his tail giving enthusiastic thumps against the antique furniture they'd carefully placed. His boundless energy seemed to absorb the sheer scale of the place, his joyful barks and snuffles filling the once-silent rooms with a vibrant, living sound. It was a symphony of their new beginning, a far cry from the hushed quiet of the city apartment they'd left behind.

They moved through the grand drawing-room, its high ceilings and ornate moldings whispering tales of a bygone era. Sunlight streamed through the tall, mullioned windows, illuminating the bare walls, which Alice already envisioned adorned with artwork and family photographs. Tom pointed out the "potential" in every nook and cranny, his imagination running wild. "This whole wall," he declared, tapping a section of plaster in the dining room, "could be custom cabinetry. Imagine it, for our china, our wine glasses..."

Alice found herself smiling, a genuine, unforced smile that reached her eyes. The lingering unease from their dealings with Mr. Abernathy seemed to recede with each step further into the house. It was like a physical shedding of old anxieties, replaced by the exhilarating weight of their new reality. The sheer size of the estate, once a source of mild intimidation, now felt like an embrace. There were so many rooms, so many corridors, so many shadowed alcoves and forgotten spaces. It was a labyrinth of comfort and privacy, a sanctuary from the outside world. The house itself seemed to breathe, a vast, old lung exhaling the scent of history and promising a future built on solid ground.

"It's even bigger than I remembered," Alice murmured, running her hand along the cool marble of the fireplace in the master bedroom. The room was vast, easily accommodating their king-sized bed, with ample space left over for a chaise lounge and a vanity. The adjoining dressing room was a dream in itself, a walk-in closet that could swallow their entire city wardrobe and then some.

"And think of the potential for Duke!" Tom enthused, as if reading her thoughts. "He'll have a field day exploring. This place is like his own personal kingdom." Duke, at that very moment, was attempting to burrow his way behind a freestanding wardrobe, his hindquarters wiggling with determined effort.

They spent the entire day in a joyous blur of unpacking and arranging. The scent of cardboard and packing tape mingled with the subtle aroma of lemon polish as they wiped down surfaces and began to fill the house with their belongings. Each item that found its place felt like an anchor, securing them more firmly in their new home. The mismatched mugs that Alice had been so concerned about were carefully arranged in the kitchen cabinets, their chipped edges a testament to shared meals and everyday life. The worn armchair that Tom had inherited from his grandfather was positioned by a window overlooking the rolling fields, a silent promise of quiet afternoons.

As dusk began to paint the sky in hues of lavender and rose, they stood on the broad, stone patio at the back of the house, a bottle of champagne chilling in a bucket of ice. Duke lay at their feet, panting contentedly, his earlier frenzy giving way to a comfortable repose. The air was cool and still, carrying the faint scent of damp earth and distant pines. The silence, so different from the city's constant hum, was profound, broken only by the chirping of crickets and the occasional hoot of an owl.

"To us," Tom said, raising his glass, his eyes sparkling with unshed tears of happiness. "To our unbelievable bargain."

Alice clinked her glass against his, her heart swelling with a mixture of relief and profound joy. "To us," she echoed, the words tasting sweet and full of promise. For now, at least, the whispers of doubt and the shadows of unease were banished, lost in the vast, embracing stillness of their new home. They were here. They were finally, undeniably here. The house, so grand and imposing, felt welcoming, a sanctuary ready to absorb their laughter, their dreams, and their lives. The sheer expanse of it, the endless rooms, the winding corridors, the secluded nooks and crannies – it all felt like an invitation to a life of unparalleled comfort and absolute privacy. They had no idea that this very expanse, this perfect hiding place, was also the ideal stage for an unseen presence, poised to make its own, unwelcome arrival, turning their haven into a gilded cage. The house, with its secrets and its silence, was ready to welcome its new occupants, unaware that it was already occupied.

The first few days in the sprawling estate were a whirlwind of organized chaos. Boxes were unpacked, furniture was positioned, and the house, which had felt so cavernous and echoing on moving day, began to fill with the comforting clutter of their lives. Alice, eager to establish a semblance of routine, set up her home office in what had been a sun-drenched morning room. Sunlight, diffused by the sheer curtains Tom had insisted they hang immediately, cast a warm, buttery glow across her antique oak desk, a piece she'd managed to acquire at a remarkable price from a local auction house just weeks before their move. She'd always dreamed of a dedicated space for her writing, a sanctuary where her thoughts could flow unimpeded. This room, with its view of the manicured gardens, felt like that dream made tangible. She arranged her notebooks, her laptop, and a small, framed photograph of her and Tom on their wedding day, the familiar weight of his arm around her shoulders a comforting presence. Duke, ever the loyal shadow, had claimed a plush dog bed in the corner, his soft snores a gentle counterpoint to the rhythmic tapping of Alice's keyboard.

It was on the third morning, amidst the settling dust of their new life, that Alice first noticed something... off. She'd reached for the carton of milk to pour into her coffee, a ritual as ingrained as breathing. The carton felt surprisingly light, far lighter than it should have been given that she was certain she'd filled her mug just yesterday. She tipped it, and only a meager splash dribbled out, barely enough to tinge the dark liquid. "That's odd," she murmured, her brow furrowing slightly. She distinctly remembered putting a brand new, full carton in the refrigerator. Had she used more milk than she thought? It seemed unlikely; she was a creature of habit with her morning brew. Perhaps, she reasoned, it was just a trick of the light, a momentary lapse in her perception of weight after the sheer physical exertion of the move. The sheer size of the house, the constant planning and arranging, could easily play havoc with one's senses. She shrugged it off, a tiny, almost imperceptible wobble in the edifice of her certainty, and poured her coffee black.

Later that day, while she was engrossed in reviewing a manuscript for a client, a subtle aroma began to permeate the air. It was a faint, acrid scent, reminiscent of stale cigarette smoke. Alice lifted her head, sniffing the air suspiciously. Neither she nor Tom smoked. They hadn't for years, and the thought of it was almost abhorrent to them now. She looked around the room, her gaze sweeping over the antique furniture, the plush rug, the pristine white walls. There were no ashtrays, no discarded butts, no lingering evidence of anyone having indulged. The scent was elusive, ghost-like, appearing and disappearing like a phantom. She walked over to the window, pushing aside the heavy velvet curtains, and inhaled deeply. The fresh air, carrying the scent of damp earth and blooming roses from the garden, seemed to push the odd smell away. "Must be a residual smell from the previous owners," she mused aloud, though she recalled the house having a distinct, clean scent when they'd first viewed it. Mr. Abernathy had assured them it had been thoroughly cleaned and aired out. Perhaps a tenant had lived here years ago, and the smell had been trapped in the very fabric of the house, only now being coaxed out by the warmth and activity of new occupants. It was a plausible explanation, one that allowed her to slot the anomaly neatly into the box of 'explained.'

These minor inconsistencies, easily dismissed in isolation, were like microscopic fractures appearing in the smooth veneer of her reality. They were the first almost imperceptible tremors before a more significant upheaval. The milk, the smell – they were tiny cracks, easily patched over with logical explanations born of fatigue and the disorienting nature of such a significant life change. Alice, a pragmatist by nature, was adept at compartmentalizing, at finding the rational explanation for almost anything. The move had been stressful, exhilarating, and exhausting, all at once. It was perfectly understandable that her mind, stretched thin by the demands of the transition, might play tricks on her. She was simply readjusting, recalibrating to her new environment.

That evening, as they sat down for dinner, a simple pasta dish they'd managed to assemble from the still-partially unpacked kitchen, Tom mentioned something equally peculiar. "Did you notice that the lights in the east wing hallway were on when we got back from the grocery store?" he asked, his brow furrowed in a mirror of Alice's earlier confusion. "I'm almost certain I turned them all off before we left."

Alice paused, her fork halfway to her mouth. "No, I didn't notice. I just followed you inside. But you're right, I thought I'd switched off all the lights in that section. It's so easy to forget in a house this size." She tried to inject a casual tone into her voice, but a subtle unease began to coil in her stomach. Two oddities in one day, and now a third. They were small things, trivial even, but their confluence felt... significant. It was like finding a single, misplaced chess piece; insignificant on its own, but unnerving when you realized the board was still set.

Tom, ever the optimist, waved a dismissive hand. "Probably just us being tired. We're still getting used to the layout, the sheer number of switches." He offered her a reassuring smile, but Alice could see a flicker of the same unease in his eyes. He, too, was searching for the most logical explanation, the most mundane answer to these tiny intrusions of the bizarre. The house was a labyrinth, and it was easy to misplace a light switch, to forget a room, to be forgetful about the contents of the refrigerator. These were the imperfections that came with inhabiting such a grand, old structure. They were the quirks of a house that had stood for decades, perhaps centuries, absorbing the lives and habits of countless others.

But the milk carton incident nagged at her. It wasn't just a forgotten light switch. It was a tangible depletion of a resource, a physical impossibility that defied simple oversight. She found herself replaying the moment in her mind, picturing the carton, its familiar branding, the weight of it in her hand. It had felt lighter. There was no denying that. And the cigarette smoke – it was a scent that clung, that was difficult to entirely banish. She'd spent years trying to get the smell out of her clothes after a brief, ill-advised phase in her late teens. It was a stubborn, pervasive odor.

As the days bled into weeks, the oddities continued, no longer isolated incidents but a series of small, disquieting events that began to chip away at Alice's sense of calm. She would find drawers slightly ajar that she was certain she had closed. Books would be askew on shelves, their spines no longer perfectly aligned. Once, she distinctly remembered placing her reading glasses on the bedside table, only to find them later that evening on the mantelpiece in the drawing-room, a place she rarely ventured into during the day. Each instance, individually, was easily explained away. A draft. Duke's playful nudges. Her own forgetfulness. But collectively, they formed a disquieting pattern. They were the quiet whispers of a presence that was both unseen and unheard, a subtle manipulation of her environment designed to sow seeds of doubt and confusion.

One afternoon, Alice was in the kitchen, preparing lunch. She reached into the pantry for a jar of olives, a specific brand she favored. When she pulled it out, the lid was slightly loose, a faint seam of brine escaping onto her fingertips. She frowned. She was meticulous about securing lids. She'd learned the hard way, after a sticky jam incident, that a well-sealed jar was a happy jar. She tightened it with a decisive twist, the familiar click of the seal engaging. Then, her gaze fell on another jar, a jar of preserved lemons she'd made herself, sitting next to it. The lid on that one was also loose, just a fraction of an inch, but enough to be noticeable. A cold knot began to form in Alice's stomach. It wasn't just her own absentmindedness. This was something else.

"Tom," she called out, her voice a little sharper than she intended. "Did you open these olives and lemons?"

Tom appeared in the doorway, wiping his hands on a dishtowel. "No, I haven't been in the pantry today. Why?"

Alice held up the olive jar. "The lid was loose. And so is this one." She gestured to the preserved lemons.

Tom took the olive jar and examined it. "Hmm, that's odd. Are you sure you didn't knock it?"

"I'm sure," Alice said, her voice firm. She felt a prickle of defensiveness, a surge of indignation. It was as if her own sanity was being questioned. "I'm very careful with things like this."

Tom looked at the lemons, then back at Alice. He didn't dismiss her concerns outright, but his expression was one of gentle skepticism. "Well, it's a big house, Al. Things can shift. Maybe the vibrations from the road... or Duke getting underfoot."

Duke, who had been dozing by the back door, let out a soft snore, a gentle rumble that seemed to contradict Tom's suggestion. Alice knew her dog. He was boisterous, yes, but he wasn't clumsy enough to dislodge jar lids without significant commotion.

She decided to test her theory. She carefully unscrewed the lid of the preserved lemon jar, took out a single lemon slice, and then, with deliberate precision, screwed the lid back on. She made sure it was perfectly sealed. She then placed the jar back on the shelf, its prominent position allowing for easy observation. She didn't say anything to Tom, letting him draw his own conclusions, or rather, allowing the evidence to speak for itself.

The next morning, Alice went into the kitchen with a sense of trepidation. She walked directly to the pantry, her heart thumping a little faster than usual. The jar of preserved lemons sat in its place. She reached for it, her fingers brushing against the cool glass. And then she saw it. The lid. It was a fraction of an inch loose. The same almost imperceptible gap she had noticed the day before. Alice felt a wave of cold wash over her. It was impossible. She had tightened it with all her might. There was no draft in the pantry. No one else had been in the house overnight. Duke had slept soundly at the foot of their bed. The logical, rational explanations were beginning to wear thin, like a much-loved blanket fraying at the edges.

She stood there for a long moment, staring at the jar, a growing sense of disquiet settling deep within her bones. The house, which had promised so much comfort and security, now felt... different. It felt watchful. The silence, once a welcome balm, now seemed pregnant with unspoken things. The vastness of it, the endless corridors and hidden rooms, which had initially felt like an embrace of privacy, now seemed to suggest the potential for unseen movements, for spaces where things could happen without her knowledge or consent.

Tom found her standing there, her gaze fixed on the pantry shelf. "Everything alright?" he asked, his voice laced with concern.

Alice turned to him, her face pale. She opened her mouth to speak, but no words came. What could she say? That a jar lid had come loose on its own? That the milk carton felt lighter? That she smelled phantom smoke? It sounded like the ramblings of someone losing their grip.

She forced a smile, a brittle, unconvincing thing. "Just... lost in thought. This house is so big, sometimes I feel like I'm still discovering new corners."

Tom put his arm around her, his warmth a momentary comfort. "We'll get there, Al. We'll make it our own. It's just a matter of time."

But Alice knew, with a certainty that chilled her to the bone, that it wasn't just a matter of time. Something was already here. Something that had been here before them, and was now making its presence known in the most unsettlingly subtle ways. The unbelievable bargain was beginning to reveal its true, unsettling cost, and the first installment was a creeping sense of unease, a gnawing doubt that whispered in the quiet corners of her mind, a prelude to a terror she couldn't yet comprehend. The house was not empty. It was occupied. And the occupant was playing games.

Duke, a creature of unwavering loyalty and imposing presence, was Alice's shadow, her furry sentinel. A Rottweiler of formidable build and gentle disposition, he moved through the grand estate with a quiet dignity that belied his powerful physique. His deep, rumbling barks, usually reserved for the mail carrier or a rustling in the undergrowth that might, in his canine mind, signify a threat, were a constant reassurance to Alice. He had an uncanny ability to sense her moods, nudging her hand with his wet nose when he detected a tremor of anxiety in her voice, or settling his heavy head on her lap during moments of quiet contemplation. His presence in her home office was more than just that of a pet; it was the embodiment of security, a living, breathing bulwark against the unknown.

Alice had always been drawn to animals, but her bond with Duke was something deeper, almost primal. He had come into her life during a period of personal upheaval, a rescue dog with a past etched in fear and uncertainty. Alice, with her innate patience and boundless affection, had patiently coaxed him out of his shell, forging a connection built on trust and mutual respect. Now, in the sprawling silence of their new home, that connection was more vital than ever. Duke's watchful eyes, dark and intelligent, seemed to constantly scan their surroundings, his ears twitching at the faintest sound. He would often lie by the French doors leading to the garden, his gaze fixed on the perimeter, a silent guardian surveying his domain. Alice would sometimes catch him on the upper landing, a sentinel overlooking the main hall, his posture alert, a low growl vibrating in his chest if a car passed too close to the gates. This vigilance, while occasionally a touch overzealous, was a comforting anchor in the vastness of the unfamiliar house.

The estate, with its many rooms and long corridors, could feel isolating. The sheer size of the place, the echoing emptiness of certain wings, had initially been a source of wonder, but as days turned into weeks, and the initial excitement of the move began to wane, Alice found herself increasingly aware of the house's profound silence. It was a silence that was often punctuated by the peculiar anomalies she'd begun to notice – the misplaced items, the phantom scents, the mysteriously depleted milk carton. In these moments of creeping unease, Duke's solid, warm presence beside her was a powerful antidote. The steady rhythm of his breathing, the soft weight of him leaning against her leg, grounded her. She would often bury her hands in his thick fur, drawing strength from his steadfast loyalty.

His protective instincts were particularly pronounced when she was engrossed in her work. The hum of her laptop, the tapping of her fingers on the keyboard, seemed to trigger a heightened state of awareness in him. He would shift from his plush bed in the corner to a spot closer to her desk, his head resting on his paws, his gaze never straying far from her. If a delivery person approached the front door, his bark would be immediate and resonant, a deep, authoritative sound that left no doubt about his displeasure at the intrusion. This fierce possessiveness, this unquestioning devotion, was a constant source of comfort. It was a tangible expression of his commitment to her, a silent promise that he would protect her from any perceived harm.

Alice often found herself talking to Duke, confiding her anxieties, her hopes, and her growing bewilderment about the strange occurrences in the house. She knew he couldn't understand her words, but he seemed to grasp the emotion behind them, offering a gentle lick to her hand or a sympathetic whine. "It's just this house, Duke," she'd murmur, stroking his broad head. "It's so... big. And sometimes, it feels a little bit strange, doesn't it?" Duke would respond with a soft sigh, his tail giving a slow, reassuring thump against the floorboards, as if to say, "I'm here, and together, we'll figure it out."

The trust Alice placed in Duke was absolute. He was more than just a pet; he was a member of the family, a steadfast companion whose presence filled the house with a sense of warmth and security. His unwavering loyalty was a cornerstone of her daily life, a reliable constant in a world that was beginning to feel increasingly... off-kilter. She relied on his instincts, on his ability to detect things she couldn't. If Duke was agitated, if he whined or paced without apparent cause, Alice paid attention. She believed his reactions were an honest barometer of the house's true nature, a reflection of any genuine threat. His deep barks at the night, directed at unseen things beyond the windows, were not just noise; they were his honest assessment of the situation, his vocal declaration that he was on guard.

This profound sense of security that Duke provided was a crucial buffer against the unsettling nature of the house's subtle disturbances. When a drawer was found ajar, Alice would glance at Duke, and if he was sleeping soundly, she would attribute it to a draft or her own forgetfulness. If she smelled that faint, acrid odor, Duke's placid demeanor would often be enough to dismiss it as a lingering scent from previous occupants. His presence acted as a constant counterpoint to her growing doubts, a living embodiment of normalcy and order. He was her furry anchor, tethered to the tangible world, a world where doors were opened and closed by hands, and milk cartons were full until emptied. His steadfastness was the very definition of trust, a bond so pure and unadulterated that the mere thought of it being compromised was unthinkable.

Alice would often reflect on how fortunate she was to have Duke. He wasn't just a protector; he was an empath. He seemed to absorb her anxieties, his own calm demeanor a reflection of her own desired state. During her most intense periods of writing, when her focus was absolute, Duke would lie at her feet, a silent, breathing presence that reminded her she wasn't alone. His soft snores were a comforting lullaby, a testament to his trust in the safety of their surroundings, a safety he actively, albeit unconsciously, helped to maintain. His deep, resonant barks at anything that moved outside the walls of their home were a vocal manifestation of his dedication, a constant reminder that while she might be delving into the abstract world of words, Duke was firmly rooted in the physical reality, ever vigilant, ever ready to defend their shared space. This unwavering vigilance, this primal instinct to protect, was what made Alice feel so secure. It was a security so profound, so deeply ingrained, that she didn't even consider the possibility of its erosion. Duke was her shield, her confidant, her furry knight in shining armor, and the very foundation of her sense of safety in this grand, echoing house. His loyalty was a given, an immutable truth in her life, a truth that would soon be tested in ways she could never have imagined.

# Chapter 2: The Unseen Tenant

The subtle shifts in her environment began to coalesce, transitioning from mere oddities to a pattern that prickled the back of Alice's neck. It started, as these things often do, with the seemingly mundane, the easily dismissible. A kitchen drawer, meticulously closed after she'd retrieved a tea towel, would be found slightly ajar hours later, a dark sliver inviting speculation. A book she'd set down on the bedside table would reappear on the mantlepiece, its spine facing outwards as if posed for inspection. These were not the forgetful misplacements of a weary mind adjusting to a new, sprawling home; these were deliberate, almost playful, adjustments. Alice found herself scrutinizing her own actions, replaying the moments in her head, searching for the lapse in her own memory that must surely be the culprit. But the conviction of her own actions, the certainty of having secured a drawer or placed a book precisely, gnawed at her.

Then came the incident with the toilet. She had, just moments before, finished using the downstairs powder room. She'd flushed, of course, and the quiet gurgle had been the last sound she'd heard from it before stepping out. Yet, when she returned a short while later, drawn by a faint, almost imperceptible hum, the toilet had been flushed again. The water in the bowl was still in its final, swirling descent, a miniature vortex mirroring the growing turbulence in her stomach. There was no draft strong enough to trigger the mechanism, no seismic tremor that would explain it. Duke, who was usually quick to investigate any unusual sound, had merely lifted his head from his nap by the fireplace, his tail giving a single, perfunctory thump before he settled back down, seemingly unconcerned. This unnerved her more than the flush itself. Duke's keen senses, his unwavering vigilance, usually reacted to anything out of the ordinary. His placidity in the face of this anomaly felt like a betrayal, or worse, an acknowledgement.

The keys. Her keys. They were a constant source of frustration. Alice was a creature of habit, and her keys had a designated spot: a small ceramic bowl on the hall table, right by the front door. It was a system she'd adhered to for years, a silent pact with herself to avoid the frantic searches that derailed mornings and poisoned evenings. But in this house, the pact was repeatedly broken. She would place them in the bowl, the familiar clink of metal against ceramic a satisfying punctuation mark to her arrival. Then, hours, or sometimes mere minutes, later, she would reach for them, and the bowl would be empty. She'd find them, eventually, perched precariously on the edge of the bookshelf in the library, tucked beneath a cushion on the sofa in the drawing-room, or once, chillingly, hanging from a hook in the guest bedroom, a room she hadn't entered in weeks. Each discovery was accompanied by a fresh wave of disorientation, a feeling of being watched, of her own established order being systematically dismantled.

She started to log these occurrences, a desperate attempt to quantify the unquantifiable, to find a logical explanation within the chaos. A small, leather-bound notebook, once intended for story ideas, became her ledger of the bizarre. Dates, times, and descriptions filled its pages:

*October 14th, 2:15 PM – Drawer in study found ajar. Believed to have closed it at 1:00 PM. Duke asleep.October 15th, 8:00 AM – Keys missing from hall bowl. Found on kitchen counter. Distinct memory of placing them in bowl at 7:30 AM.October 16th, 9:30 PM – Bathroom door found open. Closed it before dinner at 7:00 PM. No one else in the house.* The entries grew, each one a tiny chip away at her skepticism, a further erosion of her sense of security.

The house itself seemed to conspire against her. The grand architecture, once a source of pride and inspiration, now felt like a vast, intricate stage set. The long, shadowed corridors became pathways for unseen footsteps. The creaks and groans of an old house, which she'd initially embraced as character, now sounded like whispers, like the settling of a presence that was anything but inanimate. She would catch herself listening, straining to decipher the source of a particular sound, her heart hammering against her ribs. Was that the wind sighing through a loose pane, or something more deliberate? Was that the settling of timbers, or the soft drag of something across the floorboards above?

Duke, too, began to exhibit subtle changes in his behavior, though not in ways that immediately alarmed Alice. He would sometimes pause mid-stride in the hallway, his head cocked, his ears swiveling as if tracking something she couldn't perceive. He'd let out a low, rumbling growl, not the sharp, alert bark of a perceived threat, but a deep, resonant sound that seemed to emanate from the very core of his being, a sound of deep unease. He would then often look at Alice, his dark eyes filled with a question she couldn't answer, before shaking his massive head and continuing on, as if dismissing a phantom. These moments, though fleeting, contributed to the growing sense of disquiet. It was as if Duke, her steadfast protector, was also beginning to acknowledge the presence of something that defied his understanding, something that even his formidable instincts couldn't fully categorize or confront.

The atmosphere within the house shifted. The air, once fresh and carrying the faint scent of old wood and beeswax, began to feel heavy, charged with an unseen energy. Alice found herself constantly checking the locks, double-checking windows, her hands tracing the cool metal of the door handles with a newfound anxiety. The security she had felt, the tangible comfort Duke provided, was slowly being undermined by these escalating anomalies. It was like watching a meticulously constructed dam begin to leak, the initial trickles of water eventually becoming a torrent. The foundation of her trust in the safety of her home, a trust so absolute she had never even considered its vulnerability, was beginning to crumble. The house, her sanctuary, was transforming into a labyrinth of unease, each peculiar occurrence a signpost pointing towards a truth she was increasingly desperate to avoid. The silence that had once been a peaceful backdrop to her work now felt pregnant with anticipation, as if the house itself was holding its breath, waiting for the next act in its unseen, unsettling play.

The subtle shifts in her environment had escalated, no longer mere oddities but harbingers of something far more unsettling. Alice's mind, a place usually filled with narrative arcs and character development, was now a battleground of terrifying possibilities. The initial dismissal, the rationalization of misplaced items, had withered under the relentless onslaught of inexplicable events. The meticulously closed kitchen drawer, found ajar; the book, seemingly levitated to a new position; the phantom flush of the toilet – these were not the errant thoughts of an overtired mind. They were deliberate, calculated disruptions.

The feeling of being watched, initially a faint prickle, had intensified into a palpable pressure. The silence of the sprawling house, once a welcome companion for her writing, had morphed into something else entirely. It was no longer an absence of noise but a pregnant pause, a held breath that vibrated with unseen attention. Every creak of the ancient timbers, every rustle of leaves outside the grand windows, was amplified, dissected by her increasingly frayed nerves. She found herself straining to hear beyond the ordinary symphony of an old house, listening for the dissonant note, the sound that didn't belong. The ambient stillness was no longer peaceful; it was a shroud, concealing a presence that was both infuriatingly absent and terrifyingly near.

Her thoughts began to chase themselves in circles, a desperate attempt to land on a rational explanation. A break-in? It was the most logical conclusion, of course. Someone was entering her home, moving her things, playing some twisted game. But the sheer impossibility of it all gnawed at her. How could someone move through the house so silently, so invisibly? There were no signs of forced entry, no disturbed dust motes in the sunbeams that streamed through the windows. And the nature of the movements – so subtle, so personal. It wasn't the ransacking of a burglar; it was more akin to a guest rearranging the furniture to their liking. This line of thinking, however, inevitably led her down a darker, more forbidden path. The impossibility of a physical intruder, coupled with the increasingly bizarre occurrences, began to nudge at the edges of her rational mind, whispering the word she desperately tried to suppress:

*supernatural.*

The keys, an everyday object, had become a potent symbol of her loss of control. The designated ceramic bowl on the hall table, a fortress of habit, was routinely breached. One moment they would be there, a reassuring weight in her hand, the next they would have vanished, only to reappear in some absurd location – on the mantelpiece, tucked into a forgotten hatbox, or once, chillingly, dangling from the chandelier in the dining room. Each discovery sent a fresh jolt of adrenaline through her system, a mixture of relief at finding them and renewed terror at their journey. She'd retrace her steps, her mind replaying the mundane actions of her day, searching for the moment she might have absentmindedly moved them, a futile exercise in self-deception. The certainty of her own actions, the unwavering memory of placing them in the bowl, was pitted against the irrefutable evidence of their relocation.

Duke, her loyal German Shepherd, whose presence had always been a bulwark against fear, was also subtly changing. His usual boisterous energy seemed to be tempered by a pervasive unease. He would often stand at the foot of the stairs, his gaze fixed on the upper landing, a low, guttural growl rumbling in his chest, a sound Alice had never heard him make before. It wasn't a warning bark, but a sound of deep, primal apprehension. He would stare into empty corners, his ears twitching, his body tense, as if tracking something invisible to her. He'd then turn to Alice, his large, intelligent eyes filled with a disquiet that mirrored her own, as if asking for an explanation she couldn't provide. These moments, when Duke, her protector, seemed as unsettled as she was, chipped away at her remaining sense of security. His confusion was a mirror to her own, a confirmation that something was indeed amiss, something that even his formidable instincts couldn't categorize or combat.

Alice found herself spending more time in the library, the room that had once been her sanctuary. She'd sit for hours, ostensibly working, but in reality, she was listening, observing, her senses on high alert. The hushed atmosphere, the scent of aged paper and leather bindings, usually so comforting, now felt heavy, charged with an invisible static. She would stare at the rows of books, wondering if one of them had been moved, if a page had been turned by unseen hands. The polished surfaces of the antique furniture seemed to gleam with a new, watchful intensity. She started to perceive shapes in the shadows, fleeting movements at the periphery of her vision that dissolved when she turned to look directly.

The psychological toll was becoming immense. Sleep offered little respite. Nightmares, vivid and disturbing, plagued her, featuring disembodied whispers, the sensation of being touched by icy fingers, and the suffocating feeling of being trapped. She would wake abruptly, her heart pounding, the silence of the house now amplified by the echoes of her subconscious fears. She'd lie there in the darkness, straining her ears, half-expecting to hear the soft scuff of footsteps, the rustle of fabric, the whisper of breath. The grand bedroom, with its high ceilings and ornate furniture, began to feel like a gilded cage, its opulence a cruel mockery of her growing unease.

Her writing, the very purpose for her move to this grand estate, had stalled. The creative flow, once effortless, was now choked by a suffocating anxiety. The characters on her pages felt distant, their fictional struggles trivial compared to the terrifying reality unfolding around her. She would stare at the blank screen, her mind a whirlwind of fear, unable to conjure even a single coherent sentence. The house, which had promised inspiration and solitude, was now a constant source of distraction, its silence a screaming testament to her burgeoning paranoia.

She tried to rationalize it. Stress, she told herself. The solitude of the country, the pressure of a deadline, the sheer magnitude of the house – it was all getting to her. She started to meticulously document her days, filling a small notebook with every minor anomaly, a desperate attempt to impose order on the chaos.

*October 20th, 10:00 AM – Teacup left on desk found in sink. Distinct memory of placing it by the typewriter.October 20th, 6:00 PM – Bedroom door, which I had left slightly ajar, found closed. No one else in the house.* Each entry was a small admission of defeat, a testament to the growing chasm between her perception and the presumed reality of her situation.

The feeling of being intruded upon, of her privacy being violated in the most intimate way, was a constant hum beneath the surface of her thoughts. It wasn't just about objects being moved; it was the implication of presence. Someone, or

*something*, was in her house, breathing her air, observing her. She began to feel a profound sense of vulnerability, a terrifying realization that her sanctuary was no longer secure. The locks on the doors, the sturdy windows – they were no longer a comfort but a flimsy barrier against an enemy she couldn't see or understand.

She would find herself standing in the middle of a room, a vague sense of unease settling upon her, an instinct telling her that something was out of place, that a subtle shift had occurred while her back was turned. It was like a phantom limb sensation, a premonition that something had been touched, rearranged, acknowledged. She started to develop small rituals to combat this feeling: always closing doors firmly, always aligning objects on surfaces, a futile attempt to assert her will against an unseen force that seemed to delight in undoing her efforts.

The house, with its labyrinthine corridors and echoing rooms, began to feel like a character in its own right, an ancient, sentient entity that was playing a game with her. The shadows seemed to deepen, to lengthen, to coalesce into suggestive forms when she wasn't looking directly. The dust motes dancing in the shafts of sunlight appeared to form fleeting patterns, like messages she couldn't decipher. The grand fireplace in the drawing-room, with its imposing stone surround, felt like a watchful eye, its dark opening a mouth waiting to speak.

Alice found herself craving human interaction, a desperate need to ground herself in the reality of others. But the nearest village was miles away, and her work demanded solitude. She'd pick up the phone, her finger hovering over the dial, wanting to call a friend, to confide in someone, but the words always caught in her throat. How could she explain the phantom movements, the unsettling silences, the growing conviction that she was not alone? She could already hear the gentle concern in their voices, the subtle implication that she was overstressed, perhaps even imagining things. The fear of being dismissed, of being labeled as hysterical, kept her isolated in her growing dread.

The realization was dawning, slow and terrifying: the threat was not external. It wasn't a burglar with a crowbar or a ghost with chains. It was something more insidious, a subtle infiltration of her reality, a dismantling of her sanity from within. The house was not just a passive setting; it was an active participant, and she was its sole audience. The intruder's shadow was not cast from outside the walls, but from somewhere deep within the very fabric of her existence, a haunting presence that was slowly, inexorably, claiming her. The psychological torment was the true horror, the slow erosion of her certainty, the chilling awareness that the most terrifying voids were often the ones closest to home.

Alice's resolve solidified, a fragile shield against the encroaching dread. The comfort she once found in her new home had evaporated, replaced by a prickling awareness that she was no longer the sole occupant. The inexplicable events, once dismissed as errant thoughts or minor oversights, had coalesced into a chilling narrative. Her writer's mind, usually adept at weaving intricate plots, was now trapped in a feedback loop of fear and desperate attempts at logical deduction. She needed proof, tangible evidence that this was more than just a breakdown of her own psyche.

The first step was a systematic invasion of her own sanctuary. Armed with a steely determination, she began a thorough inspection of the house's perimeter. Every window was scrutinized, each pane examined for hairline fractures or tell-tale scuffs that might indicate tampering. She ran her fingers along the frames, feeling for any looseness, any gap that could admit an unwelcome visitor. The results were dishearteningly consistent: the windows were as secure as the day they were installed, the glass unblemished, the seals intact.

Next, she moved to the doors. The heavy oak front door, with its imposing iron hinges, was a fortress in itself. She tested its sturdiness, pushing and pulling with all her might, but it remained steadfast. The locks, all antique but robust, clicked with satisfying finality when engaged. She meticulously checked the smaller entrances – the back door leading to the overgrown garden, the service entrance near the kitchens – each one a testament to the house's original construction, seemingly impenetrable. She even examined the small, decorative grilles over the seldom-used basement windows, ensuring no small hand or tool could have possibly pried them open. The sheer lack of any discernible point of entry was, in its own way, more terrifying than finding evidence of a break-in. It implied an intruder who defied the laws of physical access, or worse, an intruder who had already found a way in, a way she hadn't yet discovered.

Her investigation then turned inward, a more invasive exploration of the house's hidden veins and arteries. Alice had always been drawn to the history of old buildings, the layers of lives lived within their walls. Now, that fascination was tinged with a desperate urgency. She recalled the estate agent's brief mention of "unusual architectural features" and the slight hesitation in his voice. She began to systematically explore the less-trafficked areas, the forgotten pockets of the sprawling residence.

The attic was her first target. A narrow, creaking staircase, hidden behind a discreet panel in the upstairs hallway, led her into the cavernous space. Dust motes, disturbed by her intrusion, swirled like spectral dancers in the single beam of light filtering through a grimy dormer window. The air was thick with the scent of aged wood, mothballs, and the faint, metallic tang of disuse. Old furniture, draped in white sheets that resembled silent, hunched figures, littered the floor. Trunks, their clasps rusted shut, hinted at forgotten heirlooms and untold stories. Alice moved with cautious steps, her flashlight beam cutting through the gloom, illuminating cobwebs that hung like macabre decorations. She examined every corner, every shadowy recess, half-expecting to find a hastily discarded tool, a hidden stash, or some other sign of recent occupation. But the attic, in its profound stillness, offered only the whisper of wind through unseen cracks and the persistent drumming of her own heart. It was a place of memories, yes, but not of present occupation.

The basement was a different beast altogether. A steep flight of stone steps descended into an echoing darkness, a place that felt colder, more primal, than the attic. The air here was damp and carried the earthy scent of soil and something else, something indefinable and faintly unpleasant. The stone walls seemed to weep moisture, and the floor was a uneven mosaic of packed earth and rough-hewn flagstones. Alice moved cautiously, her footsteps swallowed by the oppressive silence. This was a warren of disused storage rooms, a forgotten wine cellar, and the hulking, dormant furnace that was the house's central nervous system. She explored each cramped space, her flashlight beam probing the corners, the ceiling, the floor. She found old tools, remnants of past repairs, and the occasional scurrying rodent, but nothing that suggested a human presence, recent or otherwise. The only disturbance was the natural decay of time, the slow surrender of inanimate objects to the elements.

It was as she was about to retreat from the oppressive dampness of the basement that her attention was drawn to a section of the wall behind a stack of old lumber. It wasn't a deliberate discovery, but rather a shift in the ambient temperature. A faint, almost imperceptible draft, colder than the rest of the basement air, seemed to emanate from that specific spot. Intrigued, Alice began to move the heavy planks of wood, her muscles straining with the effort. As more of the wall was revealed, she noticed something peculiar. The mortar between the stones in this particular section seemed different, perhaps newer, or less disturbed than the surrounding areas. And then, she saw it. A faint scuff mark, almost invisible in the dim light, on the stone itself, as if something had been scraped against it.

Her breath hitched. This was the first anomaly she'd found that wasn't easily explained by age or neglect. She pressed her hand against the cold stone. It was solid, immovable. But as her fingers traced the outline of the stones, she felt a subtle difference in temperature. One particular stone felt warmer than the others, a faint, almost imperceptible heat radiating from its surface. It was a sensation so subtle, so easily dismissed, that she would have overlooked it had she not been so hyper-aware of every minute detail. She pressed her ear against the stone. Silence. Yet, the feeling of

*presence* that had been a vague unease in the rest of the house seemed to coalesce here, a concentrated point of unseen energy.

Driven by a growing conviction, Alice began to search for other interstitial spaces. She recalled the maze-like corridors of her childhood home, the hidden cupboards behind ornate paneling, the forgotten nooks within the walls. Her exploration became more granular, more obsessive. She tapped on walls, listening for hollow sounds, a technique she'd read about in mystery novels. She examined the intricate wainscoting in the drawing-room, running her fingertips along its carved surfaces, searching for hidden latches or seams. She spent hours in the library, not reading, but studying the intricate joinery of the bookshelves, the seemingly solid walls behind them.

It was in one of the smaller guest bedrooms, rarely used and even more rarely entered, that she found another clue. The room was dominated by a large, antique wardrobe. As she opened its doors, a musty smell wafted out, accompanied by the distinct scent of cedar. But it wasn't the smell that caught her attention. It was the back of the wardrobe. While the rest of the wood was dark and aged, a section of the back panel appeared slightly lighter, almost as if it had been recently replaced or treated. Intrigued, Alice pushed against it. It didn't budge. She then ran her hand over the surface, feeling for any imperfections. Her fingers brushed against a small, almost invisible seam.

With growing excitement, she searched for a tool. A long, thin letter opener from her writing desk was perfect. She carefully inserted the tip of the opener into the seam and gently pried. There was a soft click, and a section of the back panel, no larger than a shoebox, swung inward, revealing a dark, narrow cavity within the wall.

Alice's heart hammered against her ribs. This was it. This was the confirmation she had been desperately seeking. She shone her flashlight into the cavity. It was small, barely large enough for a person to squeeze into, and filled with dust and what looked like dislodged plaster. But it was the faint warmth that emanated from the cavity, a palpable warmth that defied the cool air of the room, that sent a shiver of both fear and exhilaration down her spine. It was as if the space itself retained a lingering residual heat.

She reached into the cavity, her fingers brushing against something soft. She pulled it out. It was a small, intricately carved wooden bird, its wings outstretched as if in flight. It was beautiful, delicate, and utterly out of place. It wasn't something she recognized as belonging to the house's existing décor, nor did it appear to be an antique in its own right. It felt... new, yet strangely old. And as she held it, she felt a faint vibration, a subtle thrumming that seemed to resonate from the bird itself.

Her gaze returned to the cavity. She noticed a few more disturbances in the dust, a scattering of fine particles that suggested recent movement. She also detected a faint, almost imperceptible scent –

something akin to old paper and lavender, a scent that was both comforting and deeply unsettling in this context. It was the scent of a hidden life, a secret existence playing out within the walls of her home.

This discovery was a turning point. It transformed her unease into a concrete suspicion. The house was not just old; it was actively hiding something. The secure locks and windows were a misdirection. The true point of access, the hidden ingress, was woven into the very fabric of the building. And within these hidden spaces, she sensed a presence, not just a vague feeling, but a tangible disturbance, a residual warmth that spoke of a recent occupant. The wooden bird in her hand was a calling card, a tangible artifact left behind by the unseen tenant. The question was no longer

*if* someone was in the house, but *who* and *why*. And more importantly, how could she possibly confront a presence that moved through shadows and concealed itself within the very bones of her home? The exploration had yielded answers, but each answer only deepened the mystery, and amplified the chilling realization that she was sharing her life with a ghost, a very real, very hidden entity.

The smooth, cool surface of the wooden bird still hummed with a faint, phantom vibration in Alice's palm. It was a tangible thing, a delicate artifact born from a hidden space, a stark counterpoint to the formless dread that had plagued her for weeks. But the cavity, and the bird within it, were just the beginning. The meticulous nature of her search, fueled by a desperate need for validation, had honed her senses to an almost unbearable degree. The house, once a sanctuary, was now a vast, echoing landscape of potential clues, each corner and crevice a canvas upon which an unseen tenant had left their subtle imprint.

It started small, almost imperceptible, easily dismissed as her own fatigue or an overactive imagination. The half-eaten sandwich, for instance. She'd found it on the kitchen counter one morning, a single, neat slice of ham and cheese nestled between two pieces of whole wheat bread. It was the kind of simple, unpretentious meal she herself might make for a late lunch, but she distinctly remembered clearing the counter the night before. There had been no visitors, no late-night snacks indulged in by a restless mind. Her husband, Mark, was away on a business trip, his absence a heavy silence in the house that usually offered a strange kind of solace. Yet, there it was, a half-eaten meal, a silent testament to a recent, unauthorized presence. She'd stared at it, her stomach clenching, before quickly wrapping it in cling film and shoving it into the bin, a primal instinct to erase the evidence, to pretend it hadn't happened. But the image, the sheer effrontery of it, remained seared into her mind.

Then came the scent. It was faint, elusive, a whisper of something unfamiliar that tickled the edges of her awareness. She first noticed it in their bedroom, a subtle shift in the air, a departure from the familiar blend of lavender, old linen, and Mark's faint, ever-present scent of sandalwood. This was different. It was sharper, more distinct, a musky, almost spicy aroma that reminded her vaguely of an expensive cologne, but one she'd never encountered before. She'd sniffed the air again, her head tilted, trying to pinpoint its source, but it was as ephemeral as smoke. She'd checked the wardrobe, the drawers, even Mark's discarded suit from his last trip, searching for a stray bottle or a lingering trace. Nothing. It was a phantom scent, one that seemed to permeate the very fabric of the room, appearing and disappearing without logic or reason. She'd chalked it up to a trick of the air currents, a peculiar quirk of the old house's ventilation system, but the disquiet it stirred remained, a subtle undercurrent of unease.

The discarded cigarette butt was more concrete, a physical manifestation of her intruder's trespass. She'd discovered it tucked away in the furthest corner of the overgrown rose garden, a place so neglected that even she rarely ventured there. It was nestled amongst the thorny stems of a particularly wild specimen, almost hidden from view. A single, filter-tipped cigarette, still bearing the faint imprint of lips, its tip stained with a dark, dried residue. It wasn't hers, and Mark was vehemently anti-smoking. The shock of finding it was visceral. It implied someone had been lurking in the garden, perhaps observing the house, perhaps waiting. The sheer carelessness of leaving it behind, a tangible piece of evidence, was as unnerving as the act itself. It wasn't the furtive, hurried act of a common burglar, but the casual discard of someone who felt entitled to be there, someone who considered this space their own.

These were not the hallmarks of a ghost, of a spectral presence confined to the realms of the supernatural. These were the intimate, mundane details of a human life, carelessly, or perhaps deliberately, left behind. The half-eaten sandwich spoke of hunger, of a need to sustain oneself within the confines of her home. The cologne hinted at an attempt at personal grooming, a desire to maintain a semblance of normalcy. The cigarette butt was a vice, a habit indulged in without thought or concern for discovery. They were the subtle but undeniable imprints of a living, breathing person who had been moving through her house, using her amenities, breathing her air, and leaving behind the detritus of their existence.

The shift in Alice's fear was profound. The nebulous dread, the fear of the unknown, the supernatural, was being replaced by a far more chilling, far more immediate terror: the fear of a human threat. This was not a phantom haunting her walls; this was someone walking her floors, someone who could, at any moment, be just beyond a door, just around a corner. The audacity of it was staggering. To not only gain access to her home but to

*inhabit* it, to treat it as their own, was an act of supreme arrogance and violation. It spoke of a mind that operated outside the bounds of normal social convention, a mind that saw her home not as a private sanctuary, but as a resource, a place to be exploited.

She began to revisit the earlier anomalies with this new, terrifying perspective. The sounds she'd dismissed as the settling of an old house – the faint creaks on the stairs, the rustling in the walls – now seemed to take on a new meaning. Were they the sounds of someone moving in the shadows, of someone navigating the hidden spaces she had so recently discovered? The warmth she'd felt from the stone in the basement, the lingering heat in the hidden cavity – could that be the residual warmth of a human body, of someone recently present?

Her writer's mind, though currently a battlefield of fear, began to churn, not with fantastical plotlines, but with chillingly plausible scenarios. This intruder was not a brute, not someone who would smash and grab. This was someone with immense patience, with an almost surgical precision in their movements. They had found ways into the house, ways that bypassed conventional security. They had moved through the spaces unseen, unheard, leaving behind only these fleeting, intimate traces. They were not just an unseen tenant; they were a phantom inhabitant, a ghost made flesh.

The sheer stealth involved was the most unnerving aspect. How had they managed to eat a sandwich without her hearing them? How had they moved through the house, accessing the hidden cavity, without leaving a more substantial trace? The thought of someone being in the same rooms as her, perhaps even watching her, while she went about her daily routines, sent shivers of ice down her spine. She recalled the moments she'd felt a prickling sensation on the back of her neck, a feeling of being observed, which she had attributed to her own paranoia. Now, she knew it was not paranoia; it was the heightened awareness of a hunted animal.

The fear was no longer an abstract concept; it was a cold, hard knot in her stomach, a constant tension in her shoulders. The house, once her refuge, had become a gilded cage, its beauty and history now overshadowed by the chilling knowledge that it was a shared space, a territory occupied by an invisible, yet undeniably human, presence. The subtle imprints were not just clues; they were declarations of ownership, a silent, terrifying message that her home was no longer hers alone. The writer in her, accustomed to crafting narratives, was now living one, a dark, suspenseful tale where the protagonist was increasingly aware that the villain was not a figment of her imagination, but a very real, very dangerous person lurking within the very walls she called home. The question was no longer about proving the existence of an unseen tenant, but about surviving the reality of an all-too-seen, albeit stealthy, invader. The subtle imprints were becoming a terrifying roadmap, and Alice was desperately trying to decipher it before she became another lost chapter in the story of this unseen occupant.

The silence in the house had taken on a new quality, no longer merely the absence of sound, but a heavy, expectant stillness. Alice found herself listening not just for the creaks and groans of the old structure, but for the subtle shifts in Duke's behavior. Her normally vigilant German Shepherd, a creature of keen senses and unwavering alertness, had begun to exhibit a peculiar calmness that gnawed at her. Duke, the dog who would usually erupt into a frenzy of barks at the slightest rustle of leaves outside or the distant rumble of a car, now seemed... indifferent.

It started with the noises. The soft thud from the attic that had once sent Duke scrambling to the top of the stairs, hackles raised, now elicited only a languid stretch and a soft sigh. A sudden clatter from the kitchen, the kind that would have him barking at the door, would see him merely lift his head, his large, intelligent eyes surveying the room before returning to his nap. This wasn't the usual contented sleep of a well-exercised dog; this was a deep, almost drugged repose, punctuated by slow, even breaths. Alice would watch him, her heart a tight knot of unease. Was he simply growing accustomed to the strange occurrences, his initial alarm dulled by their recurrence? Or was something more sinister at play, something that dulled his very instincts?

One evening, as Alice sat in the living room, poring over old blueprints of the house, trying to decipher the logic behind the hidden cavity, Duke, who had been asleep by the fireplace, stirred. He rose slowly, not with his usual athletic grace, but with a deliberate, almost meditative slowness. He padded across the rug, his paws making no sound, and stopped a few feet from the wall opposite the fireplace. Alice watched him, intrigued. He didn't look at her, didn't react to the faint hum of the refrigerator or the ticking of the grandfather clock. His entire focus seemed to be on the plaster and lathe of the wall.

He stood there for several minutes, his body utterly still, his gaze fixed. Then, he began to sniff. It wasn't the frantic, searching sniffs of a dog trying to identify a new scent. This was a slow, deliberate inhalation, his nostrils flaring as he drew in the air directly from the surface of the wall. He moved his head, tracing an invisible path along an imaginary line, as if reading a script written in scent. Alice's breath hitched. He was sniffing at the very section of wall where she had discovered the concealed space, the space that had yielded the wooden bird. But there was no growl, no whine of distress, no indication of alarm. There was only this strange, intense focus, a quiet investigation that felt unnervingly intimate.

She remembered the first time this had happened. A few days after finding the bird, she'd been in the hallway, dusting the antique console table, when Duke had appeared at her side. He'd walked past her, straight to the wall near the staircase, and begun his peculiar sniffing ritual. She'd dismissed it then as an odd quirk, perhaps a phantom scent clinging to the wall from some long-forgotten incident. But now, seeing it again, so close to the site of her discovery, it felt significant.

"What is it, boy?" she'd whispered, her voice trembling slightly. Duke didn't react. His tail remained still, his body locked in its focused posture. It was as if he was acknowledging a presence she couldn't perceive, a scent that spoke to him in a language she didn't understand. The absence of his usual protective barking was the most disturbing aspect. Duke was a sentinel, a furry alarm system. His silence in the face of this seemingly deliberate investigation was a deafening anomaly.

She tried to rationalize it. Perhaps the unseen presence was not overtly threatening, at least not to Duke. Perhaps whatever was in the walls emitted a scent that, while foreign to Alice, didn't trigger Duke's fear response. Perhaps it was an odor he associated with something neutral, or even something positive, in his canine world. But the nagging thought persisted: was his perceived placidity a sign of his instincts being overridden, a subtle manipulation of his senses by whatever entity inhabited her home?

The theory of a disruption of his natural instincts began to take root, a chilling counterpoint to her own burgeoning fear. If an unseen tenant could move through the house undetected, leaving behind subtle traces of their presence, could they also exert a subtle influence, a psychic fog that dulled the senses of those around them? It sounded like the stuff of speculative fiction, yet the evidence, however circumstantial, was mounting. Duke's placidity was not a sign of peace; it was a symptom of something being

*wrong.*

She recalled a specific incident from the previous night. She had been woken by a series of faint taps, like fingernails on glass, coming from the study. Her first instinct was to rouse Duke, to have him investigate with her. But he was asleep at the foot of the bed, his breathing deep and even, undisturbed by the sounds that had jolted her awake. She'd crept out of bed, a shiver tracing its way down her spine, and gone to the study. The taps had stopped as soon as she entered the room. She'd searched the windows, the walls, even the bookshelves, finding nothing. When she'd returned to bed, Duke had merely shifted, a soft murmur escaping him, before settling back into his deep slumber. He hadn't even opened his eyes.

This was not the Duke she knew. This was a Duke who slept through phantom noises, who sniffed curiously at walls that should have invoked suspicion, who seemed to exist in a state of unnatural calm. It was as if the house itself, or the presence within it, was exerting a soporific effect, a dampening of the very senses that made him her protector.

She began to observe him more closely, her eyes constantly scanning his reactions, or lack thereof. She noticed that his sniffing wasn't random. It was always directed towards specific points in the walls, particularly in the hallway and the rooms on the ground floor that bordered the older, less-used sections of the house. He would stand there, nose twitching, for extended periods, sometimes letting out a low, rumbling sound in his chest that wasn't quite a growl, not quite a purr, but something unsettlingly in between. It was a sound of contemplation, perhaps, or of a deep, internal processing of information she couldn't access.

One afternoon, while she was working in her home office, Duke was dozing in his usual spot by the French doors. Suddenly, he sat up, his ears perked. Alice's heart leaped. This was it. He'd heard something. But instead of barking, he simply turned his head towards the wall behind her desk, the wall that separated her office from the unused pantry. He began to sniff, his tail giving a single, slow wag, a gesture that Alice had come to associate with mild interest rather than alarm. He approached the wall and pressed his nose against it, his sniffing becoming more intense.

"What is it, Duke?" she asked, her voice barely a whisper. He responded with a soft huff, as if acknowledging her. He seemed to be tracing a path along the baseboard, his movements deliberate and methodical. It was as if he were mapping out the unseen territory, marking the boundaries of the intruder's domain with his own senses. The absence of fear was what unnerved her the most. A predator, a stray animal, even a strong, unfamiliar scent – anything that posed a potential threat would have elicited a defensive reaction. But this... this was different. It was calm, curious, almost accepting.

She found herself projecting her own anxieties onto his behavior. Was he trying to communicate something to her, something he couldn't articulate with barks or growls? Was his placid sniffing a coded message? Perhaps he was trying to show her where the presence was strongest, where the scent was most potent. She began to follow his gaze, to study the sections of wall he seemed so interested in. Were there subtle discolorations? Faint scuff marks? She peered closely, her writer's eye for detail now trained on the mundane canvas of her home. She saw nothing. Just plaster and paint, the familiar textures of her life.

The thought of Duke's instincts being compromised was a deeply unsettling one. He was her last line of defense, her early warning system. If his senses were dulled, if his protective nature was somehow muted, then she was truly alone. She considered the possibility of him being unwell, of some subtle neurological issue affecting his behavior. She had him checked by the vet just a few weeks prior for his annual shots, and he'd been in perfect health. The vet had commented on his excellent condition, his sharp mind. This change had been too sudden, too specific, to be a natural decline.

The peculiar behavior intensified. She started finding Duke sitting for long stretches in the hallway, facing the wall, his eyes half-closed, as if in a trance. He would remain like this for fifteen, twenty minutes at a time, utterly still, utterly silent, save for the soft rhythm of his breathing. It was as if he were meditating, communing with something beyond her comprehension. Sometimes, she would find him nudging the baseboards with his nose, a gentle, persistent pressure that suggested he was trying to dislodge something, or perhaps, to create an opening.

She recalled another incident. She'd been in the basement, sorting through old boxes, when she heard Duke moving upstairs. The usual click-clack of his nails on the hardwood floor was absent. Instead, it was a soft shuffling, a dragging sound. She'd called his name, but there was no immediate response. A surge of panic shot through her. Had he gotten stuck somewhere? Had he been injured? She'd hurried upstairs, her heart pounding, only to find him in the living room, lying on the floor, his body pressed against the wall, his nose rhythmically bumping against a specific spot near the baseboard. He looked up at her, his tail giving a slow, languid thump on the carpet, a gesture that now felt less like a greeting and more like an acknowledgment of her presence. There was no fear in his eyes, no urgency. Just a quiet, almost resigned curiosity.

The unsettling thought began to solidify: Duke wasn't just reacting to the unseen tenant; he was somehow aware of its presence in a way that bypassed his alarm protocols. He wasn't scared, but he was... engaged. He was investigating, meticulously, patiently, in a manner that mirrored Alice's own burgeoning obsession with the house's secrets. But where her investigation was driven by fear and a desperate need for answers, Duke's seemed almost... routine.

Could the unseen presence be exerting a form of subtle control, a psychic dampening that affected not just the atmosphere of the house, but the very instincts of its inhabitants? The thought sent a fresh wave of cold dread through her. If an intruder could make her dog docile, what else could they do? Could they influence her own thoughts, her own actions? She shook her head, trying to dislodge the escalating paranoia. She was a writer; her mind was prone to conjuring elaborate narratives. She needed to stick to the facts, to the tangible evidence.

But Duke's behavior was the most tangible evidence she had, albeit in its sheer strangeness. It was a deviation from the norm, a disruption of the established order of her home. The dog who was once her shadow, her constant companion in vigilance, was now a silent observer of something unseen, his focus drawn to walls that held no apparent interest for her. His peculiar behavior was not a sign of his indifference to the intrusion; it was a sign that he

*knew*. He was aware of the unseen tenant, and for reasons Alice couldn't fathom, he wasn't barking. He was observing, sniffing, and, most disturbingly, seeming to accept the presence. Was his silence a form of canine communication, a subtle warning that spoke volumes in its very stillness? Or was he, like her, being slowly, insidiously, changed by the unseen occupant of her home? The unnerving quietude of her usually boisterous dog was, in its own way, the most chilling sound in the house.

# Chapter 3: A World Within Walls

The discovery of the hidden cavity behind the bookshelf had been the crack that split Alice's perception of her home wide open. It had shifted her understanding from one of a well-loved, albeit old, family residence to a place riddled with secrets, a place that held its breath. Now, armed with the blueprints and a growing sense of unease, she was driven to uncover more. The old house, with its gabled roof and ivy-clad walls, had always felt like a character in her life, but lately, it was beginning to feel like an adversary, its stillness a deliberate deception.

She started with the attic. It was a space she usually avoided, a dusty repository of forgotten heirlooms and the occasional startled spider. But the blueprints showed a series of what appeared to be ventilation shafts, their rough outlines etched in faded ink, running not just to the exterior but seemingly

*through* the upper floors, disappearing into the mass of the building. Armed with a powerful flashlight and a thick cloth mask, Alice ascended the narrow pull-down stairs, the wood groaning in protest. The air up there was stagnant, thick with the scent of aged wood and something else, something faintly metallic, like old blood or rust.

Her flashlight beam cut through the gloom, illuminating a chaotic landscape of cobwebs and discarded furniture draped in ghostly sheets. She scanned the floorboards, her gaze sharp, searching for any deviation from the thick blanket of dust that coated everything. It was in the far corner, near a disused chimney stack, that she found it. A section of the floor, barely noticeable, seemed... cleaner. Not entirely free of dust, but with a pattern that suggested it had been disturbed. The dust was swept away in swathes, as if something had been dragged across it, or perhaps, as if a heavy object had been carefully placed and then removed.

Getting down on her hands and knees, the rough wood digging into her jeans, Alice brushed away the loose dust with her gloved hand. Beneath it, faint, dark scuff marks emerged on the wood. They were faint, almost ephemeral, but undeniably present. They didn't look like the marks of furniture being moved; they were too irregular, too scattered. They seemed to suggest a more deliberate, more cautious traversal. Her heart hammered against her ribs. This wasn't the random settling of an old house; this was evidence.

Following the direction the scuff marks seemed to indicate, she found herself at the base of the chimney. The bricks here were coated in a thick layer of soot and grime. But as she ran her hand along the masonry, her fingers brushed against something smooth, something that didn't belong. A small, rectangular piece of metal, almost flush with the brickwork, was set into the wall. It had a small, recessed handle. With a surge of adrenaline, she tugged. It gave way with a faint click, revealing a dark, narrow opening.

It was a crawlspace. Not a vast, echoing cavern, but a cramped, claustrophobic void, barely wide enough for a person to squeeze through. The air that wafted out was colder, carrying the distinct scent of damp earth and something acrid, like old insulation mixed with mold. She shone her flashlight into the abyss. It seemed to stretch, an inky blackness that swallowed the beam. The blueprints had indicated access points, but seeing one, touching it, feeling the chill emanating from it, was a different matter entirely.

This was the first of many. As she continued her meticulous search of the attic, she found two more similar access points, cleverly disguised within the architecture. One was a loose panel behind a stack of old trunks, another a section of wall that seemed to shift slightly when pressure was applied. Each revealed a similar dark maw, a promise of unseen depths. The house, she realized with a growing dread, was not a solid structure but a hollow shell, a network of interconnected spaces waiting to be explored.

Descending from the attic, her mind buzzing with possibilities, Alice moved to the main floor. The blueprints had hinted at similar hidden passages branching off from the ground floor rooms, particularly those that bordered the older, less-used sections of the house. The study, where she'd first found the bird, seemed like a prime candidate. The wall where Duke had been so intently sniffing was the one bordering the old, disused pantry.

The pantry itself was a cavernous space, its shelves bare, its walls peeling. It smelled of forgotten spices and a faint, persistent dampness. Alice spent hours in there, tapping along the walls, searching for any inconsistencies. It was in the back of the pantry, behind a thick, rotting wooden shelf that seemed to have been bolted into the wall, that she made her next discovery. The shelf, when she finally managed to pry it loose with a crowbar she'd found in the garage, revealed a dark recess. This wasn't a crawlspace in the traditional sense; it was more of a narrow alcove, a forgotten nook that seemed to lead deeper into the wall cavity.

She shone her light inside. The space was lined with rough-hewn wood, and the floor was a thick layer of compacted dirt. The air here was heavy, close, and carried a faint, musky odor that made her stomach churn. It felt ancient, undisturbed. Yet, as she examined the dirt floor, she noticed something that sent a shiver down her spine. There were faint indentations, not like footprints, but more like the marks left by something being slid or dragged across the surface. And interspersed with these marks were small, almost imperceptible wisps of what looked like dark, matted hair.

This was no ordinary forgotten space. This was a space that had been *used*. The dust was disturbed, not by time, but by presence. The realization struck her with full force: whoever, or whatever, was in the walls, they weren't just passing through. They were navigating these hidden passages, using them as their own private domain.

Her focus then shifted to the ventilation shafts. The blueprints showed a complex system, far more intricate than she had initially realized. They weren't merely for air circulation; they appeared to connect various parts of the house, forming a skeletal network beneath the surface. She found one access point in the master bedroom, cleverly concealed behind a built-in wardrobe. It was a metal grate, tarnished and dusty, but it yielded to her persistent efforts.

This was a different kind of darkness. The ventilation shaft was narrow, lined with cold metal, and eerily silent. The flashlight beam struggled to penetrate the depths, revealing only a tortuous path of bends and turns. The metallic tang she'd noticed in the attic was stronger here, mingling with the pervasive scent of dust and something else, something organic and slightly sweet, like decaying leaves. She could hear her own breath, amplified in the confined space, and the frantic thumping of her heart.

She hesitated, her hand on the cold metal. Duke was downstairs, asleep by the fire, his unnatural calm a constant, unsettling reminder of the house's insidious influence. She remembered him sniffing at the walls, his low, rumbling sounds. Was he sensing this network? Was he trying to communicate its presence? She knew, with a chilling certainty, that she couldn't ignore these hidden spaces any longer. They were the veins and arteries of the house, and whatever was within them was moving through them unseen.

She forced herself to crawl into the shaft, her body scraping against the metal. It was a terrifying experience, the darkness pressing in on all sides, the sense of being completely enclosed suffocating. She moved slowly, her flashlight beam sweeping ahead, revealing more of the metal tunnel. There were occasional, almost invisible, smudges on the interior surface, faint streaks that looked like they could have been made by a gloved hand or perhaps something more... primal. The air grew colder, and a faint draft whispered through the shaft, carrying with it the distant sound of dripping water.

She emerged, gasping for air, into another room – the downstairs guest bedroom, a room that had always felt a little too quiet, a little too vacant. The grate here was hidden behind a heavy tapestry, as if someone had deliberately tried to conceal it. The fact that these access points were not all obvious, that some had been deliberately hidden, spoke volumes. This wasn't just about finding forgotten spaces; it was about uncovering deliberate concealment.

Her investigation became a relentless obsession. She traced the lines on the blueprints, her fingers smudged with graphite, comparing them to the physical reality of the house. Each crawlspace, each hidden alcove, each seemingly innocuous ventilation shaft, was a piece of a terrifying puzzle. She discovered more access points in the basement, tucked away behind old laundry chutes, and even in the walls of the main staircase, behind a section of decorative paneling that swung inward with a soft groan.

The house was a labyrinth, its walls not solid barriers but permeable membranes, allowing passage through a hidden world. The dust was her guide, its disturbed patterns revealing the routes of passage. The scuff marks were the whispers of movement, the faint indentations the evidence of something being dragged, or perhaps, carried. And the faint, organic smells – they were the lingering scent of the unseen occupant, a phantom presence that left its mark on the very fabric of the house.

She spent days meticulously documenting each discovery, sketching the layout of the hidden passages, noting the nature of the disturbances. She found a small, tattered piece of fabric snagged on a jagged edge of metal in one of the ventilation shafts, a dark, coarse material that felt like burlap. In another crawlspace, she found a cluster of what looked like small, bird-like bones, gnawed clean. These were not the findings of a casual trespasser; they were the signs of a more deliberate, more unsettling inhabitant.

The sheer scale of the interconnectedness was overwhelming. It seemed that almost every room, every major section of the house, had some form of access to this hidden network. It was a secret world running parallel to her own, a silent, unseen domain that was being actively utilized. The realization that she was living in a house that was as much void as substance was a deeply disorienting one. The walls were no longer just walls; they were doorways, conduits, and silent witnesses to a hidden life. The house was not just a shelter; it was a trap, its hidden passages a testament to the pervasive, insidious nature of her unseen adversary. The crawlspaces weren't just dusty voids; they were the revealed arteries of a predatory presence, a stark and chilling testament to a world within walls that had finally, terrifyingly, been laid bare.

The air in the crawlspace was thick with a cloying sweetness, a scent Alice couldn't quite place, but which made her stomach clench with unease. It was a stark contrast to the metallic tang of the ventilation shafts and the damp earth smell of the deeper recesses. Her flashlight beam, though powerful, struggled to pierce the absolute darkness, its circle of light a small island in an ocean of black. She had been meticulously cataloging each entry point, each hidden passage, for days. The blueprints had been a map, but these hidden spaces were the territory, and it was here, in their suffocating confines, that the true nature of the trespasser began to reveal itself.

She had initially expected to find evidence of passage – scuff marks, disturbed dust, perhaps a dropped tool. But this was different. This was evidence of

*habitation*. In a particularly wide section of the crawlspace behind the old pantry, where the rough-hewn wood gave way to a slightly more defined alcove, her light fell upon something that made her breath hitch. It wasn't just dirt and debris. There, nestled in a hollowed-out section of the packed earth, was what looked unmistakably like a makeshift bed. A pile of old, stained blankets, matted and lumpy, had been arranged with a surprising degree of care. It was crudely constructed, functional, but it spoke of more than just a fleeting rest. Someone had slept here. Repeatedly.

The thought sent a fresh wave of cold dread through her. This wasn't a vagrant seeking shelter for a single night. This was someone who had established a base, a hidden sanctuary within the very bones of her home. The smell, she realized with a sickening lurch, was the faint, lingering odor of stale sweat and something else, something akin to unwashed wool and a hint of decay. It was the smell of prolonged, unhygienic occupation.

Her gloved fingers trembled as she reached out, not to touch, but to point her flashlight directly at the pile. Beneath the blankets, she could discern the shape of something solid, something that might have served as a rudimentary mattress or cushioning. And scattered around the edges of this makeshift bed were other objects, insignificant on their own, but chilling in their collective implication. A few crumpled wrappers, their branding faded and unidentifiable, suggesting they had been scavenged from discarded refuse. A half-eaten granola bar, long past its edible prime, its contents dry and brittle. These were not the items of a ghost; they were the detritus of a living, breathing person.

Alice forced herself to move further into the alcove, her heart hammering a frantic rhythm against her ribs. The passage narrowed again, forcing her to shimmy sideways, the rough wood scraping against her clothes. She emerged into another space, this one smaller, more confined, and it was here that the evidence of *sustained* presence became even more pronounced. The floor was littered with more debris, but this time, the items were more personal, more disturbingly intimate.

She found a pair of socks, dark and worn, the elastic at the ankles stretched and shapened by use. They were a man's socks, by the size, and the fabric was thin in places, hinting at considerable wear. The thought of these socks being worn, day in and day out, within the walls of her home, within mere feet of where she slept, was profoundly violating. They carried a faint, musty odor, a testament to their recent, albeit clandestine, use.

Beside the socks lay a small, crumpled piece of paper. Alice carefully picked it up with a pair of tweezers she'd brought, her hands still encased in their thick gloves. Unfolding it revealed a child's drawing, rendered in brightly colored crayon. It depicted a crude house, with a smiling sun and stick figures. It was a childish rendering, innocent in its execution, but its presence here, in this hidden, squalid space, was deeply unsettling. Who did it belong to? Was the intruder a man with a child? Or had he taken it? The ambiguity was more terrifying than any concrete answer. The vibrant colors seemed to mock the oppressive darkness of the space, a jarring juxtaposition that clung to Alice's senses.

Further exploration revealed a small collection of trinkets, scavenged or perhaps hoarded. A smooth, grey stone. A tarnished, inexpensive-looking earring with a chipped faux gem. A bent, almost unrecognizable toy car, its paint scraped away in patches. These weren't valuable items, but their presence suggested a desire to surround oneself with personal belongings, a need for comfort and familiarity, even in the most unconventional of environments. It painted a portrait of a life lived in the shadows, a parasitic existence that had infiltrated her home and made it its own.

The sheer intimacy of these discoveries was overwhelming. This was not a burglar looking for valuables. This was someone who had chosen to

*dwell* within her walls, to carve out a secret existence in the hidden arteries of her house. They had slept here, eaten here, and kept their meager possessions here. The intruder wasn't just passing through; he was living, breathing, *occupying* the very structure of her home.

Alice continued her painstaking search, moving from one hidden chamber to another, her flashlight beam cutting through the suffocating darkness. Each discovery served to deepen her horror. In a narrow, seldom-used ventilation shaft that ran beneath the master bedroom, she found a small, crudely fashioned pouch made of what looked like old rags stitched together. Inside, she found a handful of buttons, varying in size and color, and a few lengths of coarse thread. It was the kind of collection one might make if they were mending clothes, or perhaps, if they were gathering materials for some unknown purpose. It was domestic, yet in this context, it was utterly alien and deeply disturbing. It suggested a level of deliberate action, of planning and sustained effort to create a semblance of normalcy within this hidden world.

The most chilling discovery came in the basement, in a cramped crawlspace accessible only by pulling away a section of loose stone foundation. Here, tucked away in a corner, was a larger collection of what appeared to be discarded food items. Not just wrappers, but actual remnants of meals. The desiccated remains of a loaf of bread, its mold long since dried and flaked away. A few gnawed bones, too small and brittle to be from any animal Alice could readily identify, hinting at a meager, perhaps desperate diet. And then she saw it, half-hidden beneath a tattered piece of cardboard: a small, worn photograph, its surface scratched and faded. She hesitated before picking it up with her tweezers. It was a picture of a woman, her face indistinct with age and damage, but the image was clear enough to convey a sense of a past life. Was this someone the intruder cared for? A memory he clung to? Or was it another violation, another piece of someone else's life stolen and brought into this hidden sanctuary?

The air in the basement crawlspace was heavy with the smell of damp concrete and something else, a faint, sickly sweet odor that hinted at decay. It was here, amongst the remnants of this hidden life, that Alice felt the true weight of the intrusion. It wasn't just the physical violation of her home, but the psychological torment of knowing that someone had been living so close, so unseen, for an unknown period of time. The house, which she had always considered her sanctuary, had become a stage for a secret, unsettling drama. The walls, once solid and reassuring, now seemed to pulse with a hidden life, a testament to the unseen dweller who had made their parasitic home within them. Each discarded item, each makeshift arrangement, was a stark reminder that this was not a fleeting encounter, but a sustained, deliberate occupation. The intruder wasn't just an intruder; they were a resident, a silent, invisible tenant who had claimed the hidden spaces as their own, feeding off the unwitting hospitality of those who lived above.

The dust, usually a uniform layer of undisturbed grey across the attic floorboards, now bore a subtle roadmap. Faint trails, no wider than a fingertip, crisscrossed the space with a disturbing regularity. Alice, armed with a powerful flashlight and an even more potent sense of dread, traced these ephemeral lines. They weren't random scuffs from settling timbers or the scurrying of vermin. These were deliberate pathways, worn into the very fabric of the house by the silent tread of an unseen inhabitant. She noted their proximity to the ventilation grates, their tendency to converge near the junction of supporting beams, suggesting a preferred route, a practiced traversal. It was like finding footprints on the moon – undeniable proof of a visitor in a place that should have been entirely her own. Each faint mark was a whisper of his presence, a clue to his movements.

She began to overlay these observed trails with the house's architectural plans, mentally overlaying the dark lines on the paper with the faint smudges on the wood. The intruder, she deduced, wasn't simply moving through the house; he was using its hidden arteries, the forgotten spaces between walls, the echoing void of the ventilation system, to navigate. The crawlspaces and attics, once merely structural necessities, had become his secret highways. He moved from the basement to the first floor, then to the second, not by walking through rooms, but by slipping into the bowels of the house and emerging where he needed to be. This explained the lack of overt signs of entry or exit on the main floors. He was a ghost in the machine, a phantom operating within the building's skeleton.

The schedule, too, began to emerge, painstakingly pieced together from the subtlest of auditory clues. The faint

*thump* that sometimes disturbed her sleep around 2 AM, never loud enough to be alarming but present enough to prick her consciousness. The almost imperceptible *scrape* from the vicinity of the kitchen pantry late at night. The rhythmic *drip* that she had initially dismissed as a leaky faucet, but which, on closer inspection, seemed to emanate from a different section of the pipe network each night. These weren't random occurrences. They were the sounds of occupation, the nocturnal activities of a resident living by a different clock. He was a creature of the night, his movements synchronized with the deepest hours of sleep, when the house was at its most vulnerable, and its human occupants least aware.

Her meticulously kept logbook, filled with dates, times, and observed anomalies, started to form a pattern. The noises, while faint, were predictable. There was a window of approximately two hours, between 1:30 AM and 3:30 AM, when the majority of these subtle sounds occurred. This was his active period, his time for foraging, for maintaining his hidden domain, or perhaps, for simply observing. It was during these hours that he seemed to be most mobile, most engaged with the house. The rest of the time, a hushed stillness would descend, broken only by the natural creaks and groans of an old dwelling. This enforced quiet was, in its own way, just as unnerving as the sounds, hinting at a predator at rest, conserving energy, waiting for the opportune moment.

The placement of the personal effects she'd discovered also began to suggest a routine. The makeshift bed in the crawlspace was always oriented in the same direction. The small pile of trinkets, while seemingly random, were always found in a particular corner of the alcove, as if designated as a 'nightstand' or a personal shrine. The child's drawing, initially a source of pure terror, was consistently found tucked beneath the edge of the blankets, a silent guardian or a comforting talisman. These were not the acts of someone merely hiding; they were the habits of someone who was living, someone who was establishing a semblance of normalcy within their clandestine existence. He had carved out a niche, a territory, and he moved within it with a practiced, almost ritualistic, precision.

Alice found herself developing an unnerving awareness of the house's internal clock. She would lie awake, listening, her senses honed to an almost unbearable degree, trying to anticipate the next faint sound, the next shift in the silence. The house, once a place of comfort and security, had transformed into a complex, three-dimensional chessboard, and she was acutely aware of an invisible opponent moving across its hidden squares. The knowledge of his routines, while terrifying, also granted her a perverse sense of control. She could almost predict his path, his likely whereabouts at any given hour. This wasn't the bold strategy of a detective, but the desperate, hyper-vigilant maneuvering of prey trying to outwit its predator.

The intruder's use of the house's infrastructure was particularly ingenious. The ventilation shafts, designed for airflow, had become his personal transit system. He would slip through a grate in a disused closet, travel unseen through the metallic tunnels, and emerge in another part of the house, bypassing doors and hallways entirely. Alice had found evidence of this: a faint, metallic sheen on the dusty surface of the air filters, a subtle distortion in the metal where a panel had likely been pried open and resealed. It spoke of a methodical understanding of the building's inner workings, a knowledge that went beyond simple observation. He knew the guts of her home better than she did.

She began to map out these 'routes' as well, correlating the locations of the ventilation access points with the patterns of disturbed dust. It was a gruesome, intricate puzzle. The main living areas were largely untouched, a testament to his avoidance of direct confrontation, or perhaps, his lack of need to enter them. His domain was the interstitial space, the hidden world that existed in the negative. He was the secret tenant, the uninvited resident who paid no rent and left no forwarding address, except for the subtle clues he inadvertently left behind in the dust and silence.

The predictability of his habits was a double-edged sword. On one hand, it allowed Alice to anticipate his movements, to gauge the safest times to move about her own home. She learned to avoid certain areas during the hours she now knew he was most active. She became a creature of daylight hours, her own movements confined to the periods of his apparent inactivity. Her life began to revolve around his presumed schedule, a silent pact dictated by fear. On the other hand, this very predictability made the situation all the more chilling. It wasn't a random act of vandalism or a desperate break-in. This was a settled presence, an established pattern of occupation. He had made himself comfortable, integrating himself into the very structure of her life without her ever seeing his face.

The psychological toll of this knowledge was immense. Every creak of the floorboards, every whisper of wind through the eaves, was magnified, scrutinized. The house, her sanctuary, had become a cage, and the bars were the invisible walls of his hidden world. She felt constantly observed, even when the house was silent and still. The knowledge that he was there, somewhere within the walls, living by his own clandestine routine, was a constant, gnawing anxiety. It was the horror of the unseen, the terror of the unknown, amplified by the unsettling intimacy of his shared space. She was living with a ghost, a ghost that breathed, that ate, that slept, and that moved with a terrifying, predictable rhythm, just beyond the veil of her perception. The house, once a symbol of her independence and security, had become a testament to her vulnerability, a vessel for a haunting presence that had meticulously mapped out its own existence within its very core. The intruder's habits, once merely clues, had become the architecture of her fear.

The discovery of the mended vase was not a moment of relief, but a sharp, cold twist of dread that solidified Alice's terror into a profound, bone-deep certainty. It was a vase she had owned for years, a delicate, hand-painted piece from a trip to Italy, its ceramic glaze a vibrant turquoise studded with minuscule, almost iridescent flecks. A clumsy moment, a shelf nudged too hard during a fit of frustrated cleaning, had sent it tumbling to the floor, shattering into a dozen jagged pieces. She had been heartbroken, the fragments carefully gathered, the task of repair deemed too daunting, the original beauty irrevocably marred. The shattered pieces had been relegated to a forgotten box in the attic, a silent testament to a moment of carelessness, a broken memory.

Yet, there it was. Not on the attic floor, not among the other discarded remnants of her life, but perched on the mantelpiece in the living room, as if it had always belonged there. And it was whole. The vibrant turquoise was no longer fractured, the intricate floral pattern, previously a jagged jigsaw puzzle, flowed seamlessly across the curves of the vase. The cracks, once gaping wounds, were now invisible, the ceramic fused with a precision that defied explanation. It looked as if it had never been broken at all.

Alice's heart hammered against her ribs, a frantic bird trapped in a cage. This was not the act of a vandal, not the random destruction she had half-expected, half-feared. This was something else entirely. It was an act of restoration, of meticulous care, performed by hands that moved in the shadows, unseen and unheard. The thought sent a shiver down her spine, a cold dread that was far more potent than the fear of physical harm. Vandalism was impulsive, chaotic, a release of anger or desperation. This... this was deliberate. This was intentional. This spoke of a profound and unsettling connection to her possessions, to her life.

She approached the vase with a trembling hand, her fingertips hovering inches from its perfect surface. She could almost feel the ghost of the glue, the invisible mend that held it together. It was a miracle of repair, a testament to an almost supernatural patience and skill. But it was a terrifying miracle. Who would do this? And why? This wasn't about breaking things; it was about fixing them. It was about imposing order, about smoothing over the imperfections. It was about taking something that was broken and making it, in the intruder's eyes, whole again.

The implication was staggering. He hadn't just been passing through; he had been observing. He had seen the broken vase, noted its discarded state, and in his own twisted logic, decided to rectify the situation. He had spent time, perhaps hours, painstakingly piecing together the delicate shards, his movements so quiet, so deliberate, that they had escaped her notice. He had then placed it back, not in its original, precarious position on the shelf, but in a place of prominence, on the mantelpiece, as if presenting a gift, or perhaps, making a statement.

Alice remembered the day she had broken the vase. It had been a Tuesday, a dreary, rain-slicked afternoon. She had been overwhelmed with work, a looming deadline, and the general weight of everyday life. The clumsy accident had felt like the last straw, a fitting metaphor for her own crumbling composure. She had felt a profound sense of loss, not just of the object, but of the memory, the feeling of joy it represented. And now, this phantom had... mended it. He had, in a way, mended that broken moment for her.

The thought was deeply disturbing. It wasn't a gesture of kindness. It was an invasion. He had reached into the repository of her broken things, her discarded memories, and had decided what to preserve, what to restore. He had acted as a curator of her life, selecting an item that had been deemed beyond repair and breathing new life into it. It was an act of control, a subtle assertion of ownership over her belongings, her history. He was not just a squatter; he was a phantom curator, meticulously tending to the artifacts of her existence.

Her mind raced, replaying every subtle sound, every unexplained anomaly. Had he been in the attic that day? Had he watched her gather the shards, had he seen her put them in the box? The idea that he had been present, a silent observer of her grief and frustration, made her stomach churn. He had witnessed her vulnerability, her sadness, and had then, in his own bizarre way, decided to "fix" it.

This meticulous attention to detail extended beyond the vase. She began to recall other instances, small things she had dismissed as her own forgetfulness or the quirks of an old house. The way a stack of mail on the hall table, which she distinctly remembered leaving slightly askew, would be perfectly aligned the next morning. The stray sock, which had found its way under the sofa, mysteriously reappearing folded neatly in the laundry basket. The slightly ajar cupboard door, found shut with a quiet click. Each of these was a minor event, easily explained away. But now, seen through the lens of the mended vase, they took on a sinister new meaning.

He wasn't just moving through the house; he was tidying it. He was organizing it. He was making it, in his own warped perception,

*better*. This wasn't the messy, chaotic presence of someone simply trying to survive or hide. This was the behavior of someone who craved order, who was deeply invested in the state of things, who saw flaws and felt compelled to correct them. It was the unsettling precision of a mind that needed everything to be just so.

Alice felt a fresh wave of paranoia wash over her. If he cared about the state of her possessions, about the arrangement of her mail, what else did he observe? Did he judge her? Did he have opinions on her habits, her choices? The thought of being silently scrutinized, of having her every action, her every possession, evaluated and perhaps even corrected by this unseen presence, was profoundly violating.

She began to meticulously re-examine the vase, tracing the impossibly fine lines where the ceramic had been rejoined. She felt along the surface, searching for any tell-tale bump, any trace of residue. But there was nothing. The repair was flawless, a silent testament to his skill and his disturbing obsession. It was a work of art, a terrifying piece of evidence.

The intruder's nature was becoming terrifyingly clear. He was not merely an unwelcome guest; he was an obsessive presence. He was a phantom who not only occupied her home but also felt an intimate connection to its contents. He had the audacity, the chilling impulse, to interact with her belongings, to alter them, to "improve" them according to his own unseen standards. He was a ghost who rearranged furniture, a spirit who repaired porcelain.

This act of mending the vase was far more intrusive than any forced entry, any broken lock. It was a violation of her sense of autonomy, her right to the undisturbed integrity of her own possessions. He had taken something that was broken, something that was hers to decide the fate of, and had imposed his will upon it. He had, in effect, taken a piece of her life, a symbol of her past, and had reshaped it without her consent.

Alice found herself scrutinizing other items in her home with a newfound suspicion. Was the book on her bedside table, which she'd left face down, now closed and placed on the nightstand? Had the cushions on the sofa, which she sometimes plumped haphazardly, been smoothed into perfect rectangles? She started to doubt her own memory, questioning whether she had truly left things as she remembered, or if the intruder had already been there, making his silent, invisible adjustments.

The psychological impact was immense. The house, once her refuge, was becoming a stage for his meticulous, obsessive performances. Every object, every surface, was a potential canvas for his unsettling attentions. He was not just living within her walls; he was actively, painstakingly, engaging with the very fabric of her domestic life. He was the shadow that straightened picture frames, the unseen hand that aligned books on shelves, the silent force that repaired broken memories.

The mended vase sat on the mantelpiece, a stark, beautiful, and terrifying symbol of his presence. It was a constant reminder that he was not just hiding; he was actively participating, curating, and controlling the environment around her. His meticulous nature, once a source of faint unease, was now the chilling manifestation of a deep-seated obsession, a terrifying commitment to his unseen tenancy. He was not just an intruder; he was a phantom curator, and his work was far from finished. The silence of the house was no longer just the absence of sound; it was the pregnant pause before his next meticulous act. The dust was no longer just dust; it was a pristine canvas waiting for his careful, invisible touch. And Alice was no longer just living in her home; she was living in his meticulously curated exhibit, a prisoner of his obsessive order. The turquoise vase, once a symbol of a broken moment, was now a monument to a terrifying, pervasive control.

The chilling revelation of the mended vase had been the first crack in the carefully constructed dam of Alice's denial. She had spent days, weeks even, clinging to the notion of a lone, desperate individual seeking shelter. But the vase, so perfectly restored, whispered of something far more insidious: a presence that not only occupied her home but actively engaged with its very essence, a phantom curator meticulously tending to the relics of her life. This subtle imposition of order, this silent, invisible reshaping of her domestic landscape, had begun to gnaw at her sanity. Every misplaced item, every subtle shift in the arrangement of her belongings, now felt like a deliberate act, a coded message from the unseen inhabitant. The house, once her sanctuary, was slowly transforming into a meticulously curated diorama, and she, Alice, was merely a reluctant exhibit within it.

She had started to notice other things, small inconsistencies that, in the harsh light of the mended vase, took on a disturbing significance. A book on her nightstand, which she distinctly remembered leaving face down, would be found closed and neatly placed on the bedside table. The cushions on the sofa, often left slightly askew after her own hurried attempts at tidiness, would be found smoothed into perfect, almost military, rectangles. Had she really left that cupboard door ajar, or had he, in his silent patrol, nudged it shut with an imperceptible click? The house seemed to be breathing with a life of its own, a life dictated by an unseen hand, a will that imposed its own brand of order upon her chaos. The constant questioning, the self-doubt, began to erode her grip on reality. Was she losing her mind, or was this phantom truly engaged in a silent, relentless campaign to "improve" her life, one meticulously arranged object at a time?

The paranoia was a slow, creeping vine, its tendrils wrapping around her thoughts, constricting her breath. She found herself scrutinizing the very air she breathed, listening for the faintest whisper of movement, the slightest disruption in the pervasive silence. The intruder's meticulous nature, once a source of a vague unease, was now the chilling manifestation of a deep-seated obsession, a disturbing commitment to his unseen tenancy. He was not merely hiding; he was actively, painstakingly, engaging with the very fabric of her domestic life. He was the shadow that straightened picture frames, the unseen hand that aligned books on shelves, the silent force that repaired broken memories. The turquoise vase, once a symbol of a broken moment, was now a monument to a terrifying, pervasive control. It was a constant, gleaming reminder that he was not just living within her walls; he was curating them.

It was in the quiet hours of the afternoon, a time she usually spent immersed in her work, that the most devastating discovery of all began to unfold. A gnawing unease, a persistent feeling that something was amiss, drew her attention to the small, almost forgotten crawlspace beneath the back stairs. It was a cramped, dusty area, usually filled with forgotten boxes and the cobwebs of a neglected corner of the house. She had avoided it for months, the thought of disturbing its stillness as unappealing as the musty scent that emanated from its depths. But today, a primal urge, a visceral premonition, compelled her to investigate.

Armed with a flashlight, its beam cutting a shaky path through the gloom, Alice pushed aside a stack of old newspapers and squeezed through the narrow opening. The air was thick with the scent of damp earth and something else, something oddly familiar yet out of place. Her heart began to pound, a frantic rhythm against the suffocating silence. She swept the flashlight beam across the cluttered space, her eyes scanning for any sign of disturbance, any hint that her unseen tenant had breached this forgotten sanctuary.

And then she saw it. Tucked away behind a bulky, moth-eaten armchair, almost deliberately concealed, was a small pile of items that made her blood run cold. At first glance, they seemed insignificant, mere detritus. But as the flashlight beam settled, illuminating each object with stark clarity, a wave of nausea washed over her. There, nestled amongst the dust bunnies, were several bags of what looked like specialized dog food, a brand far superior, far more expensive, than the generic kibble she purchased for Duke. Alongside the food were an assortment of grooming tools – a fine-toothed comb, a specialized de-shedding brush, a small, soft-bristled brush that looked remarkably like it was designed for a dog's face. And then, her gaze fell upon a small, plush squeaky toy, a worn-out, slightly lopsided rabbit with one button eye missing. It was, unmistakably, a dog toy.

The realization dawned with a sickening certainty, each piece of evidence clicking into place with a horrifying precision. This wasn't just a stranger occupying her home; this was someone who had not only noticed her dog, Duke, but had actively, deliberately, engaged with him. He had been feeding Duke, grooming him, playing with him. He had been tending to her loyal companion, showering him with a level of care and attention that Alice, in her own distracted way, had perhaps been neglecting.

Her mind reeled, desperately trying to reconcile this newfound information with the image she had of Duke, her constant shadow, her furry confidant. Duke, who greeted her with ecstatic leaps and slobbery kisses every time she walked through the door. Duke, who slept curled at the foot of her bed, his soft snores a comforting presence in the dark. Duke, who was, she had always believed, utterly devoted to her.

The thought of her dog, a creature she trusted implicitly, a being whose sole purpose in life seemed to be her unwavering affection, accepting food and comfort from this intruder, was a betrayal so profound it felt like a physical blow. It shattered the illusion of safety, the fragile sense of security she had desperately tried to maintain. If Duke, her most loyal guardian, could be swayed, could form a bond with this hidden presence, then what did that say about her own judgment? What did it say about her own ability to discern truth from deception?

She pictured the scene in her mind, a horrifying tableau. The intruder, emerging from the shadows, offering Duke the premium food, stroking his fur with the specialized brush, perhaps even whispering reassurances to him in the dead of night. And Duke, his tail wagging, his eyes bright with innocent trust, accepting these clandestine gifts. It was a scenario that twisted Alice's gut, a grotesque perversion of the bond between human and animal.

She sank back against the dusty wall of the crawlspace, the flashlight beam wavering in her trembling hand. The specialized dog food wasn't just about sustenance; it was about bribery, about cultivating trust. The grooming tools weren't about hygiene; they were about a tender, intimate interaction, a calculated attempt to forge a connection. And the worn-out toy, so lovingly chosen, so clearly a favorite, was the ultimate symbol of their burgeoning friendship.

This wasn't an accidental discovery of the intruder's presence; this was a deliberate unveiling of his intimate interaction with Duke. He had sought out her dog, not as a means to an end, but as an end in itself. He had found solace, perhaps, in the uncomplicated affection of an animal, a creature who didn't question his presence, who didn't see him as a threat. And in doing so, he had inadvertently, or perhaps deliberately, alienated Alice from her own pet.

The weight of Duke's misplaced loyalty, his unwitting complicity in this strange domestic drama, was a burden Alice hadn't anticipated. She had always felt a certain reassurance in Duke's presence, a silent sentinel guarding her home. Now, that sentinel had apparently been compromised, his allegiance subtly, effectively, diverted. He was still her dog, she told herself, his love for her was surely still paramount. But the evidence in the crawlspace painted a starkly different picture, one that gnawed at her confidence, leaving her feeling exposed, vulnerable, and utterly alone.

She looked at Duke, who was now snoozing peacefully on the rug in the living room, oblivious to the turmoil he had unwittingly unleashed within her. His tail gave a soft thump against the floor as if sensing her gaze. Alice felt a pang of guilt, quickly followed by a surge of anger, then a crushing despair. How could he? How could he have allowed this?

She reached out a hesitant hand and gently stroked his head. He stirred, lifting his muzzle to lick her fingers, his brown eyes filled with the same unquestioning devotion she had always known. But now, that devotion felt tainted, tinged with the unsettling knowledge of his secret life, his secret friendships.

The intruder's care for Duke was a deeply personal violation. It wasn't just about her possessions or the order of her house; it was about her emotional core, her relationship with the one creature she believed was unequivocally hers. He had reached into the most intimate corners of her life and had somehow, in his silent, unseen way, woven himself into the fabric of her most trusted bonds.

Alice stood there, a solitary figure in the quiet house, the beam of her flashlight illuminating the dust motes dancing in the air. The specialized dog food, the grooming tools, the worn-out toy – they were not just items; they were tangible proof of an intimacy she couldn't comprehend, a betrayal she couldn't ignore. The intruder had not just invaded her home; he had infiltrated her heart, and in doing so, had left her feeling more adrift, more isolated, than ever before. The walls of her sanctuary, once a comfort, now felt like the bars of a cage, and she was trapped inside with an invisible enemy who had stolen the affections of her most faithful friend. The silence of the house, once a source of dread, was now a profound emptiness, a void where trust and security used to reside. She was no longer just sharing her home with an intruder; she was sharing it with a silent thief of loyalty, a ghost who had managed to charm her dog. The implications were chilling. If he could win Duke's affection, what other subtle manipulations was he capable of? What other aspects of her life was he slowly, insidiously, taking control of? The thought was a cold, hard knot of fear in her stomach.

# Chapter 4: The Shifting Sands of Trust

The discovery in the crawlspace had been a watershed moment, a stark, undeniable confirmation that her fear was not born of paranoia but of a tangible, encroaching reality. Yet, the weight of this knowledge pressed down on Alice with a suffocating loneliness. Her instinct, the primal urge to share the terrifying burden, led her to Tom. She needed his validation, his solid presence to anchor her drifting sanity. She found him in his study, poring over spreadsheets, the fluorescent light of his desk lamp casting a sterile glow on his focused brow.

"Tom," she began, her voice trembling, a stark contrast to the usual steadiness he associated with her. She held the worn-out rabbit toy, its single button eye staring blankly, a silent accuser. "I... I found this. And dog food. Special kind. And brushes. In the crawlspace." She laid out the evidence, her hands shaking as she presented the tangible proof of the intruder's intimate engagement with Duke. She recounted the details, the specialized brands, the meticulous grooming tools, the undeniable signs of a clandestine, affectionate relationship between her dog and the unseen inhabitant of her home. She expected a flicker of concern, a shared shiver of unease, perhaps even a call to the police. Instead, she received a sigh, a weary rub of his temples.

"Alice, darling," he said, his voice a placid murmur, devoid of any alarm. "Are you sure you're not just... overthinking things? We've moved, the house is new, it's a lot. You're stressed. And Duke, well, he's a dog. He finds things. Maybe a previous owner left them, or a neighbor's dog got in." He gestured vaguely, his eyes returning to the glowing screen. “It’s probably nothing. Just an old stash of pet supplies.”

His casual dismissal was a physical blow. “Nothing?” Alice’s voice rose, laced with a desperate urgency. “Tom, this wasn’t just some old stash. It was... it felt recent. And it was hidden. Like he was keeping it secret. He’s been feeding Duke. Caring for him. It’s like... like he’s trying to win him over.” The words tumbled out, each syllable an attempt to convey the chilling intimacy of the scene, the profound sense of betrayal. She spoke of the specialized food, the grooming tools, the worn toy, emphasizing the personal nature of these items. This wasn't a random act of vandalism or a search for shelter; this was a deliberate, tender engagement with her pet.

Tom finally looked up, his expression a mixture of impatience and weary affection. “Win him over? Alice, it’s a dog. They’re easily pleased. A bit of extra food, a new toy... Duke probably just thinks he’s found a new friend. You know how he is. Loves everyone.” He offered a weak smile, the kind one reserves for a child’s fanciful story. “You’re letting your imagination run away with you. This new place, it’s... it’s disorienting. You’re not sleeping well, are you?”

His words, meant to soothe, instead felt like a deliberate attempt to gaslight her. He was not hearing the terror in her voice; he was hearing the heightened emotions of a stressed woman. He was not seeing the evidence; he was seeing the product of an overactive imagination. The chasm between her lived reality and his perceived reality widened into an abyss. She tried again, her voice softer now, laced with a plea. “But Tom, the vase. The mended vase. You saw it.

And the way things are... subtly moved. It's not just Duke. It's him. He's here. He's been here, and he's been... taking care of things. Of

*us*." She couldn't bring herself to say "my things," because it had become more than that. It was an invasion of her very life, and he had been a willing, or perhaps oblivious, accomplice.

He finally put down his pen, turning his chair to face her fully. The expression on his face was one of paternalistic concern, not shared fear. "Alice, the vase was a shock, I agree. And yes, things can get misplaced. It happens. Especially in a house this size, when we're still settling in. But an intruder... actively caring for our dog? That's a big leap. It sounds like something out of a movie. You're letting this stress get to you. We should talk to someone. Maybe a therapist? Or a doctor, to get you something to help you sleep?"

The suggestion of therapy, of medication, of being labeled as mentally unstable, was the final straw. It wasn't just that he didn't believe her; it was that he was actively reframing her genuine terror as a symptom of delusion. He was positioning himself as the rational observer, the one who saw the "real" Alice – the stressed, overworked, slightly unbalanced wife – rather than the Alice who was staring into the abyss of a terrifying, silent invasion.

"So, you think I'm crazy?" Her voice was barely a whisper, the question heavy with the weight of her burgeoning isolation. The isolation wasn't just about being alone in the house at night anymore. It was about being fundamentally alone in her own experience, her own perception of reality. She was trapped in a narrative of terror that only she could see, while Tom remained comfortably cocooned in a world of normalcy, a world where dogs were just dogs and broken vases were just accidents.

Tom sighed, a sound that conveyed exhaustion more than empathy. "No, darling, I don't think you're crazy. I think you're under a lot of pressure. This move, my job... it's a lot for you. And this house is... it's old. It has its quirks. We all project our anxieties onto our surroundings sometimes. It's natural." He reached out, taking her hand, his touch cool and steady, a stark contrast to the frantic thrumming of her pulse. "Let's just try to relax, okay? Forget about the crawlspace. Forget about the vase for now. We'll have a nice dinner, watch a movie, and tomorrow, maybe we can go for a long walk, clear your head."

His words were a well-intentioned attempt to soothe, but they landed like stones, further burying her under the weight of her fear. He was offering comfort, but it was comfort rooted in denial, a denial that invalidated her experience. He was trying to erase her terror by dismissing its source. He couldn't grasp the chilling implication that her dog, her constant companion, the one creature she believed was purely devoted to her, had been subtly influenced, his affection potentially swayed by this unseen presence. If Duke, a being of pure, unadulterated instinct and loyalty, could be so easily swayed, what did that mean for Alice's own capacity for discernment? What subtle cues was she missing in her own life, in her own relationships, that were being manipulated by forces she couldn't comprehend?

The thought of Duke, curled at her feet, his soft snores a familiar comfort, now felt tainted. She remembered the way he would sometimes greet her with an almost frantic enthusiasm, a fervor that had always filled her with warmth. Now, a cold dread settled in her stomach. Had that enthusiasm been for her, or had it been a conditioned response, a learned behavior reinforced by clandestine treats and whispered reassurances from the shadows? The image of the intruder, offering Duke premium food and a comforting stroke, while Alice was perhaps rushing through her own interactions with her pet, preoccupied with work or the mundane stresses of life, was a painful, humiliating one. He had, in essence, become the better pet owner, at least in Duke's eyes.

She retreated, pulling her hand away from Tom's. The warmth of his touch, so readily offered, felt like an accusation. He didn't understand. He couldn't. His world was built on logic and observable facts, and her reality, increasingly, was a landscape of unsettling inconsistencies and gut-wrenching intuition. He saw stress; she saw a predator. He saw misplaced objects; she saw meticulous manipulation. He saw a dog's simple pleasures; she saw a calculated campaign of affection designed to disarm and betray.

"I can't just forget about it, Tom," she said, her voice flat, devoid of emotion. The fight had drained out of her, leaving behind a hollow ache. "It's not just stress. It's real." She looked at the worn rabbit toy still clutched in her hand. It was more than just a toy; it was a symbol of Duke's perceived betrayal, a tangible link to the intruder's intimate involvement with her pet. It was a quiet testament to the fact that her home, her sanctuary, was no longer solely hers.

Tom's gaze softened, a flicker of concern finally registering in his eyes, though it was tinged with frustration. "Alice, what do you want me to do? Call the police? Tell them a ghost is feeding the dog with fancy kibble?" He spread his hands in a gesture of helplessness, his tone laced with a subtle impatience. "We need to be rational about this."

Rationality, Alice thought, felt like a distant country she could no longer access. Her world had fractured, and the pieces no longer fit together in any coherent way. The rationality Tom clung to was a flimsy shield, incapable of protecting them from the encroaching darkness she felt so acutely. His dismissiveness wasn't just frustrating; it was actively isolating her. By refusing to acknowledge the validity of her fears, he was effectively pushing her further into the shadows, leaving her to confront the unknown alone.

She walked away, the worn rabbit toy feeling heavy in her palm. She didn't want to be rational. She wanted to be believed. She wanted to be understood. She wanted to feel safe in her own home, and the fact that she couldn't, and that the person closest to her couldn't see or validate that lack of safety, was a terrifying new dimension of her isolation. The house, which had always felt like a haven, now seemed to amplify her solitude. The silence, once a comfort, was now a suffocating blanket, punctuated by the phantom whispers of her own mounting dread. She was adrift, her anchor of trust in Tom severed, leaving her to navigate the treacherous currents of her own fear with no compass, no guide, and no one to share the terrifying journey. The realization that her deepest fears were being met with polite skepticism and suggestions of mental instability was a chilling confirmation of her aloneness. It wasn't just an intruder in her home; it was an intruder in her trust, a phantom hand siphoning away the foundations of her security, leaving her feeling utterly, terrifyingly, alone. She was an island in a sea of denial, and the waves of her fear were crashing against its shores, with no ship in sight to offer rescue.

The house, once a sanctuary, had begun to feel like a stage where a play of unsettling normalcy was being performed, with Alice as the only one privy to the actors' whispered improprieties. Tom's reaction to the crawlspace discovery had been the first jarring dissonance, a jarring note in the melody of their shared life. But it was the subsequent days, the subtle yet persistent shifts in his demeanor, that began to weave a new, more insidious narrative of unease. He had always been a creature of habit, his days a predictable rhythm of work, quiet evenings, and predictable routines. Now, that rhythm was fractured, replaced by a series of erratic beats that threw Alice off balance.

He started staying out later, his workday bleeding into the twilight hours with increasing frequency. At first, Alice attributed it to the pressures of his new role, the need to impress, to establish himself. He'd come home, his tie loosened, his shoulders hunched with a fatigue that seemed deeper than mere physical exhaustion. He would offer a perfunctory kiss, a mumbled excuse about late meetings or unexpected deadlines, and retreat to his study, the door closing with a soft click that felt like a seal on a whispered secret. The scent of stale coffee and the low hum of his computer would seep through the crack, a constant reminder of his preoccupation, his distance.

These late nights weren't just about work, though. Alice noticed other things. The faint, almost imperceptible tremor in his hands when he reached for his coffee cup in the morning. The way his gaze would dart around the room when she entered, as if he were checking for unseen observers. The sudden, uncharacteristic outbursts of frustration over trivial matters – a misplaced remote, a slightly overcooked piece of toast – that would flare up like dry tinder and then vanish as quickly as they appeared, leaving behind an awkward silence and a bewildered Alice. He'd apologize, his voice strained, offering vague explanations about stress, about being on edge. But his apologies never quite reached the point of genuine reassurance. They felt rehearsed, like lines delivered from a script he was struggling to remember.

One evening, he came home unusually early, around dusk. Alice was in the kitchen, preparing dinner, the aroma of roasting chicken filling the air. The front door opened and closed with a force that rattled the framed photographs on the hallway table. She heard his heavy footsteps, not heading towards his study, but directly towards the living room. Curious, she followed the sound. She found him standing by the large bay window, his back to her, staring out into the deepening gloom of the garden. He was dressed in his work clothes, but his jacket was slung over a chair, and his shirt sleeves were rolled up to his elbows, revealing forearms she hadn't seen in months, bare and unusually tense.

"Tom? You're home early," she said, her voice light, trying to dispel the palpable tension that seemed to emanate from him.

He didn't turn immediately. When he finally did, his eyes, usually warm and steady, held a hunted look. His face was pale, and a faint sheen of sweat slicked his brow. He blinked, as if adjusting to a sudden light. "Just... needed some air," he mumbled, his voice rough. He avoided her gaze, his eyes flicking towards the kitchen, then back to the window.

"Everything okay?" Alice took a step closer, her hand reaching out instinctively.

He flinched, a barely perceptible recoil, and then straightened his shoulders. "Fine, Alice. Just... a long day. You know how it is." He forced a smile, but it didn't reach his eyes. It was a rictus, a strained imitation of his usual warmth. He picked up his jacket, slung it over his shoulder, and began to walk towards the stairs. "I think I'll just... lie down for a bit. Feeling a bit off."

His departure left Alice standing alone in the living room, the scent of roasting chicken suddenly cloying. The way he had recoiled, the hunted look in his eyes – it was too much to dismiss as mere fatigue. It was a visceral reaction, a stark departure from the man she knew. She walked to the window he had been staring out of, her gaze following his. The garden was quiet, bathed in the muted hues of twilight. Nothing seemed out of the ordinary. The rose bushes were still, the lawn undisturbed. Yet, Tom's reaction suggested he had seen something, or perhaps, he had been seen. The thought sent a shiver down her spine. Was he being watched? Or was he the one watching?

The next few days were a tapestry of increasingly perplexing incidents. Tom began to spend more time in his study, but it wasn't the usual focused work that occupied him. Alice would hear him pacing, the sound of his footsteps a restless counterpoint to the ticking clock. Sometimes, she'd hear him on the phone, his voice hushed, urgent, and when he saw her, he would abruptly end the call, a guilty flush rising on his cheeks. He became evasive, his answers to her questions often vague and contradictory.

One afternoon, she went to the study to ask him about dinner plans. The door was slightly ajar, and she saw him at his desk, his back to her. He was wearing his reading glasses, and his head was bent low over a stack of papers, but he wasn't reading. He was meticulously tearing them into tiny pieces, his movements sharp and jerky. As she watched, he held up a fragment, his fingers hovering over it, a look of intense concentration on his face, before tossing it into the wastepaper basket. It wasn't the act of destruction itself that unnerved her, but the intense, almost ritualistic care with which he performed it. It spoke of a desperate attempt to erase something, to obliterate evidence.

"Tom?" she called out softly, pushing the door open further.

He jumped, the papers scattering from his lap. He spun around, his face a mask of alarm, quickly replaced by that forced smile. "Alice! You startled me." He quickly began to scoop up the torn pieces. "Just... clearing out some old files. Things I didn't need anymore."

"They looked like they were from your office," Alice said, her voice calm, but her mind racing. His office had strict protocols for document disposal; such a method was unheard of.

"Just some... personal notes," he deflected, his eyes darting away from hers. "Nothing important." He stood up, gathering the torn scraps in his hands. "I was just about to take these out. Don't worry about it." He clutched the pieces tightly, as if shielding them from her view, and practically fled the room, leaving Alice standing in the doorway, a cold knot of suspicion tightening in her stomach.

His disappearances became more frequent and less explainable. He'd leave the house in the morning, but wouldn't return until well after dark, sometimes not at all, claiming to have stayed at a hotel for an urgent project. He was never able to provide any concrete details about these projects, his explanations always a vague jumble of business jargon that Alice couldn't penetrate. He started to appear disheveled more often. His suits, once impeccably pressed, would sometimes be creased. His hair, usually neatly styled, would look unbrushed. There were even times, she noticed with a growing sense of alarm, when there were faint smudges of dirt on his hands, as if he had been working with soil or something similar.

One afternoon, she found him in the garage, hunched over a small, nondescript metal box. He was wearing gloves, and his movements were furtive, as if he were engaged in something illicit. When he heard her approach, he slammed the box shut, a sharp metallic clang that echoed in the confined space.

"Tom, what are you doing?" Alice asked, her voice tinged with apprehension.

He turned, his face flushed. "Just... organizing some things. Things from the move. Didn't want them getting damaged." He gestured vaguely at the box, which was plain and unadorned.

"What's in the box?" she pressed, her gaze fixed on his hands, which were still encased in the dark gardening gloves.

He hesitated for a fraction of a second too long. "Just... old tools. You wouldn't be interested." He picked up the box, his grip tight. "I need to put this away somewhere safe." He moved past her, his stride hurried, leaving Alice in the silent garage, the lingering scent of motor oil and something metallic in the air. The gloves, the secretive behavior, the metal box – it all coalesced into a disturbing picture, a mosaic of actions that didn't fit the Tom she thought she knew.

The change wasn't just in his actions; it was in his very essence. The easy laughter, the comforting presence, the unwavering certainty she had always found in him – these were eroding, replaced by a brittle facade of strained composure. He was a man walking a tightrope, and Alice could see the frayed edges of the rope, the terrifying drop below. He seemed perpetually on edge, his nerves frayed like old wiring. A sudden noise – the creak of a floorboard, the distant bark of a dog – would make him jump, his eyes widening with a fleeting panic that he quickly masked.

He started making cryptic remarks, veiled references that Alice couldn't decipher. Once, while they were watching the news, a segment about a missing person flashed across the screen. Tom's hand tightened on his glass, his knuckles turning white. "Some people just... disappear," he murmured, his voice barely audible, his gaze fixed on the flickering images. "And no one ever finds them." He then abruptly changed the subject, his face a mask of forced casualness, but the intensity of his gaze, the tremor in his voice, lingered in Alice's mind long after the news report had ended.

Another time, he was out in the garden, ostensibly weeding. Alice watched him from the kitchen window. He was kneeling, his back to the house, his movements precise and methodical. But then, he paused, looking around furtively, before pulling out a small trowel and digging a shallow hole near the fence line. He placed something small and dark into the hole, covered it quickly with soil, and then, with painstaking care, smoothed the surface, as if erasing any trace of his activity. He looked around again, his brow furrowed, before resuming his weeding. The clandestine burial, the furtive glances – it was chilling. What was he burying? And why the secrecy?

Alice found herself scrutinizing every aspect of his behavior, her mind a relentless detective, sifting through the debris of his former self for clues. She started to notice the small inconsistencies, the tiny cracks in his carefully constructed narrative. He'd talk about a meeting with a client, but when Alice casually mentioned she'd seen that client's car in their neighborhood a few days prior, Tom's explanation became flustered and vague. He'd claim to be working late at his office, but his phone records, which she'd never had a reason to check before, showed no calls made or received during those late hours.

The shift in his behavior was insidious, a slow creep of darkness that began to eclipse the man she had loved. The trust she had placed in him, once as solid as bedrock, was now beginning to crumble, replaced by a gnawing apprehension. It was no longer just the unsettling presence in the house that occupied her thoughts; it was Tom himself. The fear that had begun as a whisper in the crawlspace was now a clamor in her mind, a chilling question echoing in the silence: what secrets was Tom hiding, and why was she no longer privy to them? The man who had once been her rock, her confidant, was becoming an enigma, a stranger in her own home. His uncharacteristic behavior was not just a personal struggle; it was a new, deeply disturbing layer to the mystery that was unfolding around her, a mystery that now seemed to have its roots not in the shadows of her home, but in the heart of her marriage. The sands of trust were indeed shifting, and Alice was finding herself on precarious ground, unsure of whom – or what – to believe.

The gentle cadence of Duke's breathing, usually a comforting presence by her feet, had become a source of quiet anxiety for Alice. He still sought her out, nudging her hand with his wet nose, his tail offering a tentative thud against the floorboards when she returned home. But there was a new reserve in his affection, a subtle hesitation that hadn't been there before. It was as if a small, invisible barrier had been erected between them, a boundary she couldn't cross. He would watch her with an unnerving stillness, his deep brown eyes, once so open and loving, now holding a guarded expression, a flicker of something she couldn't quite name – concern, perhaps, or even a nascent apprehension.

This shift was most pronounced when Tom was around, particularly when he was agitated. Alice had noticed it with a growing sense of dread. Tom's recent erratic behavior, his withdrawn silences and sudden bursts of anger, had left him a coiled spring of tension. In those moments, Duke, who had always been a loyal shadow to Alice, would gravitate towards Tom. He would lay his head on Tom's lap, offering a silent, unwavering support that felt like a betrayal. Alice watched, her heart aching, as Tom would absently stroke Duke's fur, his own anxieties seeming to find a strange solace in the dog's solid presence. It was a peculiar dynamic, a palpable camaraderie that excluded her, a silent alliance formed in the face of an unseen threat that only Tom and Duke seemed to fully comprehend.

Alice tried to rationalize it. Perhaps Duke sensed Tom's distress and was simply responding to his master's emotional state. Dogs were intuitive, after all. But the instinct felt deeper, more rooted in a shared secret. There were times, sitting in the living room in the late afternoon, the house hushed and expectant, when Alice would swear she heard it – a faint, almost imperceptible scratching, a rustling sound that seemed to emanate from within the very walls of their home. At first, she dismissed it as the house settling, the wind in the eaves, or perhaps even Duke's own movements. But then she'd see Duke's head lift, his ears swivel, his body tensing as he listened intently to the very same silence she was trying to ignore. He would stare fixedly at a particular section of the wall, his posture rigid, a low growl rumbling in his chest, a sound so subtle Alice could barely register it. And when she looked at him, he would glance at her, then back at the wall, as if waiting for her to finally acknowledge what he already knew.

He was the only one who seemed to truly hear it, to react to it. Alice would point to a spot on the wall, her voice hushed, "Duke, did you hear that?" But Tom, when present, would offer a dismissive wave of his hand, a tight smile. "Just the pipes, Alice. Old house, remember?"

His words were meant to be reassuring, but they landed like stones, heavy with an unspoken dismissal. He never seemed to hear the sounds that so clearly agitated Duke, or if he did, he chose to ignore them. It was as if Duke's heightened senses were being deliberately tuned out, his awareness dampened by an unseen force, or perhaps, by Tom's own determined will.

This perceived division in Duke's loyalty was a constant, gnawing ache. Duke had been her confidante, her furry shadow since they had moved into the house. He was the one who greeted her with unbridled joy after a long day, the one who nudged her hand during moments of sadness, the one who instinctively knew when she needed comfort. Now, that unwavering connection felt frayed. When Tom was in one of his withdrawn moods, Duke would be by his side, a silent sentinel. When Alice tried to engage Duke in their usual games of fetch in the garden, his responses were a little less enthusiastic, his attention often drifting back towards the house, towards the unseen disturbances within.

One evening, as Alice sat by the fireplace, a book open in her lap but her eyes unfocused, she heard it again. A faint scuttling sound, like tiny claws on plaster. Duke, who had been dozing at her feet, suddenly sat bolt upright, his ears pricked forward. He let out a soft whine, a sound of distress, and then, instead of looking to Alice for reassurance, he turned and padded silently towards the hallway, his gaze fixed on the wall separating the living room from the master bedroom. Alice followed his movement with her eyes, her own breath catching in her throat. She could hear the faint sound too now, a whisper against the silence.

"Duke?" she whispered, her voice trembling.

The dog didn't respond. He was mesmerized, his body rigid, his tail held low. Then, he did something that sent a jolt of ice through Alice's veins. He began to scratch gently at the base of the wall, his nails making a soft, rhythmic sound. It wasn't the frantic digging of a dog trying to get to a rodent; it was deliberate, almost investigative. He paused, as if listening, then continued his soft scratching.

Alice rose from her chair, her legs feeling like lead. She moved towards Duke, her eyes fixed on the wall he was so intently studying. "What is it, boy?" she murmured, her hand reaching out to stroke his back. He flinched slightly under her touch, his focus unbroken. He nudged his nose against the wall, then looked back at her, a peculiar expression in his eyes – a mixture of pleading and urgency.

Tom appeared in the doorway of the living room, drawn by Duke's unusual behavior. He stood there for a moment, his arms crossed, his expression unreadable. Alice turned to him, her eyes wide with a desperate need for his validation, for a simple, rational explanation. "Tom, Duke is hearing something in the wall. Listen." She held her breath, straining to hear over the thumping of her own heart.

Tom listened for a moment, a faint frown creasing his brow. Then, he let out a sigh that seemed to carry the weight of his recent burdens. "It's nothing, Alice. Just the house. You're both on edge." He walked over to Duke, placing a hand on the dog's head. "Come on, boy. Let's go for a walk." He began to pull Duke gently away from the wall, but the dog resisted, planting his paws and looking back at the offending section of plaster with an insistent gaze.

"He's never done this before, Tom," Alice insisted, her voice rising slightly. "He's hearing something. I can hear it too now, faintly."

Tom's jaw tightened. He gave Duke a firmer tug. "He's just being a dog, Alice. He probably smells a mouse. Or maybe he's just bored." He forced a smile, but it was a strained, hollow thing. "Don't let it get to you." He led Duke out of the room, the dog casting a worried glance back at Alice before disappearing down the hall.

Alice remained standing by the wall, her hand pressed against the cool plaster. She could still hear it, a faint, elusive sound that seemed to mock her attempts at rationalization. Duke's reaction, his unwavering focus on that specific spot, was more convincing than any dismissal. It was a stark reminder that she was no longer the sole keeper of Duke's affections, nor the sole recipient of his loyal observations. He was divided, his instincts pulled in two directions, and that division was a mirror to the fractured trust within their home. He was a dog, yes, but he was also a barometer, and his readings were alarming, indicating a fault line running deep beneath the surface of their carefully constructed reality. The shared sanctuary of their home was being invaded, not just by an unseen presence, but by a palpable sense of unease that was beginning to erode the very foundations of their domestic peace, and Duke, her once steadfast companion, was now a living testament to this unsettling shift.

The bathroom mirror, usually a clear reflection of Alice's weary face, was now a canvas for his insidious whispers. She'd stepped out of the shower, the lingering steam clinging to her skin, and her eyes had immediately fallen upon it. In the hazy condensation, a single word had been traced, as if by a phantom finger: *Watched*. It was stark, accusatory, and sent a tremor through her already frayed nerves. She blinked, rubbed her eyes, but the word remained, mocking her attempt to dismiss it as a trick of the light or a fleeting hallucination. This was no accident. This was deliberate. He was not merely present; he was actively engaging with her, playing a game where her sanity was the prize.

Panic, cold and sharp, began to prickle at the edges of her consciousness. She spun around, scanning the small bathroom, her heart hammering against her ribs. The ventilation fan hummed its monotonous tune, the only sound besides her own ragged breathing. The window was latched, the door to the bedroom closed. There was no one there. Yet, the word

*Watched* persisted, a chilling testament to his unseen presence, a taunt that insinuated his gaze was everywhere, on her, in her home, in her very thoughts. She found herself scrutinizing the grout lines, the tiles, as if expecting to find a hidden lens, a clandestine peephole. The feeling of being observed was no longer a vague unease; it was a suffocating, tangible weight.

This wasn't the first subtle intrusion, she realized with a fresh wave of dread. A week ago, it had been the book. She'd left it on the bedside table, a worn copy of a classic novel she'd been meaning to revisit, its spine cracked and pages dog-eared. The next morning, it lay open on the coffee table downstairs, not to a random page, but to a passage detailing a character's descent into madness, their paranoia fueled by unseen forces. The underlined sentence, stark against the faded ink, read: "He could feel eyes upon him, even in the deepest darkness, and the knowledge was a slow poison." At the time, she'd dismissed it as a bookmark falling out, or perhaps Tom had been reading it. But Tom had vehemently denied touching it, his brow furrowed with a familiar frustration that Alice was beginning to doubt. Now, with the mirror's chilling inscription, the deliberate nature of these "coincidences" became terrifyingly clear.

He was testing her, pushing her boundaries, observing her reactions. It was a psychological war waged in the quiet moments, in the spaces between breaths, designed to erode her sense of security and self. He wanted her to doubt herself, to question her own perceptions, to become a prisoner within her own mind. The house, once a sanctuary, was transforming into a labyrinth of suspicion. Every creak of the floorboards, every shadow that danced in the periphery, every unexplained sound was amplified, scrutinized, and attributed to his malevolent design.

Alice found herself developing a heightened awareness, a hyper-vigilance that was both exhausting and terrifying. She started meticulously checking locks, not just on doors and windows, but on cabinets and even the drawers of her own dresser. The thought of him being able to access her belongings, to read her private thoughts through the pages of her books, was deeply unsettling. She began to feel a profound violation, a stripping away of her privacy that went beyond mere intrusion. He was not just entering her home; he was entering her mind.

The subtle manipulations extended to other senses. A faint scent of jasmine, a perfume she hadn't worn in years and that Tom detested, would occasionally waft through the house, only to vanish as quickly as it appeared. It was a scent that evoked a specific, unsettling memory from her past, a memory she rarely allowed herself to dwell on. It was as if he had scoured her past, unearthed her vulnerabilities, and was now deploying them like psychological weapons. Or perhaps it was a more primal fear – the fear of the unknown, the fear of what lies just beyond our rational grasp.

She started to notice how objects seemed to subtly shift their positions. A photograph on the mantelpiece would be tilted at a slightly different angle, a pair of scissors on her desk would be moved an inch to the left, a teacup left to dry by the sink would be found neatly placed on the draining board. These were minor alterations, easily attributable to forgetfulness or absentmindedness. But when they occurred with a disturbing frequency, and always in a way that hinted at a deliberate, almost mocking, precision, they began to chip away at her sanity. She would stare at the misplaced object, her mind racing, trying to recall if she had moved it herself. The uncertainty was the most insidious part, the slow erosion of her confidence in her own memory.

The sounds were perhaps the most pervasive form of his torment. It wasn't just the scratching in the walls that Duke had reacted to. Now, there were other sounds, faint and fleeting, that Alice could barely dismiss as the house settling or the wind. A soft, almost imperceptible whisper that seemed to brush against her ear when she was alone in a room. A rhythmic tapping, like fingernails on glass, that would cease the moment she tried to pinpoint its source. A muffled thud from upstairs when she knew Tom was out, or a soft scraping from the attic that sent shivers down her spine.

She found herself holding her breath, straining to hear, her ears becoming acutely attuned to the silence, trying to discern the unnatural within the natural. This constant state of alert was taking a toll. Sleep offered little respite. Her dreams were a jumbled tapestry of half-remembered fears, often featuring shadowy figures lurking just out of sight, whispering her name, or the chilling sensation of being watched by unseen eyes. She would wake up in a cold sweat, her heart pounding, the lingering dread of her dream clinging to her like a shroud.

Tom's reactions, or rather his lack thereof, only exacerbated her growing isolation. When she tried to articulate her fears, to explain the unsettling occurrences, he would often offer a dismissive smile, a weary sigh. "Alice, you're imagining things," he'd say, his voice tinged with a patience that was starting to feel like exasperation. "It's the stress. This house... it plays tricks on your mind." He would then proceed to meticulously check the locks, re-latch the windows, and offer a pat on her shoulder, a gesture that was meant to be comforting but now felt like a placating dismissal. He never seemed to hear the whispers, never saw the scrawled words, never felt the subtle shifts. Or perhaps he

*did*, and he was choosing to ignore them, to pretend that everything was normal. This possibility, that he was complicit in her torment, either actively or passively, was a bitter pill to swallow.

His denials, once a source of reassurance, now felt like a confirmation of her worst fears. If Tom, her anchor, her partner, couldn't or wouldn't acknowledge these disturbances, then who could she turn to? Was she truly losing her grip on reality? The intruder, by orchestrating these subtle, deniable intrusions, was isolating her, making her doubt her own sanity, and in doing so, making her utterly vulnerable. He was chipping away at the foundations of her trust – trust in her surroundings, trust in her own perceptions, and most painfully, trust in Tom.

The atmosphere in the house had become so thick with unspoken tension that it felt almost palpable. Alice found herself tiptoeing through rooms, her senses on high alert, constantly scanning for any anomaly. She would spend hours staring at the walls, listening for the faintest whisper of movement, her imagination conjuring grotesque scenarios. The comfort of familiarity had been replaced by a pervasive sense of dread. The very air seemed to hum with an unseen, malevolent energy.

One afternoon, while Alice was alone in the kitchen, preparing lunch, she heard it. A faint, metallic clicking sound, coming from the pantry. It was rhythmic, deliberate. Her blood ran cold. She froze, her hand hovering over a chopping board, her ears straining. The clicking continued, slow and steady. It wasn't the scurrying of a rodent; it was too precise, too mechanical. She could feel her heart pounding a frantic rhythm against her ribs. She knew, with a certainty that chilled her to the bone, that this was another message, another act of psychological warfare.

Slowly, silently, she moved towards the pantry door. Her fingers trembled as she reached for the handle. She hesitated for a fraction of a second, bracing herself for what she might find. Then, with a deep, shaky breath, she pulled the door open.

The pantry was a small, walk-in space, filled with shelves of canned goods, jars of preserves, and bags of flour. The clicking had stopped the moment she'd opened the door. Everything appeared normal, undisturbed. But then her eyes landed on the shelf directly in front of her. A small, tarnished silver locket, one she hadn't seen in years, a forgotten trinket from her childhood, sat perched precariously on the edge of a shelf. It wasn't just sitting there. It was positioned directly in front of a small, almost invisible hole in the back wall of the pantry, a hole she had never noticed before. And it was open.

Inside the locket, where a photograph should have been, was a tiny, folded piece of paper. Her hands shaking so violently she could barely grasp it, Alice picked up the locket. It felt impossibly cold against her skin. With fumbling fingers, she unfolded the minuscule note. The handwriting was spidery, almost illegible, but the message was chillingly clear. It contained just three words, written in a dark, almost black ink:

*I see inside.*

Alice gasped, dropping the locket. It clattered against the linoleum floor, the tiny note fluttering out. Her breath hitched in her throat. I see inside. Inside what? Inside the locket? Inside her home? Or, more terrifyingly, inside her mind? The implication was clear: he knew her deepest fears, her most private thoughts, her hidden vulnerabilities. He was not just an intruder; he was an intimate tormentor, capable of reaching into the very core of her being.

She stumbled back from the pantry, her legs weak, her mind reeling. The carefully constructed walls of her composure were crumbling. The subtle messages, the shifting objects, the phantom sounds – they were all part of a meticulously planned campaign to dismantle her sanity, to make her doubt her own reality. He was turning her home, her sanctuary, into a psychological battlefield, and she was losing. The insidious nature of his attacks was precisely their subtlety. There was no overt violence, no physical threat, just a constant, gnawing erosion of her peace of mind, leaving her feeling exposed, vulnerable, and utterly alone. The silence that followed the discovery of the locket was the most deafening of all, filled with the echoes of his unseen presence and the terrifying certainty that he was always watching, always listening, always finding new ways to breach the fragile defenses of her mind.

The weight of the locket, cold and alien in Alice's trembling hand, felt like a physical manifestation of her unraveling. The tiny, folded paper, bearing its insidious message, was proof – irrefutable proof, she had desperately hoped – that she wasn't succumbing to delusion. It was a tangible artifact of his intrusion, a shard of his malevolent presence. The urge to confront Tom, to force him to acknowledge the reality she was living, became a desperate, consuming need. She clutched the locket, the delicate metal digging into her palm, and headed for the living room, her movements jerky, her mind a tempest of fear and burgeoning suspicion.

Tom was engrossed in his laptop, the blue light casting a pale, anemic glow on his face. The usual quiet hum of the house was amplified by the frantic thumping of Alice's heart. She stood in the doorway for a moment, watching him, searching for any flicker of recognition, any sign that he was as tethered to this reality as she was. But he was lost in his digital world, his brow furrowed in concentration, the picture of normalcy. It was a normalcy that now felt like a meticulously crafted facade.

"Tom," she began, her voice a strained whisper, barely audible above the whir of the computer. He didn't look up immediately, his fingers still flying across the keyboard. Alice's resolve wavered for a fleeting instant. Perhaps he was right. Perhaps she

*was* overreacting. The thought was a siren's call, promising a return to a world where shadows were just shadows and creaks were just the house settling. But then her fingers tightened around the locket, and the chilling memory of that tiny, folded paper surged back, anchoring her to the terrifying truth.

He finally looked up, his expression shifting from mild irritation to a practiced, weary patience. "What is it, Alice? I'm in the middle of something." His tone was clipped, laced with an impatience that was becoming a familiar sting.

Alice took a deep breath, forcing herself to meet his gaze. She held out her hand, palm open, revealing the tarnished locket. "I found this," she said, her voice steadier this time. "In the pantry. It... it had a note inside." She carefully extracted the minuscule paper and unfolded it, holding it out to him.

*I see inside.*

Tom's eyes flickered from the locket to the note, then back to Alice's face. For a moment, a flicker of something – surprise? Recognition? – crossed his features. But it was gone as quickly as it appeared, replaced by a look of profound unease. He didn't reach for the note, didn't ask to examine the locket more closely. Instead, his gaze darted around the room, his pupils dilating slightly. A muscle twitched in his jaw.

"Where did you say you found this?" he asked, his voice suddenly sharper, lacking its earlier practiced calm.

"The pantry," Alice repeated, her hope beginning to dwindle. His reaction wasn't one of shared concern, of dawning understanding. It was... apprehension. A subtle, almost imperceptible shift in his demeanor that sent a new wave of cold dread through her.

He stood up abruptly, his chair scraping loudly against the hardwood floor. "Right. That's it. We need to go."

Alice blinked, taken aback by the suddenness of his declaration. "Go? Go where? What do you mean, 'that's it'?" Her voice rose, a tremor of alarm running through it. "Tom, this is serious. He's in the house. He's leaving messages, watching us."

Tom didn't meet her eyes. He was already moving towards the hallway, his movements jerky and uncoordinated. "I know, I know. Just... just grab your coat. We're leaving. Now." He seemed to be speaking to himself as much as to her, his words tumbling out in a rushed, anxious torrent.

"But... but who is 'he'?" Alice pressed, her mind struggling to keep pace with his panicked flight. "You finally believe me, don't you? You know who it is?" The question hung in the air, heavy with unspoken accusations.

Tom stopped at the foot of the stairs, his back to her. He ran a hand through his hair, his shoulders hunched. "It doesn't matter who it is, Alice. What matters is that we get out of here. This house... it's not safe." He turned, and the look on his face was not the look of a concerned husband protecting his wife. It was the look of a man caught in a trap, desperate to escape. His eyes were wide, darting, his breath coming in short, shallow gasps. There was a palpable fear radiating from him, but it wasn't fear

*for* her. It was a raw, primal fear, as if *he* was the one being hunted.

"Not safe? Tom, you're acting as if you know something," Alice said, her voice dropping to a near whisper. The suspicion that had been a faint, nagging doubt was solidifying into a terrifying certainty. His frantic insistence on leaving, his evasiveness, his palpable terror – it all pointed to something far more sinister than a stranger breaking into their home. "What are you not telling me? You know who's doing this, don't you?"

He flinched at her words, a muscle in his cheek spasming. "Don't be ridiculous, Alice. I just want us to be safe. This is... this is too much. We can't stay here." He grabbed her arm, his grip surprisingly strong, his nails digging into her skin. "Come on. We have to go. Now!"

Alice recoiled, not just from his physical touch, but from the implication of his words. His fear was contagious, but it was also deeply unsettling. He wasn't talking about calling the police, about gathering evidence, about confronting the intruder. He was talking about fleeing, about abandoning their home, as if they were fleeing from something far more immediate and personal than a phantom stalker. His panic was a red flag, a stark warning sign that something was terribly wrong, and that the problem wasn't just outside the walls of their home.

"Where are we going?" she asked, her voice barely audible. "Why are you so afraid, Tom?"

He pulled her towards the front door, his movements hurried. "Away from here. That's all that matters. Just... trust me. We need to get away from this place." His eyes pleaded with her, but there was an underlying urgency, a desperate edge to his plea that screamed of something far more than a simple desire for safety. It felt like a plea for her to overlook the obvious, to ignore the mounting evidence, to simply run.

As he fumbled with the deadbolt, Alice's gaze swept over him. The sweat beading on his forehead, the tremor in his hands, the way his eyes constantly scanned the windows, as if expecting an attack at any moment. This wasn't the behavior of a man trying to protect his wife from an unseen threat. This was the behavior of a man terrified of being discovered. His urgency, his panic, his insistence on leaving without any logical explanation – it all coalesced into a sickening realization. He wasn't just aware of the threat; he was somehow intimately connected to it. His fear wasn't for her safety, but for his own exposure. The shifting sands of trust had finally given way, revealing a chasm of deception beneath her feet. He knew. He knew who was tormenting her, and his frantic urge to flee wasn't about protection; it was about escape. And in that moment, surrounded by the suffocating silence of their home, Alice understood that the true danger wasn't just in the shadows, but in the person standing right beside her.

# Chapter 5: The Unraveling Truth

The jarring slam of the front door echoed in the sudden quiet of the house, a punctuation mark on Tom's frantic exodus. Alice stood frozen in the hallway, the metallic tang of fear and betrayal still sharp on her tongue. His desperate haste, the raw panic in his eyes – it wasn't the protective fear of a husband shielding his wife from an unseen enemy. It was the fear of a cornered animal, desperately seeking an escape route, not from a threat without, but from a truth within. The locket, still clutched in her hand, felt less like a clue to an external tormentor and more like a key to a secret locked within her own home, within her own marriage. The realization settled in her stomach like a cold, hard stone: Tom knew. And his knowledge wasn't born of shared victimhood, but of complicity, or something equally damning.

Her own fear, once a palpable entity, now coalesced into a steely resolve. If Tom was unwilling to face the truth, then she would unearth it herself. The house, which had once been a sanctuary, now felt like a stage set for a psychological drama, and she was determined to find the script. Her gaze drifted towards Tom's study, a room she rarely entered, a space he guarded with a quiet, almost imperceptible possessiveness. It was a space that, until now, had represented a harmonious division of their lives, his work and her world. But now, it felt like the repository of his secrets.

With a deliberate exhale, Alice turned, her footsteps soft on the plush carpet. The study door was unlocked, a testament to Tom's complacency, perhaps his belief that she would never dare to venture into his sanctuary. The room was a monument to his organized, meticulous nature. Bookshelves lined one wall, filled with technical manuals and dense legal texts. His desk was impeccably tidy, the surface cleared save for his laptop and a single, minimalist desk lamp. The air in the room was still, carrying the faint, sterile scent of electronics and paper.

Her hands, though steady, trembled slightly as she approached the desk. The laptop was closed, its dark screen a silent sentinel. Her heart hammered against her ribs, a frantic drumbeat against the oppressive silence. What was she looking for? A confession? A motive? A tangible link between the torment she was experiencing and Tom's increasingly erratic behavior? She didn't know, but the need to

*know* was a powerful, driving force.

Hesitantly, she lifted the lid. The screen flickered to life, displaying the familiar login screen. Tom's password. She knew it, of course. A simple, yet infuriatingly secure combination he'd chosen years ago, a blend of their anniversary and their pet's name. She typed it in, her fingers clumsy, and the desktop bloomed into existence, a landscape of organized folders and icons.

Her initial searches were broad, almost random. She navigated through his email accounts, his cloud storage, his browsing history. Hours blurred into a monotonous cycle of scrolling, clicking, and analyzing. She found mundane emails, work-related documents, and countless articles on financial markets – a stark contrast to the unsettling reality she was beginning to uncover. The sheer volume of information was overwhelming, a digital haystack where the needle of truth was likely buried deep. Frustration began to gnaw at her, the initial surge of resolve starting to ebb. Had she been too hasty in her assumptions? Was she projecting her own fears onto Tom's innocent, if slightly secretive, life?

Then, her eyes fell upon an icon tucked away in a less-frequented corner of the desktop. It was a simple folder, labeled with an innocuous string of numbers and letters that meant nothing to her. It wasn't a typical file name; it felt deliberate, almost like a coded reference. A prickle of unease, the kind that precedes a significant discovery, crawled up her spine. She double-clicked.

The folder opened, revealing a series of subfolders, each named with a date. Curiosity, now laced with a growing sense of dread, compelled her to click on the earliest one. Inside, she found a jumble of files: scanned documents, photographs, and audio recordings. The scanned documents were official reports, police incident reports, and court filings. As she began to read, her breath caught in her throat. The dates on the reports aligned with a period of time several years ago, a period that Tom had always been vague about, referencing it only as a "difficult time."

The first document she opened was a newspaper clipping, the digital image faded but legible. The headline screamed: "Hit-and-Run Driver Still at Large; Victim in Critical Condition." The article detailed a tragic accident that had occurred on a dark, rain-slicked road, a young woman struck by a speeding vehicle that had then fled the scene. The victim's name was Sarah Jenkins. Alice's stomach lurched. She vaguely remembered Tom mentioning a distant acquaintance who had suffered a similar fate, but he had always been evasive about the details.

She delved deeper into the folder, her hands shaking so violently she could barely hold the mouse. There were photographs of a damaged car, the front end mangled, a faint red smear on the grille. There were audio recordings, snippets of conversations where Tom's voice was tight with panic, discussing legal representation, the mounting evidence, the fear of prison. And then, she found it. A scanned copy of a police report, complete with Tom's signature. He had been the driver. He had been the hit-and-run driver.

The world tilted on its axis. This wasn't just a secret; it was a crime. A horrific, life-altering crime that Tom had kept buried for years. The implications slammed into her with the force of a physical blow. His evasiveness, his anxiety, his sudden outbursts of paranoia – it all clicked into place with a sickening finality. He wasn't afraid of a phantom stalker; he was terrified of his past catching up to him. The messages, the locket – they weren't directed at her, but at him. Someone knew. Someone was threatening to expose him.

She scrolled through the remaining files, a grim fascination holding her captive. There were documents detailing plea bargains, probation terms, and community service. The accident had happened nearly five years ago. Sarah Jenkins, the victim, had survived, but her life had been irrevocably altered. She was left with severe injuries and a mountain of medical debt. Alice felt a wave of nausea wash over her. She had been living with a man who had destroyed another person's life and then systematically buried the truth.

The full weight of the betrayal settled upon her. Every shared laugh, every intimate moment, every whispered promise – it was all tainted by this monstrous secret. The "difficult time" he'd spoken of wasn't a period of personal struggle; it was the aftermath of his crime. His obsession with security, his paranoia about being watched – it wasn't a symptom of her imagined torment, but a genuine fear of discovery. The unseen threat wasn't a delusion; it was the looming shadow of his past, and the people who knew he was responsible.

She stumbled back from the desk, her legs weak, her mind reeling. The study, once a symbol of his ordered life, now felt like a tomb, filled with the ghosts of his deceit. The locket, still in her hand, was no longer a piece of evidence against an unknown assailant. It was a symbol of Tom's desperate attempt to control the narrative, to placate a blackmailer, to silence the truth. The message "I see inside" took on a chilling new meaning. It wasn't about her mind; it was about his secrets, the ones he desperately tried to keep hidden.

Her gaze fell on Tom's phone, lying on a small side table. If the computer held his past, what did his phone hold? With trembling fingers, she picked it up. It was locked, of course. But Tom, in his haste and his belief in his own security, had left his charger plugged in. And beside it, almost as an afterthought, lay a small, leather-bound notebook.

Alice's heart pounded a frantic rhythm against her ribs. This was it. The ultimate confession, perhaps. Or at least, the breadcrumbs leading to it. She picked up the notebook. It felt surprisingly heavy, its pages filled with a dense, almost illegible scrawl. Tom's handwriting was notoriously neat, almost calligraphic. This, however, was hurried, jagged, a reflection of a mind under immense pressure.

She flipped through the pages, her eyes scanning the words. Dates, times, cryptic notations. "Payment due." "Contacted again." "Increased demands." And then, a name. "S.J." Sarah Jenkins. The recurring entries detailing interactions with her, the mounting pressure, the fear of exposure. It wasn't just about the hit-and-run itself; it was about the ongoing repercussions, the demands for compensation that had clearly escalated over the years, culminating in a threat to reveal everything if he didn't comply. The locket, the anonymous messages – they were all part of this insidious extortion.

Her blood ran cold. The torment she had been experiencing, the feeling of being watched, the inexplicable occurrences in the house – were they a product of Tom's escalating paranoia, his attempts to create diversions, or were they a direct result of his desperate attempts to placate his blackmailer? Had Sarah Jenkins, or someone acting on her behalf, orchestrated these events to further torment Tom, to drive him to confession, or simply to make his life a living hell? The twisted logic of it all was almost too much to bear.

She found entries detailing clandestine meetings, hushed phone calls, and large sums of money transferred from hidden accounts. Tom had been living a double life, a life of constant fear and deception, all stemming from that one fateful night. The pressure had clearly been building, driving him to the brink of madness. And now, it had all come crashing down. The locket found in the pantry, the cryptic message – it was a final, calculated move by the blackmailer, designed to shatter Tom's carefully constructed world and force his hand.

Alice sank onto the plush armchair, the notebook clutched in her numb fingers. Her mind raced, trying to piece together the fragmented reality. Tom's fear was real. His secrecy was justified, in his eyes. But his actions, his deception, his failure to confide in her – that was a betrayal of a different order entirely. He had allowed her to believe she was losing her mind, that she was the victim of some unseen force, all while he was wrestling with a very real, very dangerous secret from his past.

She thought back to his frantic insistence that they leave the house. It wasn't about protecting her from a stalker; it was about him fleeing from the consequences of his actions, from the inevitable exposure. He was running, not from a phantom, but from a ghost he himself had created. The messages weren't just a threat to Tom; they were a threat to their entire life, a life built on a foundation of lies.

The implications were staggering. If Tom was being blackmailed, then the person behind it knew his address, knew his routine, knew his deepest fears. And they had clearly escalated their tactics, using the locket and the message to directly torment Alice, to use her as a pawn in their game. The realization that she had been unwittingly drawn into Tom's past transgressions, made a victim of his deceit, was almost unbearable.

She looked back at the computer, the open folder a gaping wound on the screen. The scanned documents, the photographs, the audio files – they were irrefutable evidence of Tom's crime. This was no longer about a marriage in crisis; it was about a criminal act and its devastating consequences. Her perception of Tom, of their life together, had been irrevocably shattered. The man she thought she knew had been a stranger all along, a stranger haunted by his past.

A profound weariness washed over her. She had come searching for answers about a stalker, and had instead unearthed a much darker, more complex truth. The unraveling had begun, not with a subtle intrusion, but with a devastating revelation about the man she loved. The path forward was uncertain, fraught with danger and the wreckage of her shattered trust. But one thing was clear: she could no longer pretend. The truth, however painful, had to be confronted. And in the silent study, surrounded by the ghosts of Tom's past, Alice knew her journey into the heart of darkness had only just begun. She had discovered Tom's secret, and in doing so, had unearthed a terrifying new reality. The question was no longer who was tormenting her, but what she would do with the knowledge of the man she had married.

The sterile silence of the study was a stark contrast to the tempest raging within Alice. The digital trail, meticulously unearthed from the depths of Tom's private life, painted a picture far more sinister than she could have ever imagined. It wasn't a phantom tormentor playing games; it was a methodical, chilling form of extortion. The hit-and-run. The words swam before her eyes, the newspaper clipping a stark testament to a crime buried for years, a crime that had irrevocably shaped the man she thought she knew. Tom wasn't a victim of a deranged stalker; he was the perpetrator of a devastating act, and now, he was a prisoner of his own past.

Her hands, still trembling from the shock of discovery, now moved with a desperate urgency across the keyboard. The folder, aptly named with a string of seemingly random characters, contained not just evidence of the accident, but a chilling chronicle of Tom's subsequent torment. Scanned documents detailed financial transactions, payments made under duress, each entry a silent scream of desperation. There were encrypted emails, their digital fingerprints pointing to an anonymous entity, a shadowy figure who had gained access to Tom's darkest secret and was now ruthlessly exploiting it.

Alice navigated through the maze of digital correspondence. The tone of the messages was icy, devoid of emotion, yet laced with an undeniable menace. They were curt, demanding, leaving no room for negotiation. "The deadline is approaching," one read, the simple sentence carrying the weight of unspoken threats. Another, more explicit, stated, "Payment is insufficient. Your silence has a price, and you are not paying enough." These weren't ramblings of a madman; they were the calculated pronouncements of a blackmailer.

Her stomach churned as she pieced together the timeline. The demands had started subtly, a gradual escalation of pressure. Initially, they focused on financial compensation, a way for the blackmailer to profit from Tom's guilt. But as the payments continued, the demands grew bolder, more intrusive. The anonymous party began to insinuate themselves into Tom's life, not just financially, but psychologically. They knew details, intimate details, about Tom and Alice, details that no stranger could possibly possess. This was how they had gained access to the house, how they had been able to orchestrate the unsettling events that had plagued her for weeks.

A cold dread settled over Alice as she realized the terrifying truth: the intruder wasn't an unknown entity. The man living in their walls, the unseen tenant who had been a constant source of fear and paranoia, was the blackmailer. He was not merely an opportunistic intruder; he was the orchestrator of her torment, using her own fear as a weapon against Tom. The locket, the misplaced items, the whispers in the dark – they were all part of his elaborate scheme to break Tom, to extract every last ounce of fear and compliance from him.

She scrolled through a series of chillingly impersonal messages, each one a fresh wave of horror. "The wife is getting suspicious," one read, followed by a smug emoticon. "Make sure she stays occupied. Distraction is key." Tom had been aware, acutely aware, that Alice was being manipulated, that she was being used as a pawn in his desperate game. His frantic attempts to reassure her, his dismissive explanations, his insistence that she was imagining things – it was all a calculated performance, a desperate attempt to maintain the illusion of normalcy while the real threat lurked just out of sight, in the very fabric of their home.

The evidence was undeniable. Tom had been feeding information, and likely money, to the person living in their home. The blackmailer had leveraged his knowledge of the hit-and-run, the ultimate sin, to gain leverage over Tom. And in his terror, Tom had succumbed. He had allowed this stranger into their lives, into their sanctuary, and had actively participated in his own destruction, and by extension, hers. The weight of this betrayal was crushing. It wasn't just about

Tom's past crime; it was about his complicity in the present terror, his active role in allowing Alice to be subjected to psychological torture.

She found further evidence of Tom's desperation. Transcripts of hushed phone calls, recordings of his strained voice, pleading, bargaining, confessing his fear. He had tried to reason with the blackmailer, to appeal to any shred of humanity, but there was none. The anonymous party reveled in Tom's misery, their messages dripping with a perverse sense of power. "You have no choice," one chilling missive declared. "Confess, and you go to prison. Comply, and you live in fear. Your choice."

Alice felt a wave of nausea wash over her. She thought back to Tom's increasingly erratic behavior, his sleepless nights, his jumpiness at every sound. It wasn't the anxiety of a man protecting his wife from an unseen threat; it was the gnawing terror of a man trapped by his own past, a man desperately trying to keep a lid on a secret that threatened to destroy everything he held dear. His paranoia wasn't a delusion; it was a visceral, raw fear of exposure, a fear fueled by the very person he had allowed to infiltrate their lives.

The implications sent a fresh shiver down her spine. If the blackmailer was the intruder, then he knew their home intimately. He knew their routines, their weaknesses, their vulnerabilities. He had been watching her, observing her reactions, meticulously crafting each step of his plan to sow discord and fear. And Tom, in his misguided attempt to protect himself, had inadvertently facilitated it all. He had been too consumed by his own guilt and fear to recognize the immediate danger lurking within their own walls.

She found a series of fragmented audio files, recordings that seemed to document confrontations. Tom's voice, strained and desperate, arguing with a muffled, distorted voice that Alice could only assume was the blackmailer's. The exchanges were short, brutal, punctuated by Tom's pleas and the blackmailer's chillingly calm threats. "You owe me," the distorted voice would say, time and again. "And I will collect, one way or another."

Alice closed her eyes, trying to process the enormity of what she had discovered. The narrative of a stalker was a fabrication, a carefully constructed deception designed to both control Tom and isolate Alice. The blackmailer had wanted Tom to believe that the threat was external, that he was protecting his family, while in reality, he was complicit in inviting the predator into their midst. This twisted game had been played out in the quiet corners of their home, in the shadows of their marriage, for weeks, perhaps even months.

The locket, once a symbol of mystery, now represented a clear and present threat. It was a message, not from a stranger to Alice, but from the blackmailer to Tom, a taunt, a reminder of his power, a signal that he was in control. And the message "I see inside" wasn't a cryptic warning to Alice about her own perceived mental state; it was a direct, chilling statement to Tom, a reminder that the blackmailer had access to his deepest fears, his most damning secret.

She felt a profound sense of pity for Tom, quickly followed by a surge of anger. He was a victim, yes, but he was also a man who had made a terrible mistake and then compounded it with a decade of lies and deception. He had allowed his guilt to consume him, to paralyze him, to the point where he was willing to sacrifice his wife's peace of mind, and their marriage, to protect his own secret. The man she had loved, the man she had trusted, was a fractured soul, haunted by a crime and manipulated by a ruthless opportunist.

The implications of this revelation were vast and terrifying. The blackmailer was not just after Tom's money; he was after control, after inflicting pain, after reveling in the chaos he had created. And Alice, unknowingly, had been caught in the crossfire. She had been a pawn in a dangerous game, her sanity questioned, her fears dismissed, all while the real architect of her torment was living under the same roof, his presence a constant, insidious threat.

Alice's gaze swept over the tidy desk, the organized bookshelves. This room, once a symbol of Tom's ordered life, now felt like the epicenter of their unraveling. Every meticulously placed book, every perfectly aligned pen, now seemed to mock her. They represented a facade, a carefully constructed illusion of control that had been shattered by a single, horrific truth. Tom's carefully curated life was a house of cards, and the blackmailer had been systematically blowing them away, one by one.

She returned to the computer, her fingers flying across the keyboard with renewed purpose. She needed more. She needed to understand the full extent of the blackmailer's demands, the timeline of their intrusion, and most importantly, if there was any way to fight back. The fear that had once paralyzed her was now being replaced by a cold, hard resolve. She had uncovered the truth, and now, she had to face the consequences. The man living in their walls was not just a criminal; he was a direct threat to her safety and her sanity. And Tom, her husband, had been complicit in allowing him to exert that threat. The realization was a bitter pill to swallow, but one she knew she had to digest. The unraveling had just begun.

The weight of the files on the desk felt like an anchor, dragging Alice down into the murky depths of deception. The sterile silence of the study, once a sanctuary of intellect and order, now vibrated with the echoes of a truth so grotesque it threatened to suffocate her. She had expected a phantom, a ghost in the machine, a disturbed individual. She had braced herself for a narrative of external threat. Instead, she found a meticulously orchestrated symphony of terror, conducted by a man she had welcomed into their lives, and played out by the man she had vowed to love and cherish. The hit-and-run, a ghost from Tom's distant past, was not merely a source of guilt; it was a weapon. And she, Alice, had been the unwitting target of its venom.

Her hands, usually steady, now trembled as she scrolled through the digital abyss. The stark reality of Tom's payments, the chillingly precise dates and amounts, confirmed the worst. He hadn't been paying off a phantom stalker; he had been feeding the serpent in their midst. The encrypted messages, cold and precise, were not the ramblings of a madman but the calculated pronouncements of a blackmailer, a puppeteer pulling Tom's strings with the frayed threads of his darkest secret. "The wife is getting suspicious," one message had read, followed by a smug emoticon. Alice felt a phantom chill crawl up her spine. Tom had known. He had known she was being manipulated, used as a pawn in his desperate game, and he had done nothing. His reassurances, his dismissals of her fears, had been a performance, a desperate attempt to maintain the illusion of normalcy while the real threat lurked, not outside, but within the very walls of their home.

The locket, once a symbol of tender remembrance, now felt like a brand of shame. It wasn't a lost item; it was a deliberate message, a taunt from the blackmailer to Tom, a stark reminder of his power, his intrusive knowledge. "I see inside," the inscription had whispered to her, a cryptic warning. Now, it resonated with terrifying clarity: a direct, chilling statement to Tom, a confirmation that the blackmailer had access to his deepest fears, his most damning secret. The intruder, the unseen tenant, the source of her suffocating fear, was the blackmailer himself. He wasn't an opportunistic trespasser; he was the architect of her torment, a ruthless exploiter of Tom's guilt, using her own fear as leverage. The misplaced items, the whispers in the dark, the unsettling feeling of being watched – all part of an elaborate scheme to break Tom, to extract his compliance, his terror, drop by agonizing drop.

Alice's gaze drifted to the meticulously organized bookshelves, the pristine desk. This room, a testament to Tom's ordered life, now felt like the epicenter of their unraveling. Every perfectly placed book, every aligned pen, mocked her with its illusion of control. Tom's carefully curated existence was a house of cards, and the blackmailer had been systematically dismantling it, one by one. The evidence was irrefutable. Tom had been feeding information, money, and his very sanity to the man living within their walls. The blackmailer had leveraged the hit-and-run, the ultimate sin, to gain absolute dominion over Tom. And in his terror, Tom had capitulated. He had allowed this predator into their sanctuary, complicit in his own destruction, and by extension, hers. The betrayal was a physical blow, a crushing weight that stole her breath. It wasn't just about Tom's past crime; it was about his active role in her present terror, his complicity in allowing her to be subjected to a prolonged campaign of psychological torture.

She found more fragments of Tom's desperation: audio recordings of hushed phone calls, his voice strained, pleading, bargaining, confessing his fear. He had attempted to appeal to the blackmailer's humanity, a futile endeavor. There was none. The anonymous party reveled in Tom's misery, their messages dripping with a perverse sense of power. "You have no choice," one missive declared, a chilling pronouncement. "Confess, and you go to prison. Comply, and you live in fear. Your choice." Alice felt a wave of nausea. Tom's increasingly erratic behavior, his sleepless nights, his jumpiness at every sound – it wasn't the anxiety of a man protecting his wife from an unseen threat. It was the gnawing terror of a man trapped by his past, desperately trying to keep a lid on a secret that threatened to obliterate everything he held dear. His paranoia wasn't a delusion; it was a visceral, raw fear of exposure, a fear masterfully stoked by the very person he had welcomed into their home.

The implications were vast and terrifying. The blackmailer wasn't just after Tom's money; he was after control, after inflicting pain, after reveling in the chaos he had sown. And Alice, unknowingly, had been caught in the crossfire, a pawn in a dangerous game, her sanity questioned, her fears dismissed, all while the true architect of her torment resided under the same roof, his presence an insidious, constant threat. The thought of him watching her, observing her reactions, meticulously crafting each step of his plan to sow discord and fear, sent a fresh shiver down her spine. Tom, in his misguided attempt to protect himself, had inadvertently facilitated it all, too consumed by his guilt and fear to recognize the immediate danger lurking within their own walls.

The fragmented audio files were the most harrowing. They documented confrontations, Tom's voice strained and desperate, arguing with a muffled, distorted voice that Alice recognized, with a sickening lurch, as the blackmailer's. The exchanges were short, brutal, punctuated by Tom's pleas and the blackmailer's chillingly calm threats. "You owe me," the distorted voice would say, time and again. "And I will collect, one way or another." Alice closed her eyes, the enormity of the situation crashing down on her. The narrative of a stalker had been a fabrication, a calculated deception designed to control Tom and isolate her. The blackmailer had wanted Tom to believe the threat was external, that he was protecting his family, while in reality, he was a willing accomplice in inviting the predator into their lives. This twisted game had played out in the quiet corners of their home, in the shadows of their marriage, for weeks, perhaps months.

A profound sense of pity for Tom washed over her, quickly followed by a surge of searing anger. He was a victim, yes, but he was also a man who had made a terrible mistake and then compounded it with a decade of lies and deception. He had allowed his guilt to consume him, to paralyze him, to the point where he was willing to sacrifice her peace of mind, their marriage, to protect his secret. The man she loved, the man she trusted, was a fractured soul, haunted by a crime and manipulated by a ruthless opportunist. The unraveling had begun, not with a bang, but with the quiet, devastating click of a digital discovery.

She returned to the computer, her fingers flying across the keyboard with a renewed, almost desperate, purpose. She needed more. She needed to understand the full extent of the blackmailer's demands, the timeline of their intrusion, and most importantly, if there was any way to fight back. The paralyzing fear that had consumed her for weeks was slowly being replaced by a cold, hard resolve. She had uncovered the truth, and now, she had to face the consequences. The man living in their walls was not just a criminal; he was a direct threat to her safety and her sanity. And Tom, her husband, had been complicit in allowing him to exert that threat. The realization was a bitter pill to swallow, but one she knew she had to digest.

The silence in the study thickened, pregnant with unspoken accusations and the lingering scent of digital decay. Alice leaned back, her gaze fixed on the flickering cursor on the screen, a tiny beacon in the encroaching darkness. The information she had unearthed was a Pandora's Box, and she had pried it open with trembling, determined hands. Every file, every email, every audio snippet was a shard of glass reflecting a shattered reality. Tom's confession, when it came, would be less about admitting guilt and more about the desperate plea of a man drowning in the consequences of his own making. He had been a prisoner of his past, and now, he was also a prisoner of the present, held captive by the very entity he had allowed into their lives.

The air in the room felt heavy, charged with an almost palpable tension. It was the kind of tension that precedes a storm, the quiet before the inevitable deluge. Alice could feel the foundations of her marriage cracking, the carefully constructed edifice of their shared life crumbling around her. The man she thought she knew, the man she had built a life with, was a stranger, a man haunted by a decade-old secret and paralyzed by fear. His actions, once incomprehensible, now made a terrible, chilling kind of sense. His evasiveness, his frantic attempts to dismiss her fears, his growing paranoia – it was all a desperate attempt to maintain control of a situation spiraling out of his grasp. He wasn't protecting her; he was protecting himself, and in doing so, he had exposed her to a danger far greater than any she had imagined.

Her mind replayed Tom's hushed phone calls, his strained whispers. The fear in his voice had been palpable, raw, and utterly terrifying. It wasn't the fear of an innocent man trying to protect his family; it was the fear of a guilty man desperately trying to appease his tormentor. He had been negotiating, bargaining, begging for his freedom, his secret. And the blackmailer, a shadowy figure lurking in the periphery of their lives, had held all the cards. The audio recordings were particularly brutal. The distorted voice, devoid of any human warmth, had been a constant, chilling reminder of the power it wielded. "You owe me," it had repeated, a mantra of Tom's impending doom.

Alice felt a profound sense of disconnect, as if she were observing her life from a great distance. The intimacy she had shared with Tom, the shared dreams, the everyday moments, all seemed tainted now, corrupted by the corrosive secret that had festered beneath the surface. She looked at her hands, still bearing the faint imprint of the keyboard keys, and felt a surge of anger, hot and sharp. He had allowed this to happen. He had opened the door to their home, to their lives, and invited the predator in. And he had done so, not out of some misguided attempt to protect her, but out of a desperate, selfish need to protect himself. The betrayal was a bitter draught, far more potent than any of the fear she had experienced.

The implications stretched out before her, a dark and uncertain future. The blackmailer knew their routines, their habits, their vulnerabilities. He had been observing them, learning them, using that knowledge to amplify their fear and sow discord. And Tom, in his desperate attempt to manage the crisis, had only exacerbated it, unwittingly fueling the blackmailer's manipulative tactics. He had been so consumed by his own guilt and the threat of exposure that he had become blind to the immediate danger, allowing it to fester and grow within their own home.

She imagined the blackmailer, a phantom presence in the house, listening, watching, a voyeuristic predator feeding on their fear. The thought sent a fresh wave of revulsion through her. He had been in their bedroom, their kitchen, their living room, a silent observer, a constant threat. And Tom had known. He had known, and he had said nothing, leaving her to navigate a minefield of manufactured terror, her sanity questioned, her fears dismissed, all while the real architect of her torment was just a breath away. The silence of the house, once a source of comfort, now felt suffocating, pregnant with the unseen presence of their tormentor and the heavy burden of Tom's deception. The unraveling was far from over; it was just beginning.

The carefully calibrated campaign of terror, which had so effectively played on Tom's deep-seated guilt and Alice's burgeoning anxiety, was evolving. The intruder, sensing Tom's capitulation, was shedding the guise of subtlety. His interventions, once confined to the periphery of their lives – a misplaced object, a faint creak in the floorboards, a chill that had no source – were now bleeding into the stark reality of their days. The fear he had so expertly cultivated was no longer a creeping vine; it was an encroaching tide, and Tom, paralyzed by the threat of exposure, was allowing it to consume them both.

Alice, though still grappling with the raw shock of her discovery, was beginning to notice the shifts, the subtle escalations that her previous paranoia had overlooked. It wasn't just the disarray in the study anymore; it was a creeping unease that permeated every corner of their home. She found a single, dark feather resting on her pillow one morning, a stark, almost theatrical gesture that sent a ripple of disquiet through her. It was too deliberate to be accidental, too pointed to be dismissed. It felt like a signature, a macabre calling card left by an unseen hand. Tom had flinched when she'd shown it to him, his eyes darting to the windows as if expecting an accusation to materialize from thin air. He'd mumbled something about a bird getting in, his voice too quick, too dismissive, a familiar pattern of deflection that Alice was now learning to recognize.

Then came the music. A low, melancholic piano melody, barely audible at first, would drift through the house at odd hours of the night. It wasn't from any radio or speaker they owned. It seemed to emanate from the very walls, a phantom serenade that underscored the oppressive silence and preyed on their nerves. Alice would lie awake, straining to identify its source, her heart pounding a frantic rhythm against her ribs. Tom would stir beside her, a restless sleeper, his breathing shallow and uneven. He never acknowledged the music, never commented on it. He would simply pull the blankets tighter, a physical manifestation of his desperate desire to retreat from the encroaching reality. Alice began to understand that these were not random occurrences; they were calculated moves, designed to amplify Tom's fear and, by extension, hers. The intruder was no longer content to be a silent observer; he was actively engaging, asserting his dominance, his growing boldness a testament to Tom's crumbling resolve.

The items left behind became more personal, more insidious. A small, tarnished silver locket, identical to the one Alice wore every day, appeared on the kitchen counter one morning. It was empty, devoid of any photograph, but its presence was a chilling echo of her own cherished possession. It was a violation, a profound intrusion into her personal space, a symbol of how intimately the intruder had studied their lives. Alice felt a cold dread coil in her stomach. This wasn't a random act of vandalism; it was a targeted message, a deliberate act of psychological warfare. She confronted Tom again, the locket clutched in her trembling hand. "Where did this come from, Tom?" she'd asked, her voice tight with a fear that was no longer based on vague unease but on concrete, terrifying evidence. He'd paled, his gaze skittering away from hers. "I... I don't know," he'd stammered, the familiar lie a bitter taste on her tongue. "Maybe it fell out of your bag. Maybe you dropped it somewhere and someone returned it." His explanation was flimsy, transparent, a desperate attempt to maintain the illusion of normalcy that was rapidly disintegrating.

The intruder's tactics were becoming more sophisticated, more deeply personal. He was no longer just creating disturbances; he was actively manipulating their environment, inserting himself into their shared existence. One evening, as Alice was preparing dinner, she noticed that the spice rack, usually meticulously organized, had been rearranged. The small jars were out of order, and the salt and pepper shakers, which always sat side-by-side, were placed at opposite ends of the counter. It was a minor detail, easily overlooked, but to Alice, it was another tremor in the foundation of their reality. It was a subtle, yet unmistakable sign that someone had been in their kitchen, had touched their things, had deliberately altered their domestic landscape. She remembered the phantom chills, the feeling of being watched that had plagued her for weeks. Now, she knew it wasn't her imagination. It was the tangible presence of their tormentor, growing bolder, more brazen with each passing day.

Tom's behavior had become a constant source of alarm. He was a shadow of his former self, perpetually on edge, his eyes hollow and shadowed. He would jump at the slightest sound, his hands would tremble as he reached for his coffee cup, and he would often stare out of the window for long stretches, his expression a mask of profound despair. He was a man drowning, and he was pulling Alice down with him. She saw the glint of fear in his eyes when she mentioned a strange noise or an odd occurrence, a fear that was far deeper and more pervasive than she had initially understood. It wasn't just the fear of an external threat; it was the suffocating dread of a man trapped by his own transgressions, a man whose deepest secret was being systematically weaponized against him.

The evidence of the intruder's increasing confidence was becoming undeniable. The subtle disturbances were evolving into more direct psychological assaults. Alice found a photograph of herself, taken from a distance, tucked inside her favorite book. It was a candid shot, one she didn't recall being taken, and the angle suggested it had been captured from within their own home, perhaps from a concealed vantage point. The image itself was innocuous, but its placement, its intimate violation of her privacy, was deeply disturbing. She felt a prickle of unease crawl up her spine. This wasn't just about Tom's past anymore; it was a direct assault on her sense of security, her very autonomy within her own home. The intruder was no longer content to manipulate Tom from the shadows; he was beginning to make his presence felt more overtly, his actions escalating with chilling precision.

The fear had begun to seep into their shared life, a corrosive agent eating away at the bonds of their marriage. Alice found herself scrutinizing Tom's every word, his every gesture, searching for hidden meanings, for the tell-tale signs of his complicity. His evasiveness, his increasingly strained attempts to reassure her, no longer soothed her; they confirmed her suspicions. He was not protecting her from an external threat; he was desperately trying to contain the fallout of his own carefully guarded secret, a secret that was now being used as a weapon against them both. The intruder, sensing Tom's weakening resolve, was becoming bolder, his actions more audacious, his endgame drawing nearer. The carefully constructed facade of their normal lives was shattering, revealing the terrifying reality that had been lurking beneath the surface.

The subtle, almost imperceptible disturbances had begun to morph into something far more tangible, far more menacing. One afternoon, Alice discovered that her keys, which she always kept in a specific bowl by the front door, were missing. She searched the house frantically, her anxiety spiking. Tom, when she asked him, simply shrugged, feigning ignorance. "Maybe you left them in your car, Al," he suggested, his voice lacking conviction. Hours later, the keys reappeared, not in the bowl, but neatly placed on her bedside table, a silent, unsettling message. It was a violation of her personal space, a chilling reminder that her movements, her routines, were being observed, monitored. The intruder was no longer content with mere psychological games; he was actively demonstrating his ability to infiltrate their lives, to manipulate their possessions, to assert his physical presence within their home.

The music, too, had become more pronounced. What was once a faint, phantom melody now had moments of jarring clarity, the notes echoing through the silent house with an almost mocking precision. Alice would hear it when she was alone, a mournful piano piece that seemed to seep from the walls themselves. She'd tried to trace its origin, tiptoeing through empty rooms, listening intently, but the source remained elusive, a phantom composer in their midst. Tom, when she'd mentioned it, would dismiss it as her imagination, his gaze darting nervously towards the windows, as if expecting the phantom musician to materialize. This escalating boldness, this willingness to directly intrude upon their senses, was a clear indication that the intruder was pushing the boundaries, testing Tom's limits, and growing increasingly confident in his control.

The intruder's actions were no longer just about sowing discord; they were about asserting dominance. He was demonstrating his intimate knowledge of their lives, their habits, their fears. Alice found a wilting rose, a deep crimson bloom, placed on her car seat one morning. It was a stark contrast to the vibrant blooms in her garden, a morbid, almost ominous gesture. It was a symbol of beauty corrupted, of something living rendered lifeless, a chilling reflection of the way her own peace of mind was being systematically destroyed. Tom's reaction to the rose was even more telling. He had visibly recoiled, his face draining of color, his hand flying to his mouth as if to stifle a cry. His fear was palpable, a raw, visceral terror that Alice was beginning to understand was rooted in a far deeper secret than she had initially imagined.

The carefully orchestrated campaign was reaching its climax. The intruder, emboldened by Tom's continued compliance and Alice's growing distress, was no longer content to operate solely in the shadows. His intrusions were becoming more audacious, more blatant. He was weaving his presence into the fabric of their visible reality, transforming their home into a stage for his escalating endgame. The subtle disturbances had given way to more direct interactions, a chilling escalation that signaled a shift in power, a tightening of the noose around Tom's neck. The carefully constructed world Alice had believed in was not just unraveling; it was being systematically dismantled by an unseen hand, a hand that was growing increasingly daring, increasingly bold. The hidden world within the walls was no longer a secret; it was a tangible, terrifying force that was beginning to bleed into their lives, blurring the lines between reality and the intruder's malevolent design. The silence of their home was no longer a comfort; it was a tense, expectant hush, pregnant with the unspoken threats and the ever-growing boldness of the man who had become their unseen, terrifying tenant.

The illusion of safety, once a comforting blanket, had been ripped away with the ferocity of a predator's claw. Alice stood in the center of their living room, the late afternoon sun casting long, distorted shadows that seemed to writhe with unseen life. This house, this sanctuary they had painstakingly built, this symbol of a new beginning, now felt like a gilded cage, its bars forged from Tom's silence and the intruder's insidious presence. Every creak of the floorboards, every whisper of the wind against the windowpanes, was no longer a familiar sound of home, but a sinister punctuation mark in a narrative of escalating terror. The warmth she had once felt radiating from these walls had curdled into a pervasive, bone-chilling cold that had nothing to do with the temperature. It was the icy touch of betrayal, the stark realization that the very foundation of her peace had been built on a lie, and that the man she had entrusted with her life was not only aware of the danger but had, in his own way, facilitated it.

She looked at Tom, who sat slumped in his armchair, a hollow-eyed effigy of the man she thought she knew. His gaze was fixed on some point beyond the window, a place that held only darkness and his regrets. His helplessness, once a source of pity, now felt like a complicity that gnawed at her. He was a prisoner, yes, but he was also the jailer, a unwilling accomplice to their tormentor. His secret, whatever it was, had become a monstrous entity, feeding on their fear, growing stronger with every passing hour. And Alice, the innocent bystander caught in the crossfire, was left to navigate a labyrinth of deception and dread, armed with nothing but a growing, desperate clarity. The subtle disturbances, the misplaced keys, the phantom music, the unsettling mementos – they were no longer just random acts of a disturbed individual. They were the deliberate, calculated steps of someone who knew their lives intimately, someone who had been given access, perhaps even encouraged, by the man sitting across from her.

The weight of this realization was crushing. It wasn't just the intruder's malevolence that she had to contend with; it was Tom's profound failure, his betrayal of their shared trust. He had allowed this to happen. He had, by his silence and his fear, invited this darkness into their home. The thought was a physical blow, leaving her breathless and nauseated. Her mind replayed countless moments, reinterpreting his anxious glances, his evasive answers, his increasingly erratic behavior. What she had once dismissed as stress, as guilt related to his work, or even as a nascent form of mental fragility, now coalesced into a terrifying, undeniable truth. He was being blackmailed, manipulated, and his fear of exposure had rendered him incapable of protecting them, of protecting

*her*.

The house, once a haven of domesticity, had transformed into a stage for psychological warfare, and Alice found herself the unwilling protagonist in a play she hadn't auditioned for. The intruder wasn't just a presence; he was an architect, meticulously designing their misery, using Tom's vulnerability as his blueprint. The small, almost imperceptible changes she had begun to notice – the spice rack rearranged, the salt and pepper shakers deliberately separated, the keys moved from their designated spot – were no longer just unsettling anomalies. They were calculated gestures, designed to chip away at her sense of normalcy, to sow seeds of doubt and unease that would blossom into full-blown paranoia. These weren't the random acts of a vandal; they were the deliberate manipulations of someone who understood the power of domestic disruption, someone who knew that the most effective way to break a person was to destabilize the very ground they stood on.

She remembered the single, dark feather on her pillow, a detail she had initially dismissed as a strange but harmless occurrence. Now, it felt like a taunt, a dark omen delivered with surgical precision. And the locket, an exact replica of her own, placed so brazenly on the kitchen counter, was a chilling testament to the intruder's intimate knowledge of her life, her possessions, her very identity. It was a violation on a level she hadn't fully comprehended at the time, a psychic intrusion that bypassed physical barriers and lodged itself directly into her sense of self. Tom's flinching reaction, his desperate attempts to brush it off, now screamed of a deeper, more complicit fear. He knew why it was there. He knew the significance of its placement. And his inability to confront it, to explain it, was a confession in itself.

The phantom piano music, once a faint, melancholic hum, had begun to punctuate the silence with an unnerving clarity. It wasn't just a sound; it was an emotional landscape, a soundtrack to their unraveling lives. Alice would lie awake, straining to pinpoint its source, her heart a frantic drum against her ribs. She'd followed the notes, tiptoeing through darkened hallways, her breath catching in her throat with every shift in volume, every subtle change in melody. But the source remained elusive, a phantom artist performing solely for their torment. Tom's dismissal of it, his mumbled suggestions of an overactive imagination, now sounded like a desperate plea to maintain the illusion, a desperate attempt to keep the cracks in their reality from widening into chasms. He knew it was real, and he knew it was part of the torment.

Then there was the photograph, tucked inside her favorite novel, a candid shot taken from a distance, suggesting a hidden vantage point within their own home. The image itself was innocuous, a snapshot of her walking in the garden, but its placement was a violation of the most profound kind. It was a reminder that their privacy was a myth, that their sanctuary had been breached, and that the intruder was not merely observing from afar, but was deeply embedded within their lives. The realization that this was not just about Tom's past, but about a direct, personal assault on her sense of safety, sent a shiver of pure terror down her spine. She was not merely a victim of circumstance; she was a target, and the intruder's intentions were becoming increasingly clear and terrifying.

The subtle shifts in their environment had escalated into a palpable sense of dread. The wilting rose on her car seat, a stark contrast to the vibrant blooms in her garden, was not a romantic gesture, but a morbid symbol. It spoke of decay, of beauty corrupted, of life extinguished. It was a deliberate mirroring of her own inner state, a grim testament to the way her peace of mind was being systematically destroyed. Tom's visceral reaction to the rose – his paleness, his stifled gasp – confirmed that this was not just an arbitrary act of aggression, but a message deeply rooted in their shared past, a past he had kept hidden from her. His terror was not just fear of the intruder; it was the terror of a man confronted by the tangible consequences of his buried transgressions, consequences that were now bleeding into their present and threatening their future.

The house was no longer just a structure of brick and mortar; it was a psychological battleground. Every object, every shadow, every silence seemed to hum with a hidden menace. Alice found herself scrutinizing every detail, every misplaced item, every odd sound, searching for the pattern, for the logic behind the escalating terror. She saw how Tom's fear had paralyzed him, how his desire to protect his secret had made him vulnerable, and how that vulnerability had been ruthlessly exploited. The intruder had not only breached their home but had also infiltrated their marriage, turning Tom's guilt into a weapon and Alice's trust into a tragic casualty. The illusion of safety had not merely been shattered; it had been systematically dismantled, brick by painstaking brick, by a predator and a compromised husband.

She looked at the framed wedding photo on the mantelpiece, a frozen moment of happiness and commitment. It felt like a relic from another lifetime, a testament to a happiness that was now irrevocably tainted. The man in the photo, beaming with a future he seemed so sure of, was a stranger to the broken, terrified man slumped in the armchair. And Alice, standing before it, felt a profound sense of loss, not just for the present, but for the past that had been so effectively rewritten by Tom's deception. The shared history they had built was now overshadowed by the hidden narrative, a narrative of fear and complicity that had brought them to this precipice.

The intruder's escalating boldness was a clear indication of Tom's capitulation. The fear that had once held Tom captive was now a leash, and the intruder was tightening it with every passing day. Alice could feel it in the air, a palpable tension that made breathing difficult. The house, which had once echoed with the laughter of their shared life, now resonated with a chilling silence, broken only by the phantom music or the unsettling creak of a floorboard that signaled an unseen presence. This was not just about fear; it was about control. The intruder was asserting his dominance, not just over Tom, but over their entire lives, and Alice was trapped in the epicenter of his meticulously crafted torment.

Her own fear, though ever-present, was beginning to be overshadowed by a cold, sharp resolve. The confusion and anxiety that had plagued her were starting to give way to a grim clarity. She understood now that the threat was not external and easily vanquished; it was woven into the very fabric of their lives, a tangled knot of secrets and fear. Tom's betrayal cut deep, a wound that festered alongside the fear of the intruder. He had not protected her; he had endangered her, all for the sake of a secret that was now unraveling their world. The realization that her own husband, the man who had sworn to protect her, was inextricably linked to their tormentor was a bitter pill to swallow.

The once familiar rooms now felt alien, each corner holding a potential threat, each shadow a lurking danger. The comfort of their shared life had been replaced by a gnawing suspicion, a constant vigilance that drained her energy and frayed her nerves. She looked at Tom again, her gaze sharp, dissecting the lines of worry etched on his face. He was a man drowning, and his struggle was pulling her down with him. But she was a strong swimmer, and she would not go under without a fight. The innocence she had once possessed, the naive trust she had placed in him, was gone, replaced by a steely determination to survive.

The intruder was no longer a shadow in the periphery; he was a tangible force, his presence felt in the altered objects, the unsettling sounds, the pervasive atmosphere of dread. He had orchestrated a symphony of terror, and Tom's silence was the conductor's baton. Alice, however, was beginning to compose her own melody, a song of defiance. She understood that her home, their sanctuary, had become a prison, but she refused to remain incarcerated. The illusion of safety was gone, replaced by a stark, terrifying reality, and in that reality, she knew she had to find a way to escape, not just the intruder, but the suffocating web of deceit that had ensnared them both. The path ahead was dark and treacherous, but for the first time, Alice felt a flicker of agency, a desperate resolve to navigate the unraveling truth and reclaim her life from the encroaching darkness.

# Chapter 6: The Confrontation

The air in the study was thick with a silence that had become suffocating. It wasn't the peaceful quiet of an empty room, but a tense, expectant hush, as if the very furniture held its breath. Tom sat hunched over his desk, the single lamp casting a harsh glow that did little to illuminate the darkness pooling in the corners of his eyes. He'd been staring at the sealed envelope for what felt like hours, its stark white against the polished mahogany a beacon of his impending doom. It had appeared on his desk sometime after Alice had finally retreated to the bedroom, the click of her heels on the hardwood floor a fading echo of her growing suspicion. He hadn't heard it arrive, hadn't seen anyone. It was simply there, a silent, undeniable testament to the predator's increasing boldness.

He traced the crisp edges of the envelope with a trembling finger. The paper felt unnervingly smooth, almost silken, a stark contrast to the rough, calloused hands that had likely delivered it. This wasn't the anonymous, unsettling disruption of before. This was direct. This was personal. This was the culmination of the games, the psychological warfare, the slow, agonizing erosion of his peace. He knew, with a certainty that chilled him to the bone, that this contained not a request, but a command. An ultimatum. The word itself tasted like ash in his mouth. He had danced on the edge of disaster for so long, a tightrope walker blindfolded, and now, the ground had given way.

His mind raced, a frantic hamster on a wheel of dread. What could the intruder possibly want now that hadn't already been subtly implied? The money? He'd paid. The silence? He'd maintained it, a grim, obedient dog. The compliance? He'd offered it, his every action a testament to his subjugation. But this felt different. This felt like a final demand, a point of no return. He imagined the intruder's face, hidden behind a mask of smug satisfaction, watching him, waiting for him to crack. He could almost hear the low, insidious chuckle, the whispered taunts that had haunted his waking hours and stalked his dreams.

He finally forced himself to tear open the envelope. Inside, a single, neatly folded sheet of paper. No threatening doodles, no crude scribbles. Just typewritten words, precise and chillingly clear. His breath hitched as he read. It was a demand, not for money, but for action. A specific action. An action that involved Alice.

*"You have played your part admirably, Tom. Your fear has been a delicious appetizer. But the main course requires your active participation. Alice knows something is wrong. Her questions are becoming too pointed, her gaze too discerning. You cannot afford for her to discover the full truth. She must be... removed from the equation. Tonight. Bring her to the old boathouse by the lake. Do not call the police. Do not tell her anything. If you fail, or if she is not with you, the consequences will be far more severe than anything you have experienced thus far. And know this: I will be watching. Always."*

The words swam before his eyes. Boathouse. Lake. Remove her from the equation. The blood drained from his face, leaving him feeling clammy and nauseous. This was it. The ultimate betrayal. He, who had sworn to protect her, to cherish her, was being ordered to deliver her, his wife, his love, into the hands of this monster. The sheer depravity of the demand sent a wave of revulsion through him, so potent it threatened to buckle his knees. But beneath the revulsion, a colder, more primal fear began to coil in his gut. The fear of what would happen if he refused. The fear of the "consequences far more severe." He saw Alice's face in his mind – her trusting smile, the way her eyes crinkled when she laughed, the way she still looked at him, despite everything, with a flicker of hope. He couldn't do it. He

*couldn't.*

He reread the note, his gaze darting between the words, searching for a loophole, a misinterpretation, anything that could offer an escape. But there was none. The instructions were brutally clear. And the implied threat, the unseen eyes of the observer, was suffocating. He was trapped. A pawn in a game he had unknowingly initiated, and now, the stakes were Alice's life. His past sins, the secret he had so desperately tried to bury, had finally unearthed their monstrous offspring, and it was demanding the ultimate sacrifice.

He crumpled the note in his fist, the paper crinkling loudly in the oppressive silence. His heart hammered against his ribs like a trapped bird. He had to make a choice. A choice between his own survival, however tainted, and Alice's safety. The thought of her, unsuspecting, vulnerable, walking into a trap he himself had set, was unbearable. But the thought of the intruder's retaliation, the utter destruction he was capable of, was equally terrifying. His entire life had been built on a foundation of evasion, of sweeping things under the rug, of prioritizing his own comfort and reputation above all else. Now, that cowardice was about to cost him everything.

He looked at the framed photograph on his desk, a picture of him and Alice on their wedding day. They were so young, so full of promise. He remembered the absolute certainty he had felt then, the unwavering conviction that he would always keep her safe. That man, that earnest, hopeful groom, felt like a ghost from another life. The man sitting here now was a hollow shell, a man consumed by fear and guilt. And the intruder knew it. He had played on it, exploited it, and now, he was using it to orchestrate his ultimate revenge.

He imagined confessing to Alice, telling her everything. The shame was a physical weight, crushing him. He had built their life on a lie, and the truth, when it finally came out, would shatter her completely. But even that confession felt like a betrayal. He had kept her in the dark, protected her from the truth of his past, and now, that protection had become a weapon against her.

He stood up, his legs shaky. He had to go to her. He had to try and find a way out of this, a way to protect her. But how? How could he protect her from a threat that was inextricably linked to him? How could he fight an enemy who knew his every weakness, who had infiltrated his home, his life, his very thoughts?

He walked towards the bedroom door, his hand hovering over the doorknob. The faint sound of Alice's breathing, even and steady, was a sharp contrast to the frantic thumping of his own heart. He could hear the soft rustle of her turning over in bed, a small, innocent sound that now seemed fraught with danger. He was about to shatter her peace, to drag her into the abyss he had created. The weight of that knowledge was almost unbearable.

He opened the door slowly, the creak of the hinges sounding like a gunshot in the silent house. Alice stirred, her eyes fluttering open in the dim light. "Tom?" she murmured, her voice soft with sleep. "Is everything alright?"

He stood in the doorway, a silhouette against the dim hallway light, unable to meet her gaze. The words of the ultimatum, the demand for her to come to the boathouse, felt like a poison on his tongue. He swallowed hard, his throat dry. He couldn't tell her the truth. Not yet. He had to buy time, to find another way. But the intruder's threat loomed, a specter over their every word, their every move. He had to pretend, to act, to lure her into the trap without her knowing. The thought was a fresh wave of nausea. He was a monster, a willing accomplice in his own wife's potential demise.

"Just... checking on you," he managed, his voice raspy. "Couldn't sleep." He stepped into the room, the floorboards groaning under his weight. He avoided her eyes, his gaze fixed on the patterned duvet. "The air is so still tonight," he lied, his voice carefully modulated. "I thought we could... maybe go for a walk. Clear our heads." He hated himself for the deception, for the sickening contortion of his love into a tool of manipulation.

Alice sat up, a slight frown creasing her brow. "A walk? Now? Tom, it's late." Her voice held a hint of her growing suspicion, a subtle undertone he'd become acutely aware of. She was no longer the naive Alice of a few weeks ago. The subtle disturbances, the palpable tension that had settled over their home like a shroud, had not escaped her. Her eyes, usually so full of warmth, now held a flicker of something watchful, guarded.

"I know, I know," he said, forcing a weak smile. "But I can't seem to settle. And the lake... it's always so peaceful at night. We could just sit by the water for a while. It might help us both relax." He tried to inject a casualness into his tone, a tone he hadn't possessed in weeks. It felt like a betrayal of his very being. He watched her closely, searching for any sign that she suspected.

She studied him for a long moment, her gaze sharp, assessing. He could feel the weight of her scrutiny, the unspoken questions swirling between them. "Are you sure you're okay, Tom?" she asked, her voice softer now, but still laced with an undercurrent of concern that he knew was rapidly morphing into suspicion. "You've been acting... off."

The directness of her question was a physical blow. He wanted to confess, to spill everything, to beg for her forgiveness. But the image of the typed words, the implied threat, flashed in his mind. He couldn't. Not yet. "Just a lot on my mind with work," he deflected, a well-worn excuse that was rapidly losing its credibility. "You know how it is."

She didn't respond immediately, her silence stretching, amplifying the tension in the room. Then, she sighed, a soft, weary sound. "Alright, Tom," she said, her voice resigned. "A walk. But if you start acting strange, we're coming straight back." She swung her legs out of bed, her movements fluid and graceful, a stark contrast to his own jerky, uncertain actions. As she reached for her robe, her eyes flickered to the hallway, then back to him. There was a subtle tension in her shoulders, a guardedness that hadn't been there before. She was aware that something was wrong, deeply wrong. And he, Tom, was the source of her unease.

He followed her out of the bedroom, his mind a whirlwind of conflicting thoughts and fears. The boathouse. The lake. He had to get her there. He had to survive. But how could he live with himself if he didn't? The ultimatum had presented him with an impossible choice, a Sophie's Choice orchestrated by the devil himself. And he knew, with a chilling certainty, that whatever he decided, the consequences would be devastating. The game had reached its endgame, and the prize was not victory, but survival, a survival that felt increasingly hollow and tainted. He was walking a tightrope over an abyss, and the intruder held the knife, ready to sever the rope at any moment. And Alice, his beloved Alice, was walking with him, utterly unaware of the precipice beneath her feet.

The stark reality of the note, a cold, brutal demand, had stripped away any remaining pretense of agency. Tom was no longer a man trying to protect his family; he was a puppet, his strings held by an unseen, malicious hand. The boathouse. Alice. The words echoed in his mind, each syllable a hammer blow against his conscience. His initial instinct, a primal urge to shield Alice from the encroaching darkness, warred with the paralyzing fear of the intruder's wrath. He replayed the ultimatum, searching for any ambiguity, any sliver of possibility that would allow him to circumvent the horrific directive. But the intruder's words were precise, devoid of mercy. *"Tonight. Bring her to the old boathouse by the lake. Do not call the police. Do not tell her anything. If you fail, or if she is not with you, the consequences will be far more severe than anything you have experienced thus far."*

The threat was palpable, a suffocating blanket of dread that left no room for deviation.

He paced the study, his footsteps a frantic rhythm against the polished wood. Alice was asleep, oblivious to the precipice that yawned beneath their seemingly stable world. He pictured her face, her trust, her unwavering belief in him. To betray that trust, to willingly lead her into danger, felt like an act of unimaginable evil. Yet, the alternative – the vague but terrifying "far more severe consequences" – gnawed at him, a constant, gnawing fear that threatened to consume him entirely. He had always been a man who prioritized self-preservation, who avoided confrontation, who swept his transgressions under the rug. This situation, however, was beyond any rug. This was a reckoning.

A desperate, half-formed idea began to crystallize in his mind. It was reckless, bordering on insane, but it was

*his* idea, a deviation from the intruder's script. If he couldn't refuse, perhaps he could manipulate. Perhaps he could use the intruder's own game against him. He wouldn't simply lead Alice to the boathouse like a sacrificial lamb. He would go, but he would go prepared. He would not be unarmed, not in spirit, at least. He would try to gather evidence, something, anything, that could expose this tormentor and ensure Alice's safety. It was a fool's errand, he knew, a defiant flailing against an opponent who had orchestrated every move so far. But the thought of passive compliance was a poison he could no longer stomach.

He crept back to his desk, his eyes scanning the dimly lit room as if expecting the intruder to materialize from the shadows. He needed a weapon, not for violence, but for deterrence, for a desperate flicker of resistance. His gaze fell upon a heavy antique letter opener, its silver handle cool and solid in his hand. It was hardly a match for whatever force he was up against, but it was something. He slid it into the waistband of his trousers, the metal a cold, reassuring weight against his skin.

Next, he needed a way to document the encounter, should it come to that. His phone. He checked its battery – thankfully, fully charged. He opened the voice recorder app, his thumb hovering over the record button. This was it. His gambit. A desperate attempt to reclaim a sliver of control, to turn the tables on his tormentor. He would feign compliance, but he would also be documenting, observing, looking for any slip-up, any weakness in the intruder's meticulously constructed plan. He would use the very intimacy of the situation, the supposed trust he was being forced to betray, to his advantage.

He returned to the bedroom, his heart pounding a frantic tattoo against his ribs. Alice was still asleep, her breathing soft and even. He stood over her for a long moment, the guilt a physical ache in his chest. How could he do this? How could he ask her to walk into a potential trap, even with his flimsy plan of defense? But the note's threat, the specter of "far more severe consequences," loomed large. He couldn't risk Alice's life by outright defiance. He had to try something, anything, to mitigate the danger.

He gently shook her awake. "Alice," he whispered, his voice rough with emotion. "We need to go for a walk."

She stirred, her eyes blinking open in the dim light. "Tom? What is it? It's so late." Her voice was laced with sleep, but also with that familiar, growing unease. She had felt it, the shift in their lives, the palpable tension that had settled over their home like a persistent fog.

"I know, I know," he murmured, trying to keep his voice steady. "But I... I think I saw something. Out by the lake. Near the boathouse." The lie felt like a betrayal of its own, a desperate attempt to mask the true horror of the situation. He couldn't bring himself to tell her the actual reason. Not yet. He was trying to buy time, to create an opening.

Her brow furrowed. "Saw something? What are you talking about?" She sat up, her movements quicker now, more alert. The sleepiness had vanished, replaced by a cautious curiosity that was quickly morphing into apprehension.

"Just a flicker of movement. I don't know," he improvised, his mind racing. "I thought maybe... maybe someone was there. It felt... wrong. I want to check it out. Just to be sure. We'll be quick." He kept his tone casual, almost dismissive, as if he were simply indulging a momentary curiosity. He needed her to agree, to come with him without suspicion.

Alice studied him, her gaze sharp. He could feel her dissecting his words, his demeanor. She knew he was hiding something. "Tom, you're scaring me," she said softly. "What's really going on?"

He took a deep breath, forcing himself to meet her eyes. "Nothing is going on, Alice. I'm just being overly cautious. This whole thing... it's been unsettling. I just want to make sure everything is safe. Please. Come with me. We'll just take a quick look." He tried to project an air of weary concern, of a husband trying to reassure his wife. It was a performance, and he was playing the role of a lifetime, a role he knew he was destined to fail.

A long moment of silence stretched between them, filled only by the sound of their breathing and the distant chirping of crickets. Alice's gaze remained fixed on his, searching. He could see the conflict in her eyes – the instinct to trust him, warring with the dawning realization that something was gravely wrong. Finally, with a sigh that seemed to carry the weight of all their recent anxieties, she nodded. "Alright, Tom," she said, her voice barely a whisper. "We'll go. But if you act strange, we're turning back immediately. Do you understand?"

"I understand," he lied, the words tasting like ash in his mouth. He felt a wave of revulsion wash over him. He was a coward, a liar, a man who would sacrifice his wife's peace, perhaps even her safety, for his own survival. But he was also, in his own twisted way, trying to protect her. He had to believe that.

He grabbed his phone, discreetly activating the voice recorder as he tucked it back into his pocket. The letter opener felt like a burning ember against his hip. He would not go to the boathouse as a victim.

He would go as a man armed with desperate hope and a flawed, dangerous plan. As they stepped out of the house, the night air felt unnaturally still, pregnant with an unseen menace. The moon, a sliver of bone in the inky sky, cast long, distorted shadows that danced with his growing fear. He knew, with a chilling certainty, that this was a gamble destined to fail, a desperate gambit born of terror and guilt. But it was the only gambit he had.

The damp night air clung to them like a shroud as Tom and Alice approached the old boathouse. Each crunch of gravel under their feet sounded unnaturally loud in the oppressive silence. Tom's hand, slick with sweat, instinctively tightened around the cool metal of the letter opener tucked in his waistband. He could feel Alice's apprehension radiating beside him, a palpable wave that mirrored his own churning dread. Her whispered questions, "Are you sure you saw something, Tom? It's so dark," were met with his strained reassurances, each word a fragile shield against the truth he was keeping from her. He kept his phone in his pocket, the recorder a silent, unseen witness to the unfolding horror. He was playing a dangerous game, a tightrope walk over an abyss of unknown terror, and with every step, the ground felt more unstable.

As they neared the weathered structure, a faint light flickered within, barely a beacon against the encroaching darkness. It was an invitation, or perhaps a lure, and Tom's heart hammered against his ribs. He could feel Alice tense beside him, her breathing shallow. "It's... it's lit up," she whispered, her voice trembling. "Someone's there."

Tom swallowed, his throat dry. This was it. The moment he had both desperately sought and deeply feared. He forced himself to maintain a semblance of calm, to project an air of cautious investigation rather than outright panic. "Stay behind me, Alice," he instructed, his voice a low growl. He took another step forward, his eyes fixed on the sliver of light escaping from under the warped wooden door. The metallic scent of decay, of stagnant water and forgotten things, wafted out, mingling with an unsettling, unfamiliar odor – something sharp and acrid, like old blood and fear.

He pushed the door open slowly, the hinges groaning in protest. The interior of the boathouse was a cavern of shadows, sparsely illuminated by a single, bare bulb hanging precariously from a frayed wire. Dust motes danced in the weak light, disturbed by their intrusion. The air was thick, heavy with an oppressive stillness. Against one wall, an old, decaying rowboat lay half-submerged in the murky water that filled the far end of the structure, its ribs exposed like a skeletal figure. Nets, tangled and rotting, hung from the ceiling like macabre decorations.

And then, he saw him.

He was standing near the back, almost swallowed by the gloom, but the light caught the glint of his eyes. Not just any eyes, but eyes that seemed to bore into Tom, dissecting him, judging him. There was no warmth, no humanity in them, only a chilling, predatory intelligence. He was silhouetted against the deeper darkness, a figure of pure menace. Tom's breath hitched. This was not the spectral presence he had imagined, the disembodied voice that had held him captive for days. This was flesh and blood, a man, a tangible embodiment of his deepest anxieties.

Alice gasped, a small, choked sound that ripped through the silence. Tom felt her grab his arm, her fingers digging into his skin with a desperate grip. He could feel her entire body trembling, a violent tremor that communicated a terror far greater than his own. She had seen him, too. The unseen architect of their nightmare, the phantom who had haunted their waking hours and their dreams, was now a visible, terrifying reality.

The intruder took a slow step forward, his movements unnervingly deliberate. He was not tall, perhaps of average height, but there was an aura of power about him that seemed to distort the very air around him. His face, now beginning to emerge from the shadows, was unremarkable in its features, yet profoundly unsettling. It was a face that seemed to have been sculpted from indifference, devoid of any discernible emotion beyond a chilling, calculated amusement. His eyes, a pale, washed-out blue, held a gaze that was both penetrating and unnervingly vacant, like the eyes of a predator that had long ago shed any pretense of empathy. A faint, almost imperceptible smile played on his lips, a cruel twist that sent a fresh wave of ice through Tom's veins.

"Well, well," the intruder's voice was a low, gravelly rumble, strangely devoid of the menace that his presence exuded. It was a voice that could belong to any man, yet in this context, it was laced with a sinister undertone, a subtle mockery that underscored the power imbalance. "You've brought her. Precisely as instructed. I must say, I'm impressed, Tom. You're a surprisingly obedient little puppet."

The word "puppet" landed like a physical blow. Tom felt a surge of defiance, a desperate need to break free from the invisible strings that bound him. But the sight of Alice, her face ashen, her eyes wide with unadulterated terror, anchored him. He couldn't afford to be reckless. Not now. He could feel the recorder in his pocket, a faint warmth against his thigh, a fragile hope of evidence, of retribution.

Alice, however, was not as controlled. Her initial shock seemed to be giving way to a raw, primal fear that threatened to overwhelm her. She finally spoke, her voice a thin, reedy sound that barely carried. "Who... who are you?" she managed to ask, her gaze locked on the intruder, her body rigid with apprehension.

The intruder's smile widened, revealing teeth that were surprisingly white and even. He seemed to relish her fear, to feed on it. "Who I am is not important, Alice," he said, his tone almost conversational, as if they were discussing the weather. "What is important is what you are here for. And what will happen if you don't comply." He turned his gaze back to Tom, his eyes narrowing slightly. "You haven't told her anything, have you, Tom? Any foolish ideas about resistance?"

Tom forced himself to meet his gaze. "No," he lied, his voice tight. "She knows nothing. I told her I saw something suspicious. That's all." He felt the weight of Alice's disbelief, her dawning understanding that he had lied to her, not just about seeing something, but about the very nature of their predicament. The betrayal, he knew, was a wound that might never heal, but it was a sacrifice he felt compelled to make.

The intruder let out a soft chuckle, a dry, rustling sound. "Good boy, Tom. Obedience is the key to survival, you see. And you, Alice," he turned back to her, his eyes seeming to probe her very soul, "you are to be very, very quiet. Your husband has made arrangements for your safety. All you need to do is follow his lead. And mine."

Alice swallowed hard, her eyes darting from the intruder to Tom, searching for answers, for reassurance that he couldn't give. She was trapped, not just by the intruder, but by Tom's deception. The terror in her eyes was not just of the man before them, but of the husband who had brought her here, who had lied to her, who had placed her in this terrifying situation.

"What... what do you want?" Alice finally managed to stammer, her voice barely above a whisper.

The intruder's gaze flickered towards the decaying rowboat, then back to Alice. A cold calculation settled in his eyes. "That, my dear Alice, is a conversation for another time. For now, your role is simple. You are here. Tom has fulfilled his part of the agreement. And now," his gaze swept over them both, a palpable threat in its intensity, "we will see how well you both play your parts."

He took another step closer, and the acrid scent grew stronger, sharper. Tom's hand instinctively went to the letter opener in his waistband. He could feel Alice tense beside him, her gaze fixed on the intruder's hands. He was wearing thin, dark gloves, and his fingers were long and unnervingly still.

"There's something you need to understand, Tom," the intruder said, his voice dropping to a lower register, the amusement gone, replaced by a chilling seriousness. "I don't like surprises. And I don't like being disobeyed. You've been given a very clear set of instructions. And while you've followed them thus far, one false move, one hint of defiance, and the consequences will be... considerable." He let the threat hang in the air, unspoken but understood. He was not just threatening them; he was taunting them, enjoying the palpable fear that radiated from them.

Tom felt a prickle of something beyond fear. It was anger, a hot, simmering rage that was fueled by the intruder's smug arrogance, his blatant manipulation. He wanted to lash out, to grab the letter opener and lunge, to do

*something* to reclaim some semblance of control. But he knew, with a sickening certainty, that it would be a fatal mistake. The intruder was not a man to be underestimated. He was calculating, ruthless, and clearly, he had planned this meticulously.

Alice, despite her obvious terror, seemed to be gathering a sliver of strength. Her fear was still evident, but it was no longer the paralyzing terror of the unseen. Now, it was a fear of a tangible threat, a fear she could focus on, perhaps even fight against. "What do you want from us?" she repeated, her voice a little stronger this time, though still laced with apprehension.

The intruder turned his full attention to her, and for the first time, Tom saw something flicker in those pale eyes – a hint of something akin to possessiveness, a disturbing, proprietary interest. It was a look that made Tom's stomach churn with a fresh wave of dread. This wasn't just about an extortion or a power play. There was something far more personal, far more twisted at play here.

"What I want is for you to be quiet," the intruder said, his voice softening in a way that was far more menacing than his earlier threats. "For you to be still. For you to understand that your life, and your husband's life, are now in my hands. I have watched you, Alice. I have observed your every move. And now, you will observe mine."

He gestured vaguely towards the back of the boathouse, towards the murky water. "There are... arrangements that need to be made. Preparations. And you, Tom, will assist me. You will do exactly as I say, and you will ensure that Alice remains silent and compliant. Understood?"

Tom nodded, unable to speak, the words catching in his throat. He felt a wave of nausea wash over him. He was complicit. He had brought Alice here, had lied to her, and now he was being forced to cooperate with her tormentor. The weight of his actions, the terrible choices he had made, pressed down on him, threatening to crush him.

The intruder's smile returned, a chilling confirmation of his victory. "Excellent. Now, Tom, come with me. Alice, you will stay right where you are. Do not move. Do not make a sound. If you do," he let his gaze drift pointedly towards the dark corners of the boathouse, "the consequences will be... immediate and irreversible."

He turned and walked towards the back of the boathouse, his movements fluid and silent. Tom hesitated for a fraction of a second, his eyes meeting Alice's. He saw a flicker of understanding, a desperate plea for him to be careful, to find a way out. He gave her a curt nod, a silent promise he wasn't sure he could keep, and then followed the intruder into the deeper shadows, the faint light of the single bulb casting long, distorted shadows that seemed to mock their desperation. The recorder in his pocket felt both like a lifeline and a terrible burden. He was walking deeper into the trap, but perhaps, just perhaps, he was also gathering the pieces of the weapon that would eventually set them free. The confrontation had begun, not with a bang, but with a chilling whisper, and the unveiling of a face that was far more terrifying than any shadow. The nightmare had a name, a form, and a voice, and it was inextricably linked to Alice, to Tom, and to the suffocating darkness of that forgotten boathouse.

The air in the boathouse, once thick with the scent of decay and stagnant water, now crackled with a different kind of fetidness – the sharp, metallic tang of fear and spilled adrenaline. Tom, his hand still hovering near the letter opener, felt a sudden, sickening lurch as the intruder's demeanor shifted. The amused predator had receded, replaced by something colder, harder. The chillingly conversational tone evaporated, leaving behind a raw, primal aggression.

"You think this is a game, Tom?" the intruder's voice was no longer a gravelly rumble, but a low, guttural snarl that sent shivers down Tom's spine. His eyes, those pale, vacant pools, narrowed, and a flicker of something akin to disgust crossed his features. "You think you can bring me here, record our little chat, and then waltz away with your evidence? You overestimate your intelligence, and you underestimate my patience."

Before Tom could even process the accusation, the intruder moved. It wasn't a hurried, panicked lunge, but a swift, economical burst of violence, honed by practice and a chilling disregard for consequence. His left hand shot out, not towards Tom's chest or face, but towards the letter opener tucked into his waistband. The grip was like steel, wrenching the improvised weapon free with a surprising lack of effort.

Tom, caught off guard, instinctively recoiled, his eyes widening in dawning horror. The intruder didn't hesitate. The letter opener, a flimsy defense against a determined attacker, became a terrifyingly effective instrument. A sharp, tearing sound ripped through the heavy air as the metal blade sliced across Tom's forearm, just above the elbow. Tom cried out, a choked gasp of pain and disbelief, his hand flying to the wound as a hot, viscous stream of blood erupted, soaking his sleeve and splattering onto the damp concrete floor.

"No!" Alice's scream was a raw, animalistic sound, a desperate plea that seemed to echo in the confined space. She lunged forward, her own terror momentarily eclipsed by the sight of Tom's injury, but a harsh command from the intruder froze her in her tracks.

"Stay put, Alice," he hissed, his voice laced with menace. He turned his attention back to Tom, a cruel smile playing on his lips. "You disobeyed, Tom. You brought the recorder. You showed me you weren't as compliant as I'd hoped. This is the price for your foolishness." He gestured with the bloodied letter opener, the glint of the blade catching the dim light. "And it's just the beginning."

The pain was blinding, a searing agony that threatened to engulf Tom's senses. He stumbled back, his legs weak, his breath coming in ragged gasps. He could feel the blood pulsing, a steady, relentless drain that was sapping his strength. He looked at Alice, her face a mask of terror, her eyes wide with unshed tears, and a wave of guilt washed over him, colder than the pain. He had brought her into this. He had put her in harm's way. And now, he was the first to fall.

The intruder advanced, his movements deliberate, unhurried. He seemed to savor Tom's vulnerability, the way he swayed, the way his grip tightened on his bleeding arm. "You thought you were so clever, didn't you?" he taunted, his voice dripping with disdain. "Playing detective. Gathering your precious evidence. But you're not a detective, Tom. You're a victim. And you're about to become a pawn in a much larger game."

With a sudden, brutal thrust, the intruder shoved Tom hard. Tom stumbled backward, his heel catching on an unseen obstacle. He fell with a sickening thud, the damp concrete jarring against his already injured arm. The letter opener clattered uselessly from his grasp, skittering across the floor. He tried to push himself up, his hands slipping on the wet, bloodied concrete, but the intruder was already upon him.

He straddled Tom's chest, the weight of him pinning Tom to the ground. The smell of his sweat, mixed with the acrid odor that clung to him, was overwhelming. Tom could feel the rough texture of the intruder's clothes against his face, could hear his ragged breathing. The letter opener was back in the intruder's hand, held point-down, aimed directly at Tom's exposed throat.

"This is where it ends for you, Tom," the intruder whispered, his voice low and chillingly calm. "No more games. No more defiance."

Alice watched, paralyzed by horror. The scene unfolding before her was a nightmare made manifest, a visceral, brutal reality that shattered any remaining illusions she held. Tom, her husband, the man she loved, was being systematically broken, and the helplessness was a crushing weight. Her breath hitched, and a silent scream built in her chest. She was next. The realization hit her with the force of a physical blow, jolting her out of her stunned paralysis.

But as the intruder's focus remained on Tom, a spark ignited within Alice. It wasn't courage, not yet. It was a desperate, primal instinct for survival. She saw the raw, unadulterated violence in the man's eyes, the utter lack of remorse. She saw her husband bleeding, helpless, and something within her snapped. The fear remained, a constant thrumming beneath her skin, but it was no longer the dominant force. It was being shoved aside by a fierce, protective rage.

The intruder raised the letter opener, its point hovering inches from Tom's skin. Tom squeezed his eyes shut, a silent prayer escaping his lips. This was it. The end.

But then, a sound. Not a scream this time, but a harsh, guttural cry that ripped through the tense silence. Alice, fueled by a surge of adrenaline she didn't know she possessed, had grabbed the nearest heavy object – a thick, waterlogged wooden oar leaning against the wall. With a force born of desperation, she swung it with all her might, aiming for the intruder's head.

The oar connected with a sickening thwack, not directly to his head, but glancing off his shoulder. He roared in pain and surprise, his grip on Tom faltering for a critical instant. The letter opener clattered to the floor as he staggered back, momentarily disoriented.

"You little bitch!" he snarled, his voice raw with pain and fury. His attention snapped to Alice, his eyes blazing with a renewed, terrifying intensity.

Tom seized the opportunity. With a surge of strength he didn't know he had, he shoved himself out from under the intruder, scrambling away on his hands and knees, his injured arm throbbing with every movement. He didn't look back, his only thought to put distance between himself and the enraged attacker.

Alice, her heart hammering against her ribs like a trapped bird, didn't wait for him. She dropped the oar and turned to flee, her eyes scanning the dimly lit boathouse for an escape route. The dim light, which had seemed so oppressive before, now felt like a cruel mockery, offering visibility but no clear path to safety.

The intruder, recovering quickly from the blow, let out a guttural roar and lunged after Alice. His movements were swift, predatory, his rage a palpable force. He was no longer toying with them. The veneer of control had cracked, revealing the savage animal beneath.

Alice, her lungs burning, stumbled towards the open doorway. She could hear his footsteps pounding behind her, gaining ground. She risked a glance over her shoulder and saw him closing the distance, his face contorted with a primal fury. He was reaching for her.

Just as his fingers brushed against her jacket, Alice did something instinctive. She veered sharply to the left, towards the murky water that filled the far end of the boathouse, towards the decaying rowboat. It was a desperate, illogical move, a last-ditch gamble.

The intruder, expecting her to run for open ground, was momentarily thrown off balance by her unexpected maneuver. He stumbled, his momentum carrying him forward. Alice, her eyes fixed on the dark water, threw herself to the side, landing with a splash in the frigid, foul-smelling liquid.

The intruder, caught off guard, plunged forward, his arms flailing. He didn't fall in completely, but his legs and lower body were submerged in the stagnant water, sending ripples and disturbing the debris that floated on its surface. He cursed violently, the sound echoing in the boathouse.

Tom, who had managed to reach the doorway, watched the scene unfold with a mixture of terror and desperate hope. He saw Alice struggling in the water, her clothes heavy, her movements hampered. He saw the intruder trying to regain his footing, his rage now mixed with a grudging surprise.

The intruder, his face a mask of fury and disgust, pulled himself out of the water, dripping and furious. He glared at Alice, who was now scrambling towards the far wall, trying to find purchase on the slippery, algae-covered concrete.

"You think that will save you?" he spat, his voice hoarse. He looked at his bloodied arm, then back at Alice, a cold, calculating glint returning to his eyes. The initial burst of raw anger seemed to have subsided, replaced by a chilling, methodical resolve.

He turned his attention back to Tom, who was still dazed by the blow and the blood loss. "And you, Tom," he said, his voice regaining its unsettling calm, "you're not done yet."

He advanced on Tom, who instinctively recoiled. The fear was back, but this time, it was a cold, calculated fear, amplified by the knowledge that the intruder was not only strong and violent, but also cunning and deeply disturbed. Tom could feel the recorder in his pocket, a silent witness, a sliver of hope in the encroaching darkness. He had to survive. For Alice. For himself. He had to find a way to fight back, not with brute force, but with the knowledge he had gained, with the evidence he had captured. The confrontation had escalated beyond anything he could have imagined, and the violent climax was just beginning.

The frigid water, thick with the stench of rot and something vaguely chemical, offered a momentary, albeit disgusting, sanctuary. Alice's lungs burned, her limbs felt heavy as lead, but the immediate threat of the intruder's grasp had receded. He stood at the edge of the murky pool, a figure of dripping, enraged fury, his pale eyes fixed on her with a predatory intensity that promised no quarter. His face, contorted by a mixture of pain from the oar blow and sheer, unadulterated wrath, was a mask of primal rage. The veneer of calculated menace had shattered, revealing the savage beast beneath.

He cursed, the sound a guttural rasp that echoed unnervingly in the cavernous boathouse. He clawed at his sodden clothes, his movements jerky, agitated. The cold water, he clearly found, was an affront, a degradation he wouldn't tolerate. Alice used the precious seconds he was occupied to scramble further along the wall, her fingers scrabbling for purchase on the slick, algae-coated concrete. Every inch gained was a victory, a testament to the raw, unthinking instinct that had taken root within her. The Alice who had cowered in the shadows, consumed by paranoia and a gnawing dread, was gone. In her place was a creature driven by a singular, desperate imperative: survive.

Tom, his arm bleeding profusely, his body wracked with pain, watched from the relative safety of the doorway. His breath hitched with every surge of movement from Alice, with every guttural roar from their attacker. He was a spectator to a fight for life, a fight he had inadvertently ignited. Guilt warred with a desperate hope, a hope that Alice, the woman he loved, the woman he had promised to protect, would somehow prevail against this monstrous force. He tried to push himself to his feet, to move, to offer some semblance of support, but his legs trembled, his vision swam. He was too weak, too injured. He could only watch, a helpless observer, as the final act of this horrifying tableau unfolded.

The intruder finally extricated himself from the water, shaking his limbs like a wet dog, sending droplets of foul water spraying across the damp floor. His glare shifted from the water to Alice, his eyes narrowing into slits of pure malice. "You think that'll save you?" he spat, his voice hoarse and rough. He glanced at his bloodied arm, then back at Alice, and a chillingly familiar coldness began to seep back into his gaze. The incandescent rage, though still simmering beneath the surface, was being tempered by a calculating, almost surgical, resolve. He had been inconvenienced, humiliated even, but not defeated. Not by a long shot.

He turned his attention back to Tom, who was still trying to gather his wits, his body protesting every movement. "And you, Tom," he said, his voice regaining that unnerving, measured tone, the one that had underscored his every threat, "you're not done yet." He took a step towards Tom, his gait deliberate, predatory. The brief surge of animalistic fury had passed, replaced by a chillingly methodical approach. He knew he had Tom on the ropes, weakened and disoriented. This was the moment to deliver the final, crushing blow.

But Alice wasn't finished. The water had disoriented him, yes, but it had also cleared her head, sharpening her focus. As the intruder advanced on Tom, her eyes scanned the immediate vicinity, not with panic, but with a desperate, pragmatic assessment. Her gaze landed on a series of shelves lining the wall, laden with various odds and ends – rusted tools, forgotten fishing gear, and a small, tarnished kitchen knife, its handle worn smooth with age. It was a long shot, a pathetic weapon against such a formidable foe, but it was something.

The intruder was closing in on Tom, his hand reaching out, not for a weapon, but to seize Tom's already injured arm, to inflict more pain, more agony. Tom braced himself, a silent resignation settling over him. He had failed. He had brought Alice into this nightmare, and he couldn't even protect himself, let alone her. He closed his eyes, a whimper escaping his lips.

Then, a sound. Not a scream, but a sharp, metallic clang, followed by a choked gasp. Alice had moved. With a burst of speed that defied her exhaustion and terror, she had darted towards the shelves, snatched the kitchen knife, and thrown it with all her might. It wasn't a clean throw, her aim was wild, fueled by desperation rather than skill, but it found its mark. The knife, spinning erratically, struck the intruder in the shoulder, embedding itself shallowly, but with enough force to elicit a roar of pain and surprise.

He recoiled, his hand flying to the wound, his eyes blazing at Alice with renewed fury. "You bloody bitch!" he roared, his carefully constructed composure shattering once more. The brief moment of calculated calm had evaporated, replaced by an explosion of raw, visceral rage. He had been wounded, not by Tom, but by Alice, the woman he had dismissed as a mere witness.

Tom, sensing the shift, the momentary distraction, pushed himself up with a surge of adrenaline. He stumbled away from the attacker, his injured arm throbbing, his breath coming in ragged gasps. He needed to create distance, to allow Alice the space she needed to fight. He knew, with a certainty that chilled him to the bone, that if this man caught them again, there would be no second chances.

Alice didn't wait. She dropped the empty shelf space and scrambled further along the wall, her eyes darting around, searching for anything else, anything that could be used as a weapon, as a shield. The intruder, his face contorted in a mask of pure hatred, ripped the knife from his shoulder, the wound bleeding freely. He didn't seem to register the pain, only the burning desire for retribution. He lunged after Alice, his movements no longer those of a calculating predator, but of a cornered animal, desperate and dangerous.

She could hear his ragged breathing, the pounding of his footsteps behind her. The boathouse, once a place of refuge, had become a cage, a deadly labyrinth. She risked a glance over her shoulder. He was closer now, his hand outstretched, his fingers inches from her back. Panic flared, hot and sharp, threatening to overwhelm her. But then, a memory, a fleeting image of the intruder's violent reaction to the water, sparked an idea.

With a desperate surge of her remaining strength, she veered sharply, not towards the open door, but towards a large, overturned barrel that lay near the water's edge. It was a risky maneuver, a gamble, but she saw a sliver of a chance. She threw herself towards it, her body colliding with the rough wood with a jarring impact. The barrel rolled, creating a temporary barrier between her and her pursuer.

The intruder, caught off guard by her unpredictable movement, stumbled. His momentum carried him forward, and his foot caught on the rolling barrel. He bellowed in surprise and pain as he lost his balance, his arms fllailing wildly. For a horrifying instant, it looked as though he would fall into the murky water once more. But with a savage grunt, he managed to regain his footing, his eyes burning with a renewed, terrible intensity. He was now closer than ever, his enraged face mere feet away.

Alice, however, had used the barrel to her advantage. She had rolled behind it, using it as a makeshift shield, and as the intruder regained his balance, she was already moving, her hands scrabbling at the rough surface of the barrel, seeking a way to leverage herself. She saw a gap between the barrel and the wall, a narrow space, but perhaps just enough.

He was upon her, his hand reaching out, a desperate grab for her hair. Alice, with a guttural cry, pushed herself forward, squeezing through the narrow gap. She felt a searing pain as his fingernails raked across her scalp, tearing at her skin, but she was free, on the other side of the barrel.

The intruder, enraged by his failure to capture her, kicked the barrel with all his might. The impact sent it skidding across the floor, its movement jarring Alice's already battered body. But it also served to further disorient him, to push him back from her.

Alice didn't waste another second. Her eyes fell on the very thing that had brought them here: the concealed recorder. It was still in Tom's pocket. If she could get to it, if she could somehow transmit it, then this horrifying ordeal might not be for nothing. She looked at Tom, who was now staggering towards her, his face etched with pain and fear.

"Tom," she gasped, her voice raw, "the recorder."

He nodded, understanding dawning in his eyes. He fumbled in his pocket, his trembling fingers finding the small device. But the intruder was already recovering, his rage a palpable force. He lunged at Tom again, his eyes locked on the recorder.

This was it. The moment of truth. Alice saw the pure, unadulterated desperation in the intruder's eyes, the desperate need to silence Tom, to destroy the evidence. She knew, with a chilling clarity, that she had to act. There was no more room for fear, no more space for hesitation.

She saw it then, a glint of metal on the floor near the water's edge. It was the letter opener, the very weapon he had used to wound Tom. A surge of adrenaline coursed through her, sharpening her senses, lending her a strength she never knew she possessed. It was a crude weapon, a clumsy tool, but in that moment, it was her only hope.

As the intruder closed in on Tom, his hand reaching for the recorder, Alice surged forward. She didn't think. She didn't hesitate. She scooped up the bloodied letter opener, its cold metal a stark contrast to the heat of her desperate resolve. She lunged, not at the intruder's chest, but at his legs, aiming for the Achilles' heel that had been revealed when he stumbled.

Her aim was true. The letter opener, held low, struck him in the calf. It wasn't a deep wound, but it was enough. He cried out, a sharp, pained yelp, and his advance faltered. He stumbled, his legs buckling beneath him.

This was her chance. Tom, seeing the opening, pushed the recorder into Alice's hand and scrambled away, putting more distance between himself and the attacker. Alice, the letter opener still clutched in her hand, turned to face the intruder. He was on his knees, his eyes blazing with a mixture of pain and disbelief. He looked at the letter opener, then at Alice, his face a mask of fury.

"You... you won't get away with this," he stammered, his voice laced with pain.

Alice didn't reply. She saw the raw violence in his eyes, the unrepentant depravity. She knew, with a terrifying certainty, that he would never stop. He would hunt them, torment them, until they were broken. The recorder, a symbol of their desperate attempt to expose him, was now in her hands, a lifeline, a chance for justice. But first, she had to survive.

He lunged again, a desperate, half-crouching movement, his hands reaching for her. Alice stood her ground. Her fear was still there, a cold knot in her stomach, but it was no longer paralyzing. It was a driving force, a raw, primal urge to protect herself, to protect Tom. She raised the letter opener, her hand shaking, but her gaze steady.

He closed the distance, his rage a tangible force. He was within inches of her, his breath hot and foul against her face. Alice closed her eyes for a brief second, picturing Tom's face, picturing a life beyond this nightmare. Then, with a guttural cry, she thrust the letter opener forward, with all the strength she could muster.

The metal blade sank into his chest, piercing through his clothes, finding its mark. A gasp tore from his throat, a ragged, wet sound. His eyes widened in shock, then in a dawning terror. He looked down at the letter opener embedded in his chest, then back at Alice, his face paling.

He stumbled back, a hand flying to the wound, but it was no use. The life drained from his eyes, a vacant horror replacing the rage. He swayed for a moment, a broken puppet, then crumpled to the floor, his body hitting the concrete with a sickening thud. The letter opener remained lodged in his chest, a grim testament to the desperate act of survival.

Silence descended, thick and heavy, broken only by Alice's ragged gasps and the distant sound of dripping water. She stood frozen, the letter opener still in her hand, her body trembling uncontrollably. The adrenaline that had fueled her fight began to recede, leaving behind a profound exhaustion, a deep-seated shock. She looked at the body on the floor, at the still, unmoving form of the man who had threatened to destroy them, and a wave of nausea washed over her.

Tom, his arm still bleeding, stumbled towards her, his eyes wide with a mixture of relief and horror. He reached out, his hand hovering over her, unsure of what to do, what to say. He saw the blood on her hands, the wildness in her eyes, and he knew, with a crushing certainty, that nothing would ever be the same.

Alice finally dropped the letter opener. It clattered onto the concrete, its metallic ring echoing in the sudden, vast emptiness. She looked at Tom, her gaze unfocused, her body starting to buckle under the immense weight of what had just happened. The fight for survival was over, but the battle for her sanity had just begun. She had killed a man. In self-defense, yes, but the act itself was a stain, a scar that would forever mark her soul. The boathouse, once a symbol of their torment, had become the site of their desperate, brutal salvation.

# Chapter 7: The Fragile Refuge

The clang of the letter opener hitting the concrete floor was a sound that seemed to reverberate not just through the boathouse, but through the very marrow of Alice's bones. It was the punctuation mark at the end of a sentence written in blood and terror, a sentence that had taken her to the precipice of her own existence. The silence that followed was not a relief, but a heavy, suffocating blanket, muffling the frantic pounding of her own heart. The adrenaline, that potent elixir of survival, was beginning to recede, leaving behind a vast, desolate emptiness. Her limbs, once propelled by an instinct for self-preservation so fierce it felt alien, now felt leaden, unresponsive. She stood, a statue carved from disbelief and shock, her gaze fixed on the sprawled, lifeless form on the damp concrete. The man who had brought such darkness into her life, who had threatened to extinguish not only her own light but Tom's as well, was gone. And the chilling reality of it was a burden far heavier than any physical injury.

Tom, his breathing still ragged, his injured arm a throbbing testament to the brutal encounter, slowly pulled himself towards her. His face, streaked with grime and blood, was a roadmap of fear and exhaustion. He looked at her, his eyes wide, searching for something in her frozen demeanor – reassurance, sanity, perhaps even a reflection of the horror he himself felt. He reached out, his fingers trembling, stopping just short of touching her. The unspoken words hung between them, thick with the weight of what they had witnessed, of what they had done. He saw the blood on her hands, the raw, animalistic sheen in her eyes, and a profound, soul-deep certainty settled upon him: the Alice he knew, the Alice he loved, was irrevocably changed. The veneer of ordinary life had been stripped away, revealing the primal survivor beneath, and the scars of that revelation would forever remain.

Alice finally released the letter opener, her grip slackening, her fingers uncurling as if they no longer belonged to her. The weapon clattered onto the cold, unforgiving floor, its final, metallic cry swallowed by the immense quiet. She looked at Tom, her vision swimming, the edges of her perception blurring. His face seemed distant, unreal, a ghost in the dim light. Her body, no longer held rigid by the sheer force of will, began to tremble, a deep, uncontrollable tremor that shook her from her head to her toes. The fight was over, the immediate danger averted, but the battle for her mind, for her soul, had only just begun. She had taken a life. Even in self-defense, the act was a profound violation, a stain that would never truly be washed away. The boathouse, a tomb now, had also been their sanctuary, the stage for their desperate, brutal rebirth.

The air in the boathouse was thick with the coppery scent of blood, a smell so potent it seemed to cling to the back of her throat. Alice's eyes, still adjusting to the aftermath, swept across the scene, taking in the gruesome tableau with a detached horror. The body of the intruder lay sprawled near the water's edge, a grotesque parody of life. Nearby, Tom was slumped against a dilapidated workbench, his breath coming in shallow gasps, his arm wrapped in a makeshift bandage fashioned from a torn shirt. The once familiar space was now a charnel house, a testament to the violence that had erupted within its damp walls. Each stain on the concrete, each overturned piece of debris, was a stark reminder of the brutal struggle, of the sheer, unthinking will to survive that had possessed her.

She knelt beside Tom, her movements stiff and uncertain. His face was pale, his lips tinged with blue, but his eyes, though clouded with pain and shock, held a flicker of recognition, of relief. He managed a weak smile, a shadow of his usual warmth. "Alice," he whispered, his voice hoarse. "You... you did it."

Alice could only nod, her throat too tight to form words. She reached out, her hand trembling, and gently touched his cheek. His skin was cold, clammy. "Are you alright?" The question felt absurd, a gross understatement of their current predicament.

"Just... tired," he managed, wincing as he shifted his weight. "And hurt. But I'm here. We're here." He looked towards the body of the intruder, his expression hardening for a fleeting moment. "He's gone."

The finality of that statement settled upon Alice with crushing weight. He was gone. But the echo of his violence, the residue of his malice, seemed to permeate the very air they breathed. She looked down at her hands, still faintly stained with blood, and a wave of revulsion washed over her. These were the hands that had held Tom, that had clutched the recorder, that had plunged a letter opener into another human being. They felt foreign, tainted.

"We need to get out of here," Tom said, his voice gaining a fraction of its former strength. "Before... before someone else finds us."

Alice's gaze flickered to the recorder clutched in her other hand. It felt heavy, a burden and a hope all at once. This small device, the catalyst for their ordeal, was now their only weapon against the darkness that had nearly consumed them. "The recorder," she said, her voice barely above a whisper. "We have it."

Tom nodded, his eyes meeting hers with a shared understanding. "We do. And that means... we need to tell people. We need to make sure this doesn't happen to anyone else." He paused, his gaze drifting to the door. "But first, we need to survive this. We need to get help."

The immediate shock had begun to recede, replaced by a gnawing fear of what lay ahead. They were alive, but they were also exposed, vulnerable, and carrying a secret that could either save them or condemn them. The boathouse, once a place of refuge, now felt like a cage, a grim reminder of the close call they had endured. Alice surveyed the scene again, her eyes lingering on the disarray, the shattered remnants of their attempted sanctuary. The silence that had initially been terrifying now seemed to press in on her, pregnant with unspoken horrors, with the terrifying stillness of death.

She stood up, her legs unsteady, and moved towards the door, her gaze fixed on the faint light filtering in from outside. The world beyond this grim space seemed impossibly distant, a place she was no longer sure she belonged to. The violence had been primal, brutal, and in its wake, Alice felt a profound sense of alienation, as if a fundamental part of her had been irrevocably fractured. The act of survival had demanded a ruthlessness she hadn't known she possessed, and the realization of that buried ferocity was as terrifying as the intruder himself.

"We need to go, Tom," she said, her voice firmer now, a new kind of steel replacing the tremor of shock. "We need to leave this place behind. And we need to keep moving." She looked back at the body, at the stillness that had claimed it, and a shiver ran down her spine. The boathouse was a tomb, and they were its reluctant, traumatized survivors, forever marked by the echoes of violence. The fragile refuge had been shattered, leaving behind only the stark, chilling reality of what it took to endure. The aftermath was not a gentle dawn, but a stark, brutal awakening into a world forever altered.

The scent of decay and brine, once a mere backdrop to their terror, now seemed to cling to Alice like a second skin. As she helped Tom to his feet, his injured arm cradled protectively, her eyes scanned the interior of the boathouse with a renewed, almost clinical, assessment. The adrenaline had ebbed, leaving behind a bone-deep weariness, but also a clarity she hadn't possessed before. The distorted, primal fear had been replaced by a grim, pragmatic focus. She saw not just the bloodstains and the overturned furniture, but the potential hazards, the lingering threats, and the essential escape route. Her gaze, however, kept returning to the spot where the intruder had fallen, to the unsettling stillness that now occupied the space where raw, untamed malice had so recently resided. It was a profound silence, heavier than any sound, a testament to the absolute finality of death.

Tom leaned heavily against her, his breath hitching with each movement. "We... we can't just leave him here," he murmured, his voice strained. "Someone will find him."

Alice's jaw tightened. "They will," she agreed, her voice flat, devoid of emotion. "But it won't be us. We have to go. Now." The thought of lingering, of confronting the full horror of what had happened in a more tangible way, sent a fresh wave of nausea through her. She needed distance, air that wasn't thick with the stench of violence and death. She needed to put as much space as possible between herself and this place, this nightmare.

As they moved towards the doorway, the weak sunlight filtering in felt like an accusation, a stark contrast to the darkness they had just emerged from. Alice stumbled slightly, her foot catching on something unseen on the floor. She looked down, her heart leaping into her throat. It was a loose floorboard, pried up, its splintered edges glinting dully. A memory, sharp and unwelcome, pierced through her haze: the intruder's desperate scramble, his frantic search for something he had hidden, something he had feared being discovered. Her eyes widened. He had been searching for something, something he had evidently not found, or perhaps, had lost in the chaos.

"Tom," she said, her voice urgent, "wait." She knelt, her fingers tracing the edges of the disturbed floorboard. Her mind raced. What had he been looking for? Had he hidden something here? Was it related to why he had targeted them in the first place? The questions swirled, adding another layer of unease to her already frayed nerves. But the immediate need for escape overrode her curiosity. They couldn't afford to linger, to explore every dark corner of this tragic place.

With a sigh, Tom nodded his assent, leaning against the doorframe, his eyes fixed on her with a mixture of concern and unspoken anxiety. Alice pushed aside her fleeting curiosity, the instinct for self-preservation reasserting its dominance. They had the recorder. That was what mattered. The rest was just... fallout.

Stepping out of the boathouse was like stepping into another world. The air, though cool, felt clean, blessedly free of the cloying scent of blood and decay. The familiar chirping of birds, the rustle of leaves in the wind – sounds that had once been so mundane they were barely noticed – now struck Alice with a profound sense of normalcy, of life continuing, oblivious to the horror they had just endured. She blinked, her eyes adjusting to the brighter light, and for a moment, it felt as though they had simply been on a terrifying, extended camping trip, a nightmare they had somehow woken from.

But the reality quickly asserted itself. Tom's labored breathing, the throbbing pain etched on his face, the way he instinctively cradled his injured arm – these were tangible reminders that the ordeal was far from over. The boathouse, a dark, brooding presence behind them, held the grim testament to their survival, a secret they now carried within them. Alice looked at Tom, her expression softening with a tenderness that had been momentarily eclipsed by the sheer force of adrenaline.

"We need to get you to a hospital," she said, her voice firm, determined. "And then... then we deal with this." She gestured vaguely towards the recorder, its dark plastic casing a stark contrast to the vibrant green of the surrounding woods.

Tom managed another weak smile. "One step at a time, Alice. We're alive. That's the first, and most important, step." He pushed himself away from the doorframe, his movements slow and deliberate. "Let's just... get away from here. As far as we can."

As they began to walk, their footsteps crunching softly on the fallen leaves, Alice couldn't shake the feeling of being watched. It was a residual paranoia, a phantom sense of the intruder's predatory gaze, but it was there, a cold knot in the pit of her stomach. She glanced back at the boathouse, its weathered timbers looking ominously dark against the bright afternoon sky. It seemed to hold its secrets close, a silent witness to the violence that had unfolded within its walls.

The path leading away from the boathouse was overgrown, winding through dense woods. With each step, Alice felt a growing sense of detachment from the events that had transpired. It was a survival mechanism, she knew, a way to shield herself from the full impact of the trauma. But a part of her remained frozen in that moment of desperate combat, the visceral fear, the raw fight for life. She would carry those echoes with her, she suspected, for a long time to come.

Tom stumbled, and Alice immediately steadied him. His face was pale, his breathing shallow. "Almost there," she murmured, her voice a low, encouraging hum. The car, hidden deeper in the woods, felt like their only lifeline to the outside world, a temporary sanctuary before the true reckoning. She knew that once they reached it, once they contacted the authorities, their lives would be irrevocably altered. The violence they had faced, the act of self-defense, would become a public spectacle, a legal battle, a psychological entanglement they might never fully escape.

But for now, there was only the immediate need for safety, for medical attention. The woods, which had once seemed like a maze designed to trap them, now offered a sense of cover, a temporary reprieve. As they pushed through the undergrowth, the recorder felt like a lead weight in Alice's pocket, a tangible symbol of the danger they had courted and the justice they now desperately sought. The silence of the woods was a stark contrast to the cacophony of violence they had left behind, a fragile peace that felt both welcome and unnerving. They had survived, but the cost was etched deep within them, a silent testament to the fragile nature of safety and the enduring shadows of fear. The aftermath was a landscape of uncertainty, a journey into the unknown, with the weight of their experience a constant, heavy companion.

Alice's gaze, initially fixed on the ravaged scene within the boathouse, began to drift, snagging on the periphery of her vision. The immediate, visceral shock had begun to recede, not dissipating entirely, but morphing into a dull, persistent ache beneath the surface of her awareness. It was a peculiar sensation, like a phantom limb that throbbed with a pain that wasn't entirely her own. Tom's labored breathing beside her, the rough texture of the torn fabric she'd used to bind his arm, the metallic tang still clinging to the air – these were all grounding elements, stark reminders of their tangible reality. Yet, as she took a shaky breath, a subtle disquiet began to bloom in the corners of her mind, a feeling that defied rational explanation.

It started small, almost imperceptible. A faint scuff mark on the far wall, near the ventilation grate, a mark she was certain hadn't been there before. She traced its outline with her eyes, trying to attribute it to the frantic struggle, to the sheer chaos that had erupted. But it felt... deliberate. Too clean, too precise for the wild flailing of bodies and the desperate scrabble for survival. Then, her gaze landed on a small, dark object tucked beneath a stack of decaying fishing nets. A button. Not the kind that would fall off clothing in a scuffle, but a small, intricately carved button, made of a material that glinted with an almost unnatural sheen in the dim light. It was out of place, utterly alien to the grimy, utilitarian world of the boathouse. She hadn't seen it during the fight. Had Tom? She risked a glance at him. He was slumped against the wall, his eyes closed, his face a mask of pain and exhaustion. He hadn't noticed.

The feeling intensified. It wasn't just a lingering paranoia born of extreme stress, a common enough companion after such an ordeal. This felt different. It felt like... observation. As if, even in their desperate struggle, even in the aftermath, they had not been alone. The silence of the boathouse, which had been so deafening moments before, now seemed to hold a different quality. It wasn't just the absence of sound; it was the

*presence* of something listening. She found herself scanning the shadows, her eyes darting towards the small, grimy windows that offered glimpses of the dense foliage outside. Were those branches swaying unnaturally? Was that a flicker of movement in the undergrowth, too quick to be a bird, too deliberate to be the wind?

A faint, almost inaudible click echoed from the direction of the ventilation grate. Alice froze, her blood turning to ice. It was the sound of metal on metal, a delicate, precise sound that was utterly at odds with the crude structure of the boathouse. Her breath hitched. She looked at the grate, then back at the button, then at the scuff mark. The pieces, disparate and unsettling, began to coalesce into a disturbing picture. Someone had been watching. Not just the intruder they had dealt with, but someone else. Someone who had perhaps orchestrated the entire event, or at least, had been observing it with a detached, clinical interest.

The implications were chilling. If the intruder hadn't been working alone, if there was a network, a larger organization behind him, then their victory in the boathouse was far from complete. It was merely a skirmish, a single battle won in a war they hadn't even fully understood they were fighting. The recorder, clutched so tightly in her hand, suddenly felt less like a triumphant trophy and more like a dangerous piece of evidence, a beacon that had drawn unwanted attention.

She moved cautiously towards the ventilation grate, her heart pounding a frantic rhythm against her ribs. The metal was cool beneath her fingertips. She peered through the rusted mesh, her eyes straining in the gloom. The air inside was thick with the smell of damp earth and stagnant water, but beneath it, she detected a faint, acrid scent, like ozone. And then she saw it. Not an object, not a person, but a subtle distortion in the air, a shimmering that suggested a lens, a hidden camera. It was small, almost invisible, tucked away in the shadowed recess of the vent, its dark eye fixed on the very spot where the intruder had met his end.

The revelation struck her with the force of a physical blow. They had been observed. Every moment of their terror, every desperate act, had been witnessed. The intruder's attack, their brutal fight for survival, Tom's injury, her own desperate measures – all of it had been recorded, analyzed, perhaps even enjoyed, by an unseen observer. The thought sent a wave of nausea through her. They were not just survivors of a violent encounter; they were subjects in someone's grim experiment, characters in a narrative unfolding according to someone else's script.

The button. The scuff mark. The click. They were not random occurrences. They were signals, perhaps accidental, perhaps deliberate, left by someone who had been present, someone who had access. Someone who was still close. The feeling of being watched intensified, no longer a vague unease but a concrete certainty. The woods outside, which had seemed like a sanctuary just moments before, now felt like a cage, with unseen eyes peering in from every shadowed thicket.

Tom stirred, his eyes fluttering open. "Alice?" he rasped, his voice rough. "What is it?"

She tore her gaze away from the vent, forcing herself to appear calm, though her insides churned with a terrifying new understanding. "Nothing, Tom," she lied, her voice tight. "Just... checking the door. Making sure it's secure." She moved away from the vent, forcing a casualness she didn't feel into her movements. She couldn't tell him about the camera, not yet. Not when he was so weakened, so vulnerable. But the knowledge that they had been watched, that their most desperate moments had been cataloged, added a new layer of dread to their already precarious situation.

The recorder felt heavier in her pocket now, a potent symbol of their ordeal, but also a dangerous liability. It was proof, yes, but it was also a testament to their exposure. If someone had been watching them in the boathouse, it was highly probable they were still being monitored. Their escape from the boathouse, their journey through the woods, their eventual contact with the outside world – all of it could be compromised.

She looked back at the body, at the stillness that had been so terrifying and now seemed almost... insufficient. The intruder was dead, but the true threat, the unseen observer, was still out there, a ghost in the periphery, a puppet master pulling invisible strings. The fragile refuge had been breached, not just by violence, but by surveillance. And the chilling realization was that their fight for survival might have only just begun, a fight waged not just against brute force, but against an insidious, unseen enemy who held the power of observation, and perhaps, control.

As Alice and Tom stumbled away from the boathouse, the woods seemed to press in on them, the shadows deepening with an unnatural intensity. The air, which had felt so clean and liberating moments before, now felt thick with a suffocating awareness. Every rustle of leaves, every snap of a twig, sent a jolt of adrenaline through Alice's system. She couldn't shake the feeling of unseen eyes tracking their every move, of a silent, invisible audience privy to their every labored breath.

It was more than just a lingering paranoia from the encounter. It was a subtle dissonance in the environment, a sense of order that felt wrong. A branch, snapped cleanly as if by a deliberate pressure, lay across their path, a path they had just cleared. It wasn't there when they passed the first time. Then, a bird's call, sharp and distinct, repeated itself with uncanny regularity, as if a signal, not a natural occurrence. Alice paused, her hand instinctively going to the recorder in her pocket. Its weight was a cold comfort, a tangible piece of evidence, but also a stark reminder of how they had become the center of someone's attention.

Tom, leaning heavily on her, his face a pallid mask, noticed her hesitation. "What is it?" he murmured, his voice strained.

"Nothing," she said, forcing a smile that felt brittle on her lips. "Just... the woods are thicker than I remember. Easy to get turned around." But her eyes scanned the dense canopy, searching for the source of this disquiet. She saw a glint of something metallic high up in the branches of an old oak tree, too high for a bird's nest, too small for a natural formation. It caught the sunlight for a fleeting moment before disappearing. A lens? A microphone? The possibilities, each more terrifying than the last, began to cascade through her mind.

The intruder was dead. Their physical confrontation was over. But the chilling truth began to dawn: their fight was far from won. The boathouse had been a trap, yes, but it had also been a stage. And the audience was still watching. The neat, orderly snap of the branch, the rhythmic bird call, the glint in the trees – these were not random events. They were breadcrumbs, meticulously placed, designed to sow unease, to confirm their fear, to let them know that their escape was only an illusion.

They were not simply running from a dead man; they were fleeing an unseen network, a silent observer who had witnessed their every move, their every desperate act. The recorder was their only weapon, their only proof, but it was also the reason they were being so meticulously observed. It was the catalyst that had brought them to this point, and it was the very thing that ensured they remained under scrutiny.

Alice tightened her grip on Tom's arm, her resolve hardening. The fear was a cold, constant presence, but it was no longer paralyzing. It was sharpening her senses, fueling a fierce determination. They had survived the immediate threat, but now they had to survive the surveillance. They had to reach safety, not just to tend to Tom's injuries, but to expose the truth, to reveal the unseen observer before they could be silenced, before their story could be manipulated or erased. The woods, once a symbol of their brief sanctuary, now felt like a labyrinth, each rustle of leaves a whisper of danger, each glint of light a potential threat. The fragile refuge was gone, and in its place, a chilling awareness had taken root: they were never truly alone. The silence of the forest was not empty; it was pregnant with watchful eyes.

The woods, once a sanctuary, now felt like a cage, each rustle of leaves a whisper of danger, each glint of light a potential threat. The fragile refuge had been shattered, replaced by a chilling awareness: they were never truly alone. The silence of the forest was not empty;

it was pregnant with watchful eyes. Alice's every instinct screamed for them to run, to put as much distance as possible between themselves and the boathouse, between themselves and the unseen observer. The remote location, which had once offered solace, now felt like a trap, its isolation amplifying their vulnerability.

Tom, though weakened, managed to keep pace, his labored breaths a testament to his resilience. Alice's arm was a vice around him, her own fear a cold, hard knot in her stomach, but her mind was already racing ahead, planning their next move. The house, her home, was no longer safe. The very walls that had once been a symbol of security had been breached, not just by violence, but by the insidious presence of surveillance. The recorder, clutched tightly in her pocket, felt like a burning ember, a testament to what had happened, and a beacon for whoever was watching.

They needed to disappear. Not just from the immediate vicinity, but from the radar of whoever had been observing them. The woods offered a temporary cover, but they couldn't stay there. They needed a place where they could vanish, a transient haven where their faces wouldn't be recognized, where their presence wouldn't raise suspicion. The nearest town, a cluster of buildings barely visible through the dense foliage, offered a sliver of hope. It was a gamble, but staying put was no longer an option. Every shadow seemed to harbor a watcher, every sound a potential threat.

The drive from the woods was a blur of adrenaline and controlled panic. Alice kept her eyes on the road, her knuckles white on the steering wheel, while Tom, his face etched with pain, periodically winced as he shifted his weight. They spoke little, the unspoken fear a heavy blanket between them. She scanned the rearview mirror incessantly, her heart leaping into her throat with every car that appeared behind them, convinced it was the observer, coming to reclaim their prize, or worse, to silence them permanently.

As they approached the outskirts of the town, Alice's gaze landed on a nondescript motel, its neon sign flickering weakly against the darkening sky. It was the kind of place people passed through, a temporary stop on a longer journey, a place where anonymity was not just expected, but actively sought. It was perfect. A haven of transience, a temporary shell into which they could retreat and hopefully, for a few precious hours, cease to exist in the eyes of their pursuer.

"That place," she said, her voice tight, nodding towards the motel. "We'll stop there."

Tom grunted his assent, his eyes closed, conserving what little energy he had left. Alice pulled into the sparsely populated parking lot, the gravel crunching loudly under the tires, a sound that seemed to echo in the unnatural stillness. She killed the engine, and for a moment, silence descended, a fragile, temporary peace. But even in the quiet, the feeling of being watched lingered, a prickle on her skin, a whisper in the back of her mind.

She found a vacant room at the front desk, her voice deliberately low and even, betraying none of the turmoil raging within her. The clerk, a young man engrossed in his phone, barely glanced at her, his indifference a welcome balm. Alice paid in cash, her hands trembling slightly as she accepted the key card. Every interaction felt like a potential exposure, a chance for someone to notice them, to remember them.

Back in the car, she glanced at Tom. "Stay here," she instructed, her voice firm. "Just for a minute."

She walked to the room, the key card feeling alien and yet essential in her hand. The corridor was dimly lit, the carpet worn and stained, the air thick with the faint, cloying smell of stale cigarette smoke and cheap air freshener. It was the antithesis of her home, of the life she had known, yet in its very anonymity, it offered a stark, albeit temporary, sense of security.

She unlocked the door, the click echoing in the narrow space. The room was small, utilitarian, furnished with a worn queen-sized bed, a rickety dresser, and a television set that looked like it belonged to another era. But it was private. It was a space where she could shut out the world, where she could finally, for a brief moment, attempt to process the horror of the day.

She immediately went to the door, double-checking the lock, then sliding the deadbolt into place. Her gaze swept over the windows, two of them, small and grimy, overlooking a bleak expanse of asphalt and overgrown weeds. She tugged at the flimsy curtains, drawing them shut, plunging the room into a deeper gloom. Then, she moved to the bathroom, checking the small space with a thoroughness born of paranoia, peering behind the shower curtain, under the sink, ensuring there were no hidden observers, no fresh breaches.

When she returned to the main room, Tom had managed to get out of the car and was leaning against the doorframe, his face a mask of exhaustion. Alice rushed to him, her initial surge of relief at being inside replaced by a fresh wave of concern for his well-being.

"Careful," she said, guiding him towards the bed. "Don't push yourself."

He sank onto the edge of the mattress with a groan, his breath coming in shallow gasps. Alice helped him out of his jacket, her fingers fumbling with the buttons, revealing the blood-soaked bandage. The sight of it, so raw and immediate, sent another tremor of fear through her. The observer had seen it all. They had witnessed his injury, his pain, and likely, they were still aware of it.

She looked at him, her heart aching. He needed medical attention, proper care, but that would mean venturing back out, exposing them again. For now, she could only do what she could. She fetched the small first-aid kit she kept in her car, along with fresh water and some painkillers. The room, with its peeling wallpaper and its musty odor, was a far cry from the pristine environment she was accustomed to, but it was a refuge. A temporary one, perhaps, but a refuge nonetheless.

As she carefully examined Tom's wound, cleaning it gently and applying a fresh dressing, the weight of their situation pressed down on her. They had escaped the boathouse, they had evaded immediate capture, but they were far from safe. The anonymity of the motel room was a fragile shield, and the silence outside its walls was pregnant with threat. She knew, with a certainty that chilled her to the bone, that the observer was still out there, a shadow lurking just beyond the periphery of their vision, waiting. The recorder in her pocket felt like a ticking bomb, a constant reminder of what they possessed and the danger it represented.

She had to think, to plan. The adrenaline that had fueled their escape was beginning to wane, replaced by a bone-deep exhaustion, but Alice knew she couldn't afford to let her guard down. The intimacy of the horror they had experienced, the betrayal of her own home, had left deep scars. But this motel room, this anonymous box, was a chance to begin again, to regroup, to heal, and more importantly, to figure out how to fight back against an enemy they couldn't see. The anonymity of the hotel room offered a temporary balm, a stark contrast to the intimate, horrifying betrayal of her own home. She locked the door, checked the windows, and tried to breathe. This was not an end, but a desperate pause in a battle that had just begun. The recorder, a silent witness to their ordeal, lay on the bedside table, its dark casing reflecting the dim light, a potent symbol of both their vulnerability and their resilience.

The click of the deadbolt felt unnervingly loud in the stifling silence of the room. Alice leaned her forehead against the cool, solid wood of the door, a shudder wracking her frame. *Safe*, she repeated the word to herself, the sound hollow in her own ears. *I'm safe*. It was a mantra, a desperate attempt to anchor herself to a semblance of reality, to push back against the spectral echoes of the boathouse, the chilling certainty of being watched. The stale, faintly medicinal scent of the motel room was a stark contrast to the earthy, blood-tinged air she'd left behind, yet it was a welcome change. It was neutral. It was anonymous. It was, for now, a refuge from the suffocating intimacy of the horror that had unfolded in her own home.

She turned away from the door, her gaze sweeping the small space. The faded floral wallpaper seemed to hum with a silent, oppressive energy. The worn carpet, a nondescript brown, absorbed the meager light filtering through the drawn curtains. On the bedside table, the small, dark rectangle of the recorder lay accusingly, a tangible piece of the nightmare, a constant reminder of what she had seen, what she had heard. Her fingers itched to pick it up, to listen again, to find some thread, some clue that would make sense of the senseless violence. But she couldn't. Not yet. The raw wound of the experience was too fresh, the emotional fallout too devastating.

Alice sank onto the edge of the bed, the springs groaning in protest. She stared at her hands, noticing for the first time how they trembled. The adrenaline that had propelled them from the boathouse, that had fueled her desperate flight, was finally ebbing, leaving behind a profound exhaustion that seeped into her bones. Her mind, however, remained a tempest. It replayed fragments, shards of memory, sharp and unforgiving: the sudden crack of glass, the guttural roar of the intruder, the sickening thud of impact, Tom's agonized cry. Each memory was a fresh stab, a visceral reminder of their vulnerability.

The sheer audacity of it all gnawed at her. Her home, the sanctuary she had built, the place where she had felt most secure, had been invaded, violated. It wasn't just a physical intrusion; it was a brutal, soul-shattering assault on her sense of safety. The familiar objects in her living room, the worn armchair, the framed photographs, the books lining the shelves – they had all been witness to the violation, their silent presence now imbued with the chilling stain of what had occurred. And the thought that someone had been

*watching*, documenting their fear, their pain, was almost more than she could bear. It was a violation of a different, more insidious kind, stripping away not just privacy, but dignity.

Beside her, Duke stirred. He had remained a quiet presence since they had entered the room, a silent, mournful shadow. He nudged her hand with his wet nose, his dark eyes filled with a profound sadness. Alice reached out, her fingers burying themselves in his thick fur. His steady, warm weight against her leg was a grounding force, a small, tangible comfort in the midst of her swirling chaos. He had seen it too, she knew. He had sensed the danger, the malevolence that had permeated the air. His low growl had been a primal warning, a protective instinct that had been tragically insufficient against the brutal reality.

"Oh, Duke," she whispered, her voice thick with unshed tears. She buried her face in his neck, drawing in his familiar scent, a scent that spoke of loyalty and unconditional love. He offered no judgment, no questions, only a quiet, unwavering companionship. He was a survivor, too, a silent witness to the unfolding tragedy. His presence, though a stark reminder of all that had been disrupted, was also a lifeline. In his unblinking gaze, she saw a reflection of her own resilience, a silent testament to the enduring will to survive.

She closed her eyes, trying to force the jumbled images into some semblance of order. The intruder – who was he? What did he want?

The recorder... what information did it hold? Was it the reason for this brutal intrusion? Or was it merely a tool, a means to an end? Her mind grasped at straws, desperate for a logical explanation, for a way to make sense of the senseless. But logic felt like a distant, unattainable luxury. All she felt was the raw, visceral aftermath of trauma, the profound sense of violation, and the gnawing fear that this was far from over.

The silence in the room was a heavy shroud, broken only by Tom's shallow breathing from the other side of the bed and Duke's occasional sigh. Alice knew she needed to think, to strategize, but her mind felt like a tangled knot. The sheer speed of the events, the suddenness of the violence, had left her reeling. She was accustomed to order, to predictability. Her life had been a carefully constructed edifice of routine and control. Now, that edifice had been reduced to rubble, and she was left standing amidst the ruins, exposed and vulnerable.

She traced the pattern of the worn bedspread with her finger, each rough thread a small anchor. The perceived calm of the motel room was a fragile thing, a thin veneer stretched over the abyss of her fear. It was a moment of respite, yes, but it was also a moment of reckoning. A moment where the full weight of the trauma could finally begin to settle, to seep into her consciousness. She was safe, for now. But the word felt like a hollow echo. The true nightmare, she suspected, was only just beginning. The quiet hum of the motel's neon sign outside was a lullaby of sorts, a disorienting counterpoint to the internal storm raging within her. It was a fragile peace, a deceptive stillness that masked the churning chaos beneath. She was in a place of transit, a temporary stop, and she knew, with a chilling certainty, that they couldn't stay here for long. The observer, whoever they were, was out there. And they were waiting.

The transient nature of the motel room, while offering a temporary shield, did little to quell the relentless siege of Alice's anxiety. The thin walls, designed for anonymity and privacy, now felt porous, permeable to the very threats she was fleeing. Each anonymous footfall in the hallway outside sent a jolt through her system, a phantom echo of the intruder's presence. She found herself flinching at the distant wail of a siren, her mind immediately conjuring images of police cars converging, of the perpetrator being apprehended – or worse, of the perpetrator being alerted to their location. The urban symphony of the night, once a background hum, was now a symphony of potential danger. A car door slamming shut on the street below became the sound of an approaching vehicle, the rumble of a truck the approach of a pursuer. Her breath would hitch, her heart would pound a frantic rhythm against her ribs, and her eyes would dart to the door, to the window, to the gaps beneath them, seeking a confirmation of her fears.

The cheap, particleboard furniture of the room offered no solace. The wardrobe door, when opened, let out a hollow squeak that made her jump. The flimsy curtains, ostensibly drawn to block out the outside world, felt more like a flimsy veil, easily penetrated by prying eyes. She'd found herself checking the lock on the door repeatedly, her fingers tracing the cold metal of the bolt, as if willing it to become a more formidable barrier. The deadbolt, a symbol of security, had become an object of obsessive scrutiny. She'd find herself standing before it, her hand resting on the cool metal, a silent plea for it to hold, for it to be enough. The thought that someone might have a key, that the thin barrier could be bypassed with terrifying ease, was a constant whisper in the back of her mind, a cold dread that she fought to suppress.

Tom, still groggy from the blow to his head and the lingering effects of shock, seemed less attuned to the subtle shifts in the environment. He'd managed to clean the worst of the blood from his temple with a damp washcloth from the bathroom, the makeshift dressing doing little to disguise the angry purple bloom beneath. He lay on the bed, his breathing shallow and uneven, his eyes closed, but Alice suspected he wasn't truly sleeping. He was likely wrestling with his own demons, the same ones that were now holding her captive. His stillness, however, was a stark contrast to her own internal turmoil. She felt a pang of guilt for her own inability to offer him comfort, her own mind so consumed by the escalating sense of threat that she could barely register his pain beyond a surface level.

She found herself pacing the small room, a restless energy coursing through her veins. The worn carpet, once an insignificant detail, now felt like a treacherous terrain. Each step was measured, deliberate, as if a misplaced footfall might trigger an alarm. She'd find herself pausing mid-stride, straining her ears, convinced she'd heard something – a faint scrape, a muffled cough, a whisper. The silence that followed was often more unnerving than any sound, amplifying her own breathing, the thumping of her heart, making her acutely aware of her own vulnerability. Her mind was a hyper-vigilant sentinel, on constant alert for any deviation from the perceived norm. A shadow cast by the neon sign outside, flickering across the wall, could morph into a looming figure in her periphery. The drone of the air conditioning unit, a steady, monotonous sound, could morph into the low hum of an engine, the stealthy approach of an enemy.

The faces of the few other guests she glimpsed in the dimly lit corridor earlier that evening, while perfectly ordinary, now seemed to hold a hidden significance. The tired-eyed woman with the overflowing shopping bags, the young couple arguing in hushed tones, the man with the gruff demeanor who had nodded curtly in her direction – each one was cataloged and re-examined in her mind. Were they just travelers seeking a night's rest, or were they something more? Had they seen her? Had they noticed her disheveled state, the desperation in her eyes? Had they reported her presence? The paranoia was a voracious entity, feeding on every interaction, every fleeting glance, twisting them into confirmations of her deepest fears. She felt exposed, as if her inner turmoil was visible on her face, broadcast to anyone who cared to look.

Duke, sensing her agitation, had shifted from his place at the foot of the bed. He was now lying by the door, his ears perked, his body tensed. He wasn't growling, but his quiet vigilance was a mirror to her own. He was her early warning system, a furry barometer of the unseen. His stillness, punctuated by the occasional twitch of his ear, was a constant reminder that even in this supposed sanctuary, vigilance was paramount. She knelt beside him, stroking his head, his fur a familiar, comforting texture. "It's okay, boy," she murmured, her voice a low rasp. "We're safe here." But the words felt like a lie, a desperate incantation against an encroaching darkness. Duke's low whine was a subtle disagreement, a gentle correction. He knew. He felt it too – the lingering scent of the boathouse, the echo of violence, the undeniable presence of an unseen threat.

The recorder, tucked away in her purse, felt like a ticking time bomb. Its very existence was a testament to the horror, a silent witness to the unspeakable. The thought of its contents, the potential evidence of the intruder's motives, or worse, his identity, was a double-edged sword. It offered a glimmer of hope, a potential path to understanding, but it also represented a terrifying entanglement. If the intruder knew she had it, or suspected she might, they would undoubtedly come looking for it. And for her. The mundane object, designed to capture sound, had become a vessel of pure dread. She imagined him, the unseen observer, the architect of their terror, patiently waiting, calculating his next move. The notion that he might be so close, so aware of their present location, was a chilling prospect.

Alice found herself drawn to the window, despite herself. She cautiously parted the thick curtains, just a sliver, her eye pressed against the cool glass. The parking lot was sparsely populated, bathed in the sickly yellow glow of the overhead lights. A few cars sat empty, their metallic shells glinting. A solitary figure, silhouetted against the harsh light, walked briskly towards the ice machine, their back to her. For a heart-stopping moment, Alice froze, convinced she recognized the gait, the posture. It was a phantom limb twitch of her fear, a desperate, irrational leap of imagination. She held her breath, her gaze locked on the figure, until they disappeared into the side entrance of the building. A wave of relief, so potent it made her dizzy, washed over her. But it was fleeting, replaced by a fresh wave of apprehension. Had

*he* been watching her from the shadows, waiting for her to reveal herself?

The small bathroom offered a brief, if temporary, respite from the visual stimuli of the main room. The harsh fluorescent light was unforgiving, illuminating every dark circle under her eyes, every line of tension etched onto her face. She splashed cold water on her face, the shock of it a welcome distraction from the internal storm. Looking in the mirror, she saw not her own reflection, but a stranger. Her eyes, once clear and bright, were now shadowed and darting, filled with a deep-seated wariness. Her lips were drawn into a tight, anxious line. This was not the woman who had woken up that morning, full of plans and a quiet contentment. This was a woman who had been fundamentally altered, irrevocably broken by what she had witnessed. The reflection was a stark reminder of the psychological toll, the invisible wounds that ran deeper than any physical injury.

She returned to the main room, the oppressive atmosphere reasserting itself. Tom had stirred, his eyes now open, staring blankly at the ceiling. He blinked slowly, his gaze eventually finding hers. There was a dawning awareness in his eyes, a flicker of recognition, followed by a profound weariness. "Alice?" he rasped, his voice rough.

"I'm here," she replied, her own voice trembling. She sat on the edge of the bed beside him, her hand finding his. His skin was clammy, his grip weak.

"Did... did we get away?" he asked, his words slurred.

"Yes," she said, forcing a conviction she didn't feel. "We're safe. We're far away."

He nodded, a slow, pained movement. "He... he was so fast. So strong."

"I know," she whispered, her thumb stroking the back of his hand. "Don't think about it now. Just rest."

But the words "safe" and "rest" felt like cruel jests. The refuge was a fragile illusion. The boathouse, the violation, the chilling certainty of being watched – these were not distant memories to be compartmentalized. They were visceral realities, seeping into the present, poisoning every moment of perceived calm. The motel room, with its anonymous walls and flickering neon sign, was a temporary dam against a rising tide of terror. And Alice knew, with a certainty that chilled her to the bone, that the dam was already beginning to crack. The paranoia was not a passing phase; it was a new, unwelcome companion, its icy tendrils already wrapping around her heart, its whisper a constant, insidious reminder that the nightmare had followed them. Every creak of the floorboards, every distant car horn, every unknown face in the hallway, was a potential harbinger of renewed danger. The fragile refuge was already showing its seams, and the haunting fear of being found, of being discovered, was an ever-present, suffocating weight.

# Chapter 8: Echoes in the Dark

The air in the motel room, stagnant and thick with the metallic tang of cheap disinfectant, offered no comfort. Alice moved through the small space like a phantom herself, her senses on high alert, cataloging every creak of the floorboards, every distant hum of traffic. Tom's shallow breathing from the bed was a low counterpoint to the frantic thumping of her own heart. She'd tried to create a semblance of normalcy, to convince herself that this anonymous box of linoleum and particleboard was a sanctuary. But the lingering unease, the phantom echoes of the boathouse, clung to her like a second skin. It was then, amidst the sterile, impersonal scent of the room, that she caught it – a whisper, so faint she almost dismissed it as her own frayed nerves playing tricks.

It was a fragrance, distinct and unsettlingly familiar. Not the cloying sweetness of air freshener or the stale odor of cigarette smoke that often permeated such establishments. This was something else, something sharp and subtly metallic beneath an overlay of what she could only describe as an aggressive, almost cloying, spice. It was the same scent that had prickled her nostrils in her own bedroom, a phantom presence that had first alerted her to the violation of her home. It was the intruder's signature, a scent so out of place in the quiet sanctuary of her domestic life, and now, impossibly, impossibly here, in this transient haven miles away.

Her breath hitched. Her eyes, which had been scanning the room with a restless, darting gaze, now locked onto an unseen point, her mind replaying the memory with chilling clarity. The scent, so fleeting, so easily dismissed as a trick of the mind, was a physical manifestation of her deepest fear. He was here. Or, at the very least, he had been. The thought sent a jolt of pure adrenaline through her, a primal instinct screaming danger. She spun around, her gaze sweeping the room with renewed intensity. The cheap wardrobe, the stained armchair, the television screen a blank, unseeing eye – had he been in here? Had he left this spectral trace of his presence?

Her fingers, suddenly clumsy, fumbled with the zipper of her purse, her intent to retrieve the recorder momentarily forgotten. Instead, she pulled out a small, travel-sized bottle of hand sanitizer, her mind latching onto the irrational hope that she could somehow scrub away this olfactory ghost. She squeezed a dollop into her palm and rubbed her hands together vigorously, the alcohol's sharp scent momentarily overpowering, but it did nothing to erase the phantom aroma that seemed to linger in the air, clinging to the very fabric of the room. It was a scent that bypassed the rational mind, a primal trigger that bypassed logic and spoke directly to the deepest, most ancient parts of her brain.

She paced the length of the small room, her movements jerky, her breath coming in short, shallow gasps. Duke, who had been dozing fitfully by Tom's feet, lifted his head, his ears swiveling, his body tensing. He let out a low, almost imperceptible growl, a sound that vibrated in his chest and sent a fresh wave of panic through Alice. He smelled it too. The canine's heightened senses, so attuned to the subtle shifts in their environment, confirmed her deepest fears. This wasn't just her imagination. This was real. The phantom scent, whatever its origin, was a beacon, a chilling confirmation of their continued peril.

"Duke, shhh," she whispered, her voice strained, trying to soothe the dog while her own heart hammered against her ribs like a trapped bird. But the dog's unease was infectious, amplifying her own terror. She found herself compulsively sniffing the air, trying to pinpoint the source of the scent, as if by identifying it, she could somehow banish it. She moved towards the window, cautiously parting the heavy, nondescript curtains that hung like dusty shrouds. The parking lot below was a desolate expanse under the weak glow of the security lights. A few cars were scattered like fallen dominoes, their surfaces reflecting the sickly illumination. Nothing. No one. Just the vast, indifferent darkness that pressed in on all sides.

She retreated from the window, her gaze falling on the small, utilitarian bathroom. Perhaps, she thought, the scent was stronger in there. It was a flimsy hope, but it was all she had. She pushed open the door and stepped inside, the harsh fluorescent light above casting her face in stark relief. The air in the bathroom was heavy with the usual scents of soap and stale water, but as she took a deep breath, she caught it again. Faint, yes, but undeniably present. The same spicy, almost metallic aroma. It seemed to emanate from the small ventilation grate near the ceiling, a dark, perforated circle that offered no visible entry point, yet somehow felt like a conduit for this spectral intruder.

Her mind, in its desperate attempt to rationalize, latched onto the idea of a lingering residue. Perhaps the previous occupant of this room had worn the same cologne, or used a similar product. But the thought was quickly dismissed. This scent was too specific, too deeply ingrained in her memory of the violation. It was not a generic fragrance; it was a declaration, a personal mark left behind. She leaned closer to the vent, her nostrils flaring, trying to discern any further clues. Was it stronger here? Or was this just the focal point of her heightened paranoia? The sheer impossibility of it gnawed at her. How could he have gotten here? They had driven for hours, taken circuitous routes, tried to be as invisible as possible. Yet, the scent, this phantom echo of his presence, persisted.

She found herself running her hands over the cheap laminate countertop, then the porcelain sink, as if physical contact might reveal a tangible trace. Nothing. The scent seemed to be airborne, an invisible miasma that permeated the very air she breathed. It was a psychological weapon, deployed with devastating effectiveness. He didn't need to be physically present; his scent was enough to shatter her fragile sense of security, to remind her that escape was an illusion. The fear, which had been a cold knot in her stomach, now began to unfurl, its tendrils reaching out, constricting her chest.

She returned to the main room, her movements becoming more frantic. She checked the deadbolt on the door for the tenth time, her fingers tracing the cool metal, willing it to be more than just a simple lock. She peered through the peephole, her eye pressed against the lens, scanning the empty, dimly lit corridor. The muted carpet swallowed any sound, making it impossible to discern footsteps approaching or receding. The silence itself was a threat, a vast canvas upon which her imagination painted the most terrifying scenarios.

Tom stirred on the bed, a low groan escaping his lips. His eyes fluttered open, unfocused, then slowly found her. "Alice?" he rasped, his voice raw.

She rushed to his side, kneeling beside the bed. "I'm here, Tom. I'm right here."

He blinked, his brow furrowed with a pain that went beyond the physical. "What... what is it? You're trembling."

She forced a smile, a brittle, unconvincing expression. "Nothing. Just... can't seem to get comfortable." She hesitated, the words catching in her throat. How could she explain? How could she articulate the phantom scent that had sent her spiraling into a fresh wave of terror?

"You saw something?" he pressed, his gaze sharpening, even through the haze of pain and medication.

She shook her head, then nodded almost imperceptibly. "It's... it's silly, really. I thought I smelled something. Something familiar."

His eyes searched hers, a flicker of understanding in their depths. He remembered. He remembered the boathouse, the overwhelming, cloying scent that had been the first warning, the first sign of the intruder's presence. "The cologne?" he whispered, his voice barely audible.

Alice's breath hitched again, the confirmation, even from him, a physical blow. "Yes," she managed, her voice a choked whisper. "The same one. It was just... a whiff. I think it might have been in the air conditioning, or maybe a residue from the last person in here. It's probably nothing." She was trying to convince herself as much as him, clinging to the sliver of logic that might save her from succumbing to full-blown panic.

Tom's hand, surprisingly steady, reached out and found hers. His grip was weak, but the gesture was a lifeline. "We're a long way from home, Alice," he said, his voice firm despite its rasp. "He can't have followed us here. Not this far."

But the words, meant to reassure, only served to highlight the absurdity of her fear. If he couldn't have followed them, then what was the scent? A cruel hallucination, a manifestation of her shattered nerves? Or was it something more sinister, something that defied logical explanation? She looked at Duke, who was now sitting by the door, his body a coiled spring of tension, his gaze fixed on the closed door. He didn't believe it was nothing.

Alice pulled her hand away from Tom's, the need to
*do* something, to *find* something, overriding her desire for comfort. She began to systematically search the room again, her movements more deliberate this time, less frantic, more methodical.

She ran her hands along the baseboards, behind the flimsy curtains, under the edges of the worn rug. She opened the wardrobe, its hollow interior offering only the faint mustiness of old fabric. She checked the small bedside table, its drawer containing only a Gideon Bible and a hotel directory. Every surface, every nook and cranny, was examined with a hyper-vigilant scrutiny.

She found herself drawn back to the ventilation grate in the bathroom. This time, she stood on the edge of the bathtub, reaching up to touch the cool metal. There was no way in, no obvious sign of tampering. Yet, the scent seemed to be strongest here, a phantom whisper of violation in the sterile air. She closed her eyes, trying to recall the exact nuances of the cologne from her bedroom. It was a complex scent, she remembered, layered with something dark and earthy beneath the sharp spice. It wasn't a scent one would expect to find in a cheap motel room. It was the scent of someone who took a perverse pride in their presence, someone who wanted to be noticed, even in their transgression.

She opened her eyes and looked at her reflection in the cheap, framed mirror above the sink. Her face was pale, her eyes wide and shadowed. She looked like a cornered animal, her every instinct screaming to flee. The scent, whether real or imagined, had been the catalyst, the spark that ignited the tinder of her fear. It was a psychological assault, a reminder that the perpetrator's reach extended far beyond the physical boundaries of her home, far beyond the miles they had traveled. He was in her head, a constant, insidious presence.

She stepped out of the bathroom, her mind racing. What if the scent wasn't from the intruder directly, but from something he had touched, something he had carried? A piece of clothing, a personal item, left behind in a previous room, its scent clinging stubbornly to the ventilation system. It was a desperate attempt to find a logical explanation, a way to anchor herself in reality. But the lingering feeling, the visceral certainty that it was

*him*, persisted. It was the scent of his audacity, his chilling confidence.

She walked over to the small desk in the corner, its surface littered with the hotel's complimentary stationery. She picked up a pen, her fingers tracing the plastic. Was it possible that he had been in this room before them? That he had somehow known they were coming here? The thought was almost too terrifying to entertain. It suggested a level of planning, a meticulousness that went beyond random pursuit.

Duke let out a low whine, nudging her hand with his wet nose. She knelt and buried her face in his fur, drawing strength from his solid presence. "We'll be okay, boy," she murmured, her voice muffled against his warm coat. "We have to be." But even as she spoke the words, she could feel the creeping tendrils of doubt, the insidious whisper that suggested otherwise. The scent was a phantom, a ghost in the machine, but its effect was devastatingly real. It had shattered the illusion of safety, leaving her exposed and vulnerable, once again adrift in a sea of uncertainty. The echoes of the dark were not just in the boathouse; they were in the air, in her memory, and now, it seemed, in the very scent of this supposed refuge.

The sterile hum of the motel's air conditioning unit, usually a source of background white noise, now seemed to throb with an almost sentient malevolence. Alice watched Duke from the corner of her eye. He had been a shadow of himself since they'd fled the suffocating familiarity of their home, his usual boisterous energy replaced by a quiet, watchful stillness. But that stillness was beginning to fray. He'd risen from his spot by Tom's feet, his movements fluid and silent, and was now pacing the length of the room, a restless, caged predator. His powerful frame seemed to strain against the confines of the cheap linoleum, his tail, usually a barometer of his mood, held low and stiff.

He paused at the door, his broad head tilted, ears pricked forward, as if straining to catch a whispered conversation beyond the thin wood. Alice's breath caught in her throat. Had he heard something? The phantom scent had unsettled her profoundly, a visceral reminder of the violation that had driven them from their sanctuary. Now, Duke's behavior was amplifying that unease, twisting it into a knot of pure, unadulterated fear. He wasn't growling at the door, though. His attention seemed to be directed elsewhere, his large, intelligent eyes scanning the room, then flicking upwards, towards the ceiling, before settling back on the walls, his gaze unfocused, as if looking through them.

A low, guttural sound rumbled in Duke's chest, not a warning bark, but a deep, resonant vibration that seemed to emanate from his very core. It was a sound Alice hadn't heard since they'd been in their old house, a sound that had always preceded a palpable shift in the atmosphere, a tangible increase in the sense of

*wrongness*. It was the sound of him sensing an unseen presence, a hostile energy that was invisible to her human senses. The terror that had been a cold, distant observer now pressed in, hot and suffocating. She'd tried to rationalize the scent, to dismiss it as a trick of her overactive imagination, a lingering residue from a previous guest. But Duke's reaction was harder to ignore. He was a creature of instinct, his senses honed by millennia of survival, and his unease was a language she understood all too well.

He continued his patrol, his pacing becoming more agitated. He'd stop abruptly, his body tensing, then resume his circuit, his movements growing more erratic. He'd sniff the air with a low, almost mournful whine, then turn his head sharply, as if responding to a sound only he could hear. His focus seemed to shift from one part of the room to another, his nose twitching, his brow furrowed in a way that mimicked human confusion and distress. It was as if he was trapped in a phantom landscape, a battleground invisible to Alice.

Alice's gaze followed his, trying to decipher his silent communication. Was he reacting to the lingering scent? Or was there something more? The thought sent a fresh wave of dread through her. If he could sense something,

*someone*, that she couldn't, then they were even more vulnerable than she had imagined. The miles they had put between themselves and their home felt suddenly insignificant. The fear that had been a dull ache was now a sharp, insistent jab, reminding her of the predatory nature of their pursuer. He was cunning, elusive, and now, it seemed, capable of infiltrating even the most transient of spaces.

She watched Duke as he approached the wall nearest the bathroom, his nose pressed against the cheap, patterned wallpaper. He let out another low growl, a frustrated sound, and then began to scratch lightly at the surface with his paw. It wasn't an aggressive scratching, more a tentative exploration, as if he were trying to understand or communicate with whatever lay beyond. Alice's heart hammered against her ribs. Was there something in the wall? Some hidden space, some conduit that allowed this unseen presence to seep into their temporary refuge?

"Duke, easy, boy," she murmured, her voice tight with a fear she was trying desperately to suppress. She didn't want to alarm Tom further, who was already pale and shaken. But the dog's persistent unease was a tangible presence in the room, an unspoken confirmation of her own deepest anxieties. He was reacting to something, something that mirrored the phantom scent, the violation of their space, the knowledge that they were not truly safe.

Tom stirred on the bed, his eyes opening slowly. "What's wrong with Duke?" he whispered, his voice hoarse.

Alice walked over to the bed, her movements stiff. "He's just... restless," she said, choosing her words carefully. "He's picking up on... something." She didn't want to say 'fear', didn't want to plant that seed of doubt in Tom's already fragile state. But Duke's behavior was too specific, too reminiscent of their past experiences.

Duke, as if sensing the conversation, padded over to Tom, resting his head on the edge of the bed. He let out a soft whine, his dark eyes fixed on Alice. It was a look of shared understanding, a silent plea for her to acknowledge what he was sensing. He nudged Tom's hand with his nose, a gesture of comfort, but his body remained coiled, his senses still on high alert.

"He's acting like he did back at the house," Tom murmured, his gaze drifting towards the wall Duke had been investigating. "Remember when he used to just stare at that one spot in the living room? Like someone was standing there?"

Alice nodded, a shiver tracing its way down her spine. "I remember. He'd growl, too, at nothing we could see." She ran a hand through her hair, the texture feeling alien and rough. "It feels like... like it's happening again." The phantom scent, Duke's agitated pacing, his strange focus on the walls and ceiling – it all coalesced into a chilling tableau of their past trauma replaying itself in this anonymous motel room.

Duke continued his uneasy watch. He'd lie down for a few moments, his body a taut spring, then spring back up, his ears swiveling, his head cocked as if listening to a distant conversation. He'd pace again, his powerful frame a testament to his protective instincts, his instincts screaming that something was amiss. He'd occasionally let out a low, throaty rumble, directed not at the door, but at the ceiling, then the walls, as if the threat was all around them, seeping through the very fabric of their temporary sanctuary.

Alice tried to retrace their journey, to find a logical explanation for this pervasive sense of unease. They had taken backroads, avoided major highways, changed vehicles twice. They had been meticulous in their attempts to disappear. Yet, here they were, miles from home, and the specter of their tormentor seemed to have followed them, not in the flesh, but in the form of an unsettling scent and the heightened senses of their loyal companion.

She looked at the ventilation grate in the bathroom again. The phantom scent had seemed strongest there. Could it be connected to

Duke's current distress? Was there a way for something to infiltrate their room through the ventilation system? It seemed far-fetched, but in their current predicament, logic had become a fickle ally. She found herself scrutinizing every detail of the room, every scuff on the wall, every loose tile, searching for a clue, a sign that would explain the intangible threat Duke was sensing.

Duke walked over to the window, his body pressing against the glass, his nose twitching as he sniffed the air outside. He didn't bark, didn't growl, but remained there for a long moment, a silent sentinel surveying the desolate parking lot. Then, with a soft sigh, he turned away, his unease seemingly undiminished. It was as if the outside world offered no solace, no escape from the perceived threat within.

Alice returned to her methodical search of the room, her eyes scanning every inch. She checked behind the bedside table, ran her hand along the underside of the desk, even lifted the thin mattress on the bed to ensure nothing was hidden beneath. Every object, every surface, was subjected to her intense scrutiny. Duke's behavior was a constant, unnerving reminder of their past. The phantom scent had been the initial spark, but Duke's reaction was the sustained burn, the ever-present flame of their fear.

He returned to his pacing, his steps heavy with an unspoken anxiety. He'd stop at the wall, his ears pressed against it, then move on, his search for the source of his unease seemingly fruitless. It was as if he were chasing ghosts, a torment that mirrored Alice's own internal struggle. The inability to pinpoint the threat, to confront it, was almost as debilitating as the threat itself.

"He's really stressed," Tom observed, his voice laced with concern. "You think he's picking up on the smell again?"

Alice nodded, her gaze fixed on Duke. "I think so. Or something related to it. It's like... like he knows it's not just a smell. That it means something." She remembered how Duke had reacted when she'd first caught the scent in her bedroom, the low growl, the prickling of his fur, the way he had instinctively positioned himself between her and the unseen intruder. He had been aware, on some primal level, of the danger.

Duke suddenly stopped his pacing and let out a soft, almost whimpering sound. He was looking at the ceiling directly above the bathroom door, his tail giving a small, uncertain wag. Alice's gaze followed his. There was nothing there but the stained acoustic tiles, the faint shadow of the light fixture. But Duke seemed convinced. He whined again, a questioning sound, and then, to Alice's surprise, he sat down, his body still tense, and began to watch the ceiling intently.

"What is it, boy?" Alice whispered, approaching him cautiously. "What do you see up there?"

Duke didn't respond, his attention locked on the innocuous ceiling. He remained in his seated position, a silent sentinel, his every muscle tensed, his gaze unwavering. It was a vigil, a silent vigil that spoke volumes about the fear that had permeated their lives. He was waiting, watching, as if expecting something to descend from the bland expanse above.

Alice felt a tremor of apprehension. The ceiling. It was the one place she hadn't thoroughly investigated. It seemed absurd, but Duke's unwavering focus was a powerful motivator. She looked around the room, her eyes landing on the small, rickety chair that served as a bedside table. It wouldn't be enough to reach. She would need something more.

She glanced at Tom, who was watching her with a mixture of worry and resignation. "I think Duke's onto something," she said, her voice steadier than she felt. "He's fixated on the ceiling. I need to check it out."

Tom nodded slowly. "Be careful, Alice."

Armed with a newfound, albeit irrational, determination, Alice carefully moved the flimsy chair closer to the wall beneath the spot Duke was intently observing. She hesitated for a moment, then climbed onto the chair, her heart pounding a frantic rhythm against her ribs. Duke watched her, his body coiled, ready to spring into action if needed.

She reached up, her fingertips brushing against the cool, textured surface of the acoustic tiles. There was nothing immediately apparent. No marks, no damage, no sign of intrusion. But Duke's unwavering gaze was a constant pressure, a silent insistence. She pressed her fingers harder, trying to discern any subtle differences, any irregularities in the surface.

And then, she felt it. A slight give, a subtle indentation in one of the tiles, almost imperceptible to the touch. It was small, no bigger than her thumbnail, but it was there. Her breath hitched. Was this it? Was this the point of entry, the breach in their defenses? She pushed harder, and the tile shifted slightly, revealing a sliver of darkness behind it.

Duke let out a low growl, a sound of pure warning. Alice's hand froze. She was on the verge of uncovering something, but the sound from Duke was an unmistakable alarm. Whatever was behind that tile, it was something that filled their loyal protector with dread. The phantom scent, Duke's restless pacing, his focused unease – it all culminated in this single, terrifying discovery. The echo of the dark was no longer confined to the boathouse, or to her memory. It was here, lurking just beyond a thin layer of acoustic tile, a palpable manifestation of the terror that had driven them from their home. The uneasy watch was far from over. It had, in fact, just begun.

The silence in the motel room, which had been a fragile shield against the encroaching dread, began to crack under the weight of Alice's new, terrifying certainty. Duke's low growl, a sound that had become a constant, unnerving soundtrack to their flight, seemed to deepen, resonating with a primal understanding that mirrored her own dawning horror. The phantom scent, that lingering ghost of violation, now felt less like a personal haunting and more like a meticulously placed breadcrumb, a deliberate clue left by a mastermind. She had focused on the immediate threat, the man she had confronted, the brute force that had invaded their sanctuary. But his actions, his unnerving composure, his almost rehearsed movements – they now screamed of an orchestrator, a puppeteer pulling the strings from the shadows.

The sheer audacity of the intrusion, the intimate knowledge of the house's layout, the precise timing of his arrival, his apparent understanding of their routines, and most disturbingly, the almost casual way he had navigated the chaos he had unleashed – it all pointed to a level of preparation far beyond the scope of a lone wolf. This wasn't the desperate act of a burglar or the impulsive rage of a jilted lover. This was a surgical strike, executed with a chilling precision that suggested a deep, almost familial understanding of their lives, their vulnerabilities, their very essence. He had known where to look, what to find, how to manipulate their environment, and crucially, how to disappear without a trace. The back roads they had taken, the careful switching of vehicles, the deliberate avoidance of any traceable digital footprint – they were all attempts to outrun a single individual. But what if he wasn't alone? What if he was merely the most visible piece of a much larger, more sinister puzzle?

The thought settled over Alice like a shroud, cold and suffocating. Her focus had been so intensely on the man, on the immediate danger he represented. She had treated his apprehension as the end of the threat, a victory, however pyrrhic. But now, looking at Duke's unwavering vigilance, sensing the lingering tendrils of that invasive scent, a chilling clarity washed over her. Killing him, or even seeing him apprehended, wouldn't be the end. It would be like lopping off a single, venomous fang. The source of the venom, the intricate network that produced it, would remain untouched, festering, and ready to strike again. The resources he had at his disposal, the apparent ease with which he had operated, the sheer planning that had gone into his infiltration – it all suggested an accomplice, a network, a support system that had facilitated his actions and ensured his escape.

She pictured him, not as a solitary figure, but as an agent, a pawn in a game far grander and more terrifying than she had dared to imagine. His knowledge of their home, their routines, their possessions – it wasn't just observational. It was intimate. It spoke of surveillance, of detailed dossiers, of information gathered over an extended period, likely by multiple individuals. Had someone been watching them for weeks, months? Had they been mapping their lives, noting their habits, their comings and goings, their moments of vulnerability? The idea that their privacy had been so thoroughly and systematically violated by a group, rather than an individual, was a fresh layer of horror. It meant that the threat wasn't confined to a single, identifiable person. It was diffused, distributed, a hydra with multiple heads, each capable of inflicting its own unique brand of pain.

The phantom scent, so potent and unsettling, now seemed less like a personal effluvium and more like a signature, a calling card left by an entire organization. It was too specific, too deeply ingrained, to be merely the incidental odor of a single intruder. It suggested a deliberate application, perhaps a chemical agent used for tracking or intimidation, something applied with knowledge and purpose. And Duke, with his heightened senses, had picked up on it immediately, his primal instincts screaming that something was fundamentally *wrong.* He had reacted not just to a smell, but to the intent behind it, the underlying malice that it represented.

Alice's mind raced, replaying fragmented memories of the intrusion, searching for inconsistencies, for details that now pointed towards a larger conspiracy. The almost too-perfect timing of his appearance, the way he seemed to anticipate their movements, the lack of any real struggle to escape – it all suggested a well-rehearsed plan. He hadn't been surprised; he had been expected. And if he had been expected, then someone had known he was coming, and

*why* he was coming. That "why" was the linchpin, the motive that had driven this entire elaborate operation. And if there was a motive, there had to be someone pulling the strings, someone with a vested interest in their torment.

She thought of the escape route. It had been too clean, too efficient. He hadn't been trapped; he had simply... vanished. There had been no panicked scramble, no desperate attempt to break down doors or scale fences. It was as if he had known the exact moments to slip away, the precise avenues of egress that would be least observed, least guarded. This wasn't the spontaneous escape of an individual caught in a moment of panic. It was the controlled extraction of an operative, orchestrated by people who understood the environment, who had contingency plans, who were prepared for every eventuality.

The implications were staggering. They weren't just being targeted by a single, deranged individual. They were ensnared in something far more complex, something with reach and resources. The thought that their lives, their safety, were now at the mercy of an unseen network, a group that could track them, infiltrate their homes, and orchestrate such daring intrusions, was a chilling prospect. It meant that every step they took, every decision they made, was potentially being observed, analyzed, and countered. Their flight, their attempts to disappear, were likely being met with amusement, with a quiet confidence that they would eventually be caught, that their efforts were futile against such a pervasive and organized adversary.

Alice looked at Duke, his body still a taut coil of anxiety, his gaze fixed on some unseen point in the room. He was their early warning system, their primal radar. If he was still sensing something, if his unease hadn't abated, then the threat wasn't confined to the man they had encountered. It was still present, an invisible pressure, a silent hum of malevolence that permeated their temporary refuge. This wasn't just a residual scent; it was an active presence, an echo of the dark that had followed them, not as a single entity, but as a persistent, insidious influence.

The sheer amount of effort, the level of planning, the meticulous execution – it all suggested a motive that went beyond simple revenge or personal grievance. There had to be something they possessed, something they knew, something they represented that was so threatening, so valuable, that it warranted such an extensive and complex operation. Was it a piece of information? A hidden asset? Or was it something more abstract, a threat to an ideology, a disruption to a carefully constructed order? The question gnawed at her, a persistent, unpleasant itch that she couldn't scratch.

She remembered the way the intruder had moved, his eyes, not filled with rage or desperation, but with a cold, detached efficiency. He had seemed almost like a tool, an instrument wielded by a stronger, unseen hand. His purpose was clear, his objective singular, and his execution flawless. But there had been no personal animosity in his actions, no flicker of genuine hatred. It was purely professional, almost clinical. And that clinical detachment was more terrifying than any outburst of anger. It spoke of a detachment from humanity, a willingness to inflict harm without remorse, a characteristic that would be amplified in a network, where responsibility could be diffused, and accountability could be avoided altogether.

The phantom scent was a tangible manifestation of this invisible threat, a sensory clue that their instincts, particularly Duke's, were tuned to a frequency of danger that remained hidden from their conscious minds. It was like a subtle tremor before an earthquake, a faint scent that warned of an impending eruption. And the eruption, she now understood, was not a single event, but a sustained campaign, a relentless pursuit orchestrated by unseen forces.

Her gaze drifted to the ventilation grate again. Could it have been a conduit? Not just for the scent, but for information? For listening devices? For something even more insidious? The idea of microscopic surveillance, of their every word and action being recorded and relayed back to this unseen network, sent a fresh wave of revulsion through her. They were not just being hunted; they were being studied, their every move analyzed, their vulnerabilities cataloged.

The realization that the man she had encountered was merely a single node in a vast, interconnected web of darkness was a devastating blow. It stripped away the illusion of control she had clung to, the fragile hope that by neutralizing the immediate threat, they had somehow gained an advantage. Instead, they had merely revealed themselves, drawn the attention of the larger organism, and alerted it to their presence and their potential. They had, in essence, pruned a single branch, but the root remained firmly entrenched, drawing sustenance from the shadows, and preparing to send forth new, even more dangerous growths. The echoes in the dark were not individual cries; they were the resonant hum of a clandestine operation, a symphony of unseen threats that had only just begun to play its chilling overture. The motel room, once a temporary sanctuary, now felt like a trap, a small, enclosed space where the tendrils of this unseen network were already beginning to tighten their grip. She looked at Duke, his unwavering gaze, his low rumble, and knew that their fight was far from over. It had, in fact, just escalated to a level she had never anticipated.

The stale air of the motel room, thick with the scent of cheap disinfectant and desperation, began to feel like a physical weight pressing down on Alice. Duke, ever vigilant, remained by her side, a silent sentinel whose every muscle tensed at the slightest sound from beyond their thin walls. But it wasn't the mundane noises of the highway or the distant murmur of other guests that kept her on edge. It was the subtle, almost imperceptible shifts within the room itself, the uncanny echoes of the violation she had suffered, manifesting in ways that were both insignificant and profoundly unsettling.

It started with the television. She'd briefly flicked through channels earlier, searching for any news that might shed light on the man who had terrorized her, or perhaps a report on their escape, a sign that the authorities were even aware of what had transpired. She'd landed on a local news broadcast for a fleeting moment, the anchor's face a blur of concerned pronouncements, before switching to a nature documentary. Yet, an hour later, as if summoned by some unseen hand, the television flickered back to life, not to the calming imagery of migrating birds, but to the very same news channel. The anchor's voice, mid-sentence, was a jarring intrusion. Alice's hand shot out, silencing the screen with a decisive click of the remote. It was a small thing, a simple malfunction, perhaps. But the

*specificity* of it, the way it had re-selected the exact channel she had abandoned, felt... deliberate. It was a whisper of intrusion, a phantom touch on the controls, a reminder that even in this anonymous box of a room, her privacy was a fragile illusion.

She tried to dismiss it, to chalk it up to faulty electronics in a roadside establishment. But then came the key card. She'd used it to enter the room, and again a few hours later to retrieve a forgotten water bottle. As she approached the door, ready to swipe, the small, blinking light on the reader seemed to hesitate, then sputter erratically, refusing to acknowledge the card. A wave of anxiety, sharp and cold, washed over her. She tried again, her hand trembling slightly. This time, it worked, the familiar green light illuminating, the lock mechanism disengaging with a soft click. But the momentary failure, the brief refusal of a simple electronic lock, felt like another deliberate stumble in her path. It was a disruption, a tiny hiccup designed to sow doubt, to make her question her own actions, her own senses. Was she imagining things? Was the stress finally getting to her?

Duke let out a low, guttural whine, his gaze fixed on the door, as if sensing her unease. He nudged her hand with his wet nose, a silent reassurance. But his presence, usually a comfort, now amplified her paranoia. He was attuned to threats, to dangers that she, with her human limitations, might miss. And if he was sensing something, even if it was just the residual psychic residue of their pursuers, then these glitches weren't random. They were calculated. They were breadcrumbs of unease, designed to destabilize her, to chip away at her resolve.

She walked over to the window, peering through the grimy pane at the darkened parking lot. A lone pickup truck was parked under the flickering neon sign, its headlights casting long, distorted shadows. Was someone watching? Was this a surveillance tactic, a way to gauge her reaction, to confirm that she was as rattled as they intended her to be? The thought was almost absurd in its paranoia, yet it felt terrifyingly plausible. The intruder in her home had moved with such unnerving precision, such an intimate knowledge of her life, that the idea of this network, this unseen organization, extending its reach even to this nondescript motel room, was not an outlandish leap, but a logical, chilling progression.

Alice returned to the small, worn table, running her fingers over its scuffed surface. She remembered the way the intruder had moved in her home, the almost fluid grace, the eerie confidence that suggested he belonged there. He hadn't been a stranger fumbling in the dark; he had been an actor on a familiar stage. And these glitches, these small, inexplicable disruptions in the motel room, felt like extensions of that same performance. They were subtle cues, designed to keep her off-balance, to erode her sense of security, to remind her that the boundaries she thought she had established were illusory.

She thought back to her home, to the way she had felt after the break-in. It wasn't just the fear of physical harm, but the deep, unsettling feeling of being

*known*. They had known where to find the hidden safe, they had known the specific items of value, they had known her routines. It was a violation of her innermost sanctum, a testament to a level of surveillance that chilled her to the bone. And now, here, in this temporary haven, the subtle manifestations of that same invasive intelligence were beginning to surface.

The television incident replayed in her mind. It wasn't just that it had turned on; it was the

*content*. The news channel. Had there been a report about the break-in? Had they been monitoring her search for information? Or was it a more insidious message, a subtle broadcast designed to deliver a specific, unsettling piece of information, tailored to her fears? She dismissed the thought; it was too elaborate, too reliant on a level of psychic telepathy that bordered on the fantastical. Yet, the sheer improbability of it, the uncanny coincidence, gnawed at her.

Then there was the key card. It was a simple piece of plastic, programmed to interact with a specific reader. For it to fail, even momentarily, suggested a disruption in that programmed sequence. Was it a temporary deactivation? A jamming signal? Or was it something more mundane, like a power fluctuation in the room's circuitry? But if it was mundane, why had it coincided with her own heightened anxiety, with her growing suspicion that she was still being observed? The pattern, however faint, was beginning to emerge. Each anomaly, no matter how small, seemed to reinforce the idea of an external force at play, a subtle, unseen hand guiding events, manipulating her environment.

Alice took a deep breath, trying to center herself. She had to remain rational. She couldn't let these perceived glitches spiral into full-blown paranoia. But the memory of the intruder's eyes, devoid of emotion, still haunted her. He had been a conduit, a tool, and the hands that wielded him were clearly capable of orchestrating a far more pervasive form of control. They weren't just breaking into houses; they were infiltrating minds, sowing seeds of doubt and fear with every subtle manipulation.

She glanced at the small trash can by the desk. Had she seen that crumpled candy wrapper before? Or was her mind, already strained, playing tricks on her, rearranging the visual landscape of the room? It was the subtle psychological warfare that was most unnerving. It wasn't about brute force anymore; it was about wearing her down, about eroding her confidence, about making her question her own sanity. The intruder had left his mark on her home, but this... this was an attempt to leave his mark on her mind.

Duke shifted, his low growl a steady rumble in his chest. He seemed to sense her internal turmoil, his instincts picking up on the vibrations of her anxiety. Alice knelt beside him, stroking his fur. "It's okay, boy," she murmured, her voice a little shaky. "We're okay. We just need to stay alert." But even as she spoke the words, a sliver of doubt crept in. Were they okay? Or were they simply walking into the next stage of a carefully orchestrated game, a game where the rules were constantly shifting, and the playing field was any environment they dared to inhabit?

She looked at the phone on the bedside table. Had she dialed a number earlier? Had she spoken to anyone? Her memory was a blur of adrenaline and fear. Could someone have accessed the phone? Placed a listening device? The technological capabilities of their adversaries seemed boundless, capable of penetrating even the most secure spaces. The thought of their every word being intercepted, analyzed, and used against them was a suffocating prospect.

The phantom scent, that lingering olfactory ghost, had been the initial intrusion, a sensory violation that had alerted her to the presence of an external threat. These glitches, these small, inexplicable disturbances, were the follow-up. They were the psychological reinforcement, the subtle reminders that the threat was not a solitary event, but an ongoing campaign. They were designed to make her feel exposed, vulnerable, and perpetually on edge, even in the supposed safety of a locked room.

Alice stood up, pacing the confines of the room. The flickering fluorescent light above seemed to mock her with its unsteady glow, mirroring the instability she felt within. The air conditioning unit, which had been humming steadily, suddenly sputtered, emitting a brief burst of ice-cold air before resuming its normal rhythm. Another anomaly. Another small, insignificant event that, in the context of everything else, felt like a deliberate act of disruption. It was like a symphony of minor inconveniences, each note designed to jar her, to break her concentration, to prevent her from finding clarity, from formulating a coherent plan of escape.

She remembered the meticulous way the intruder had moved, the almost surgical precision with which he had navigated her home. He hadn't been rushed; he had been methodical. And that methodical approach, she now realized, extended beyond the physical act of intrusion. It was a philosophy, a methodology that permeated every aspect of their operation. They were not leaving things to chance; they were engineering every outcome, controlling every variable, even the seemingly random malfunctions of a cheap motel's amenities.

The thought settled over her like a layer of dust: they were not just being hunted; they were being played with. These glitches were not accidental; they were deliberate provocations, designed to elicit a specific emotional response. They wanted her to be afraid, to be anxious, to be on the verge of breaking. And in her brokenness, she would be more susceptible, more easily manipulated.

She sat back down, Duke's head resting on her lap. His steady breathing was a grounding force in the rising tide of her apprehension. She closed her eyes, trying to filter out the subtle disturbances, to focus on the core of the problem. The man was a symptom, not the disease. The disease was this unseen network, this pervasive influence that could manipulate electronics, create phantom scents, and sow seeds of doubt with calculated precision.

The television. The key card. The sudden gust of cold air. Each a tiny crack in the facade of normalcy. Each a reminder that they were not truly alone, that the darkness that had followed them was capable of extending its tendrils into the most mundane aspects of their existence. It was a chilling realization, a confirmation that their flight was not just about evading a physical threat, but about navigating a landscape that was being subtly, insidiously reshaped around them. The echoes in the dark were not just sounds; they were atmospheric shifts, electronic whispers, and phantom sensations, all orchestrated to amplify her fear and erode her defenses. The game, she knew, was far from over. It had, in fact, just entered a new, more unnerving phase.

The gnawing unease that had settled in Alice's gut had begun to coalesce into a terrifying certainty. It wasn't just a lingering echo of the violation she had endured; it was the palpable, chilling understanding that the pursuit had not ended. The carefully curated illusion of anonymity, the thin veneer of safety offered by the nondescript motel room, had been irrevocably shattered. Her sanctuary, she now understood with a cold dread, was merely a temporary pit stop on a relentless, unyielding trajectory. This wasn't the work of a lone, deranged individual; it was a continuation of a campaign, a sustained assault with a singular, terrifying objective. The subtle malfunctions, the phantom sensations, the disquieting echoes – they were not random occurrences. They were calculated moves in a larger, more insidious game, orchestrated by hands that had demonstrated an unnerving capacity to infiltrate and manipulate. The individual who had invaded her home was a component, a tool, but the true threat was far more pervasive, a network or an organization that operated with a chilling, almost supernatural efficiency.

Alice's gaze swept across the room, her senses now hyper-alert, scanning for the slightest anomaly, the subtlest deviation from the mundane. The way the dust motes danced in the slivers of light filtering through the grimy blinds, the rhythmic squeak of the ancient ice machine down the hall – each sound, each sight, was now scrutinized, imbued with a potential malevolence. The sheer terror of realizing that the predator had not only found her but was actively continuing its hunt, its objective undiminished, was a crushing weight. It was the sickening realization that her brief respite had been an illusion, a fleeting pause before the inevitable resumption of the chase. The feeling of being hunted was no longer a nascent fear; it was a visceral, suffocating reality. Her mind, already frayed at the edges by the recent trauma, grappled with the enormity of this persistent threat. It wasn't just about physical safety anymore; it was about the erosion of her very sense of security, the insidious understanding that no space was truly her own, no moment truly free from observation.

She looked at Duke, his ears perked, his body coiled in a state of perpetual readiness. He was more than a pet; he was a living, breathing barometer of danger, his instincts honed by countless generations to detect threats that human senses often missed. The low growl that rumbled in his chest was not directed at anything specific, but rather at the ambient tension, the unseen pressures that were beginning to suffocate the small room. It was a sound that echoed the growing dread in Alice's own heart, a primal warning that the perceived safety of their makeshift refuge was a fragile construct, easily breached. The initial break-in had been a shockwave, a violent disruption that had sent her fleeing. Now, this creeping realization – that they were still being pursued, that the danger had not receded but had merely shifted its form – was a slow, agonizing bleed.

The memory of the intruder's unnervingly calm demeanor, the precise, almost surgical way he had moved through her home, returned with vivid clarity. He had been an instrument of a larger will, a pawn in a game she was only beginning to comprehend. His actions, while terrifyingly intimate, had also felt detached, as if he were merely executing a script. And now, this unfolding scenario in the motel room felt like the continuation of that same script, the subtle disturbances designed to psychologically prepare her for whatever came next. It was a form of psychological warfare, a deliberate campaign to wear down her resolve, to isolate her in a bubble of anxiety and paranoia. The objective, she suspected, was not simply to apprehend her, but to break her, to render her pliant and compliant before the final act.

Alice walked over to the window again, her movements no longer tentative but imbued with a desperate vigilance. The parking lot, once a mundane expanse of asphalt, now appeared as a stage set, each parked car a potential hiding place, each shadow a possible ambush. The lone pickup truck, which had seemed insignificant before, now loomed as a symbol of their surveillance, its dark windows impenetrable, its presence a silent, unnerving testament to the fact that they were not hidden, not truly. The world outside their thin walls was no longer indifferent; it was an active participant in their pursuit, a vast, indifferent canvas upon which their desperate flight was being meticulously charted. The knowledge that the individuals orchestrating this pursuit possessed such a profound understanding of her movements, her anxieties, and her attempted evasions was a terrifying validation of their capabilities. They were not guessing; they were anticipating, their actions a direct response to her attempts to disappear.

She pressed her forehead against the cool glass, the faint vibration of the distant highway a stark contrast to the stillness within the room. The illusion of escape, the brief hope that she had managed to put enough distance between herself and her tormentors, was crumbling with each passing moment. The terror was not in the unknown, but in the horribly familiar. It was the chilling recognition of a pattern, a methodology that had been applied once and was now being replicated, albeit in subtler, more insidious ways. The objective remained the same: to exert control, to reclaim what they believed was theirs. And her current location, this anonymous motel room, was simply another waypoint on their map, another stage in their relentless pursuit.

The incident with the television, the inexplicable re-selection of the news channel, felt less like a malfunction and more like a deliberate, albeit subtle, message. Was it a confirmation that they were aware of her attempts to seek information about them? Or was it a more pointed communication, a carefully chosen broadcast designed to sow further discord and unease? The sheer specificity of it gnawed at her, a constant reminder that their adversaries were not just capable of tracking her, but of understanding her, of anticipating her actions and reacting to them with an almost prescient accuracy. It was a terrifying form of intimacy, this knowledge that they were not just looking for her, but observing her, analyzing her every move.

The key card refusal, though fleeting, had been another calculated disruption. It was a micro-aggression designed to undermine her confidence in the basic mechanics of her environment. A simple tool of access denied, even for a moment, served to destabilize her, to make her question the reliability of her surroundings. These weren't acts of random chaos; they were precisely timed disruptions, each one designed to chip away at her composure, to erode her sense of agency. The threat wasn't just external; it was becoming internalized, a constant hum of anxiety that threatened to overwhelm her rational thought.

Alice's thoughts drifted back to the security measures she had implemented at her home, the layers of protection that had ultimately been so easily bypassed. The sophisticated alarm system, the reinforced doors and windows – all had proven futile against the intruder's methodical approach. This new manifestation of the threat, this subtle infiltration of her temporary refuge, suggested a more advanced, more insidious form of intrusion. It wasn't about brute force anymore; it was about exploiting vulnerabilities, about manipulating the very fabric of her perceived safety. They were not just breaking down doors; they were picking locks, not with physical tools, but with an understanding of the systems themselves, and by extension, of her reliance on them.

She picked up the phone, her fingers hovering over the keypad. Had she made any calls? Had she spoken to anyone? Her memory of the immediate aftermath of the break-in was a haze of adrenaline and terror. The possibility that her communications could be monitored, that her every word could be intercepted and used against her, was a suffocating prospect. It meant that her attempts to seek help, to reach out to trusted individuals, could be feeding directly back to those who were hunting her. The isolation she felt was no longer just geographical; it was technological, a chilling realization that even her attempts to connect could be rerouted, distorted, and ultimately exploited.

The phantom scent, that initial olfactory intrusion, had been a stark, visceral warning. It had been a direct sensory assault, a violation that had transcended the physical and invaded her very perception of reality. These subsequent glitches, these minor electronic and environmental disturbances, felt like a continuation of that psychological assault. They were designed to keep her perpetually on edge, to prevent her from ever truly relaxing, from ever feeling safe.

The objective was to exhaust her, to drain her mental and emotional resources until she was too depleted to resist, too overwhelmed to strategize.

Alice walked to the small, rickety closet, opening the door to reveal the meager collection of extra towels and the industrial-sized bottle of cheap shampoo. She checked behind the hangers, a futile gesture born of ingrained paranoia. The thought that someone could have accessed this space, could have tampered with their belongings, was almost too much to bear. Yet, the possibility lingered, a persistent whisper of doubt that she could not entirely silence. The meticulous nature of the initial intrusion suggested a thoroughness that extended to every aspect of their operation. They were not prone to oversight; they were meticulous planners, and their plans likely encompassed every eventuality, including her attempts to secure even the most mundane aspects of her temporary shelter.

She recalled the way the intruder had moved with such fluid grace, as if he had an innate understanding of the layout of her home, a familiarity that suggested he had studied it, perhaps even walked through it mentally before ever setting foot inside. This same unnerving precision seemed to be at play here, in this anonymous motel room. The glitches were not random acts of electronic failure; they were carefully orchestrated disruptions, designed to achieve a specific psychological effect. They were subtle cues, placed strategically to amplify her fear and destabilize her. It was a performance, and she was the unwilling audience, trapped in a play where the script was constantly being rewritten to her detriment.

The pervasive feeling of being watched was no longer a vague suspicion; it was a concrete certainty. The illusion of invisibility, the hope that she had managed to fade into the background, had been a dangerous delusion. The threat had followed her, not necessarily in the form of the same individual, but as a continuation of the same relentless pursuit, the same unwavering objective. Her sanctuary was compromised, her privacy a distant memory. The world outside the motel room was no longer a neutral space; it was a landscape actively managed by her pursuers, a carefully constructed environment designed to control her movements, her thoughts, and her emotions. The game had intensified, and she was no longer just running; she was being herded, subtly nudged in directions that served their ultimate purpose.

Alice sat on the edge of the bed, Duke's weight a reassuring presence against her leg. The springs groaned under her slight shift, another minor annoyance in a symphony of subtle disturbances. She closed her eyes, trying to block out the perceived intrusions, to focus on what she knew for certain. The man in her home was a symptom, a manifestation of a larger, more organized force. This force was capable of tracking her, of anticipating her movements, and of manipulating her environment with an unsettling precision. The question that burned in her mind was no longer

*if* they had found her, but *how* and *why*. The initial break-in had been a violation, but this ongoing pursuit, this psychological manipulation, was a torment.

The objective, she was beginning to suspect, was not merely to apprehend her, but to psychologically dismantle her. To make her question her own perceptions, to erode her confidence in her own judgment, to render her incapable of formulating a coherent escape plan. The subtle disturbances were designed to create a constant state of hyper-vigilance, a mental exhaustion that would make her susceptible to further manipulation. They wanted her to be afraid, yes, but more than that, they wanted her to be disoriented, to be unsure of what was real and what was a manufactured illusion. The threat had followed her, and it was now actively working to undermine her very sense of self.

She looked at the small, framed print on the wall – a generic landscape that was supposed to evoke a sense of calm, but now seemed like a mockery of her situation. Even the decorative elements of the room felt like they were part of the carefully constructed illusion. Every detail, from the flickering fluorescent light to the thin, worn carpet, was part of a landscape designed to be both unremarkable and, as she was now discovering, deeply unsettling. The feeling of being hunted had permeated every aspect of her existence, transforming even the most mundane environments into potential arenas of conflict. The carefully constructed illusion of safety had dissolved, replaced by the chilling, undeniable truth: the threat was not behind her; it was beside her, within her, and all around her. The pursuit had not ended; it had merely evolved, adapting its tactics to the new environment, its objective unwavering. The echoes in the dark were growing louder, and Alice knew, with a grim certainty, that the true horror was only just beginning.

# Chapter 9: The Cycle Continues

The silence in the motel room, once a fragile balm, now felt like a taut drumskin, ready to split. Alice's breath hitched, not from fear this time, but from a sudden, sharp clarity that pierced through the fog of her own immediate peril. It had started with a flicker, a barely perceptible shift in the static that hissed from the ancient television. She'd been about to snap it off, desperate for the oblivion of blacked-out silence, when a voice, rough and low, had cut through the crackle. It was a hushed exchange, barely audible, seemingly emanating from *within* the television, or perhaps from just beyond its flickering confines. Her initial thought was that some late-night talk show or infomercial had taken an unexpectedly sinister turn. But the tone, the cadence, was wrong. Too urgent, too hushed for broadcast.

She froze, her hand hovering inches from the power button. Duke, sensing her stillness, let out a low, inquisitive whine, his head cocked. Alice shushed him, her gaze fixed on the screen, though she knew the visual was irrelevant. It was the sound, the fragmented whispers, that held her captive. She strained to decipher the words, her mind working furiously to piece together the disjointed phrases. It was like trying to reassemble a shattered mirror by the light of a dying candle – impossible, yet utterly compelling.

"...target profile matches..."

"...new acquisition... similar energy signature..."

"...relocation confirmed... twenty-four hours out..."

The words, though sparse, landed like shards of ice in her gut. Target profile. New acquisition. Relocation. These weren't the random ramblings of a talk show host. This was something deliberate. Something chillingly familiar. The phrase "similar energy signature" sent a ripple of dread through her. It spoke of observation, of analysis, of a process that went far beyond simple tracking. They weren't just looking for a person; they were looking for a

*type* of person, a resonance, a pattern. And the confirmation of a relocation... it implied a continuation, a broader operation.

Alice's eyes darted around the room, suddenly seeing it not as her refuge, but as a stage from which she had inadvertently overheard a rehearsal. The cheap laminate furniture, the worn carpet, the thin walls – they had all become conduits for a conversation that was not meant for her ears. The intruder, the phantom scents, the flickering lights, the recalcitrant key card – they hadn't been random acts of psychological warfare aimed solely at her. They had been part of a larger process, a system, and she had merely been an early test case, a beta subject whose reactions were being monitored and analyzed.

The understanding dawned with a sickening lurch. This wasn't just about her anymore. The cycle of fear and manipulation she had experienced, the terror of being hunted and violated, was not an isolated incident. It was a replicable model. The network, the organization that had sent the intruder, was not sated. It was expanding. The fear she had felt, the violation she had endured, had been a blueprint, a preparatory phase for something more. And this new target... it was the next step.

Alice's mind raced, desperately trying to anchor itself. Who was this new target? What did "similar energy signature" truly mean? Was it about their past, their vulnerabilities, their aspirations? The idea of a couple seeking a fresh start, a common thread in her own narrative before the invasion, resonated with a terrifying possibility. People who were trying to escape something, people who were rebuilding, were they the most susceptible? Were they the ones most likely to be broken, to be manipulated, to be... acquired?

The vague sense of unease she'd felt about the pickup truck in the parking lot, its dark windows an impenetrable barrier, now intensified. Had it been surveillance not just for her, but for something else? Had the network's operatives been in this very motel, or one nearby, observing, waiting, and now confirming their next move? The casual indifference of the motel's façade, its anonymity, had been its greatest asset in her eyes. Now, it seemed, that same anonymity made it the perfect breeding ground for their clandestine operations.

The overheard whispers had been brief, almost subliminal, but their implications were vast and terrifying. They indicated a level of organization and systematic planning that dwarfed her initial understanding. The intruder had been a single point of contact, a physical manifestation of their reach. But this... this was the digital, networked infrastructure of their terror. The ability to identify, profile, and target individuals remotely, to orchestrate their movements and their psychological states from afar. It was a cold, clinical efficiency that made her blood run even colder.

She remembered the intruder's unnerving calm, his almost surgical precision. It hadn't been the act of a rogue agent. It had been the execution of a protocol. And now, she was privy to the next protocol in their chilling playbook. The weight of this knowledge settled upon her, heavy and suffocating. She was no longer just the hunted; she was a witness. A witness to a terrifying, ongoing operation, a cycle that was not about to end, but was merely shifting its focus, its tentacles reaching out to ensnare new victims.

Alice rose from the edge of the bed, her movements slow and deliberate, each step a conscious effort to quell the rising panic. She walked to the window, peering through a sliver of the blinds. The parking lot was largely empty now, the night deepening. The pickup truck was gone. A small, almost insignificant detail, yet it felt like a crucial piece of the puzzle. Had they moved on? Or were they simply repositioning, their mission here complete, their sights now firmly set on the new target? The thought of them, wherever they were, continuing their predatory dance, was a visceral agony.

She considered Duke. His presence was a comfort, a warm weight against her leg, his instincts a constant, if unsettling, confirmation of danger. But he couldn't understand the nuances of what she had overheard. He couldn't grasp the chilling implication that their tormentors were not singularly focused on her, but were part of a larger, more insidious system, systematically selecting and pursuing others. He was a loyal companion, a shield against immediate physical threats, but the burden of this new knowledge, this expanded awareness of the pervasive danger, was hers alone to carry.

The urge to flee, to disappear again, warred with a nascent sense of responsibility. If she knew, if she had glimpsed the machinery of their operation, did she have a moral obligation to do something? But what could she do? Report it? To whom? Her previous attempts to seek help had been met with skepticism, with disbelief. The idea that a sophisticated, almost invisible organization was targeting people was likely to be dismissed as the delusion of a traumatized mind. Yet, the overheard conversation had been undeniably real, a stark counterpoint to the manufactured illusions she had been subjected to.

She imagined the new target, perhaps a young couple, excited about their new home, their new life, completely unaware of the shadow that was about to fall upon them. The thought sent a fresh wave of revulsion through her. The violation she had experienced, the fear, the uncertainty – it was a hell she wouldn't wish on anyone. But this organization, this network, seemed to thrive on inflicting that very hell. They fed on disruption, on the unraveling of hope, on the systematic dismantling of individuals and their lives.

Alice looked at the small, almost childish drawing of a lighthouse taped to the wall beside the television. It was meant to be a symbol of hope, a beacon in the storm. But now, it felt like a cruel joke. There was no beacon for her, no safe harbor. Only the vast, indifferent ocean of their pursuit. The overheard fragments, however, had given her a new perspective. She wasn't just the victim of a random attack. She was a witness to a crime in progress, a crime that was about to be committed again.

The realization that she was privy to information about their future actions was a heavy burden. It was a terrible knowledge, a Pandora's Box of information that she could not unhear. The cycle was indeed continuing, and the fact that she had inadvertently stumbled upon the next phase of it was both terrifying and, in a strange, desperate way, empowering. It meant they were not infallible. It meant that their plans, however meticulously laid, could be overheard, could be glimpsed, could be disrupted.

She walked back to the bed, sinking onto its edge. Duke nudged her hand with his wet nose, a simple, grounding gesture. Alice stroked his fur, trying to sort through the chaotic storm of her thoughts. The original intruder had been a predator, yes, but he had also been a signal, a harbinger of something far larger and more organized. His actions, his intrusion, had been a prelude. And the whispers she had just heard... they were the sound of the curtain rising on the next act of their dreadful play.

The details of the new target remained elusive, shrouded in the vague but potent language of their operation. Was it a house, a specific address? Or a person, a demographic? The lack of concrete information was both a relief and a source of gnawing anxiety. If she knew more, perhaps she could act. But without specifics, she was like a soldier who had overheard enemy troop movements but lacked the intelligence to pinpoint their location.

The question of

*why* this organization operated in this manner, *why* they targeted these specific individuals, gnawed at her. Was it for financial gain, for some twisted form of ideological cleansing, or for reasons that were even more profoundly inscrutable and terrifying? The lack of motive, the sheer clinical detachment with which they seemed to operate, was perhaps the most unsettling aspect of all. They were not driven by passion or rage, but by a cold, calculated efficiency that suggested a deep-seated amorality.

Alice's gaze fell upon the small, laminated hotel directory lying on the bedside table. She picked it up, flipping through its pages with a detached curiosity that belied the turmoil raging within her. The services offered, the local attractions listed – it all seemed so... normal. So mundane. And yet, beneath this veneer of normalcy, this clandestine network was operating, its eyes and ears wherever they pleased, its targets chosen with chilling precision. The contrast was stark, and it amplified her sense of unease.

She thought about the security measures she had tried to implement at her home, the layers of protection that had been so easily breached. Now, she realized, the threat was not just about physical barriers. It was about psychological vulnerabilities, about exploiting the very fabric of human trust and connection. This new target, whoever they were, would likely be caught completely off guard, their lives disrupted by an unseen force that could manipulate their environment and their perceptions with terrifying ease.

The overheard conversation had been a stark reminder that her own ordeal was not an ending, but a chapter in a much larger, ongoing narrative. The cycle was not broken. It was merely continuing, its momentum undiminished. And she, Alice, was now caught in its periphery, a silent witness to its relentless progression. The fear she had felt for herself had now expanded, a cold dread that encompassed the unknown future victims of this predatory network. The burden of her knowledge was a heavy one, a grim testament to the fact that the nightmare was far from over. It had merely found new ground, new subjects, new avenues for its insidious work. The faint static from the television, now thankfully silent, seemed to echo with the ghosts of those whispered words, a chilling reminder that the hunt was on, and she had just glimpsed the next quarry.

The fragmented whispers, once a ghostly echo in the sterile motel room, had congealed into a solid, unyielding mass in Alice's mind. It was the weight of knowing, of understanding the true architecture of her torment. It wasn't the singular madness of one deranged individual; it was a meticulously constructed edifice of fear, built brick by psychological brick, designed to dismantle, to break, to *acquire*. The intruder, the phantom scents, the flickering lights – these were not random acts of aggression, but carefully calibrated steps in a process. A process that had already claimed her, and was now, with chilling efficiency, moving on to its next mark. This realization was a corrosive acid, eating away at any semblance of safety she had managed to construct. The motel room, meant to be a temporary sanctuary, now felt like a confessional booth, where she had inadvertently overheard the sins of a far greater, more insidious entity.

She traced the condensation on the windowpane with a fingertip, the cold seeping into her skin, a stark contrast to the simmering dread that consumed her. Who were they, these architects of terror? What drove them? The whispered words – "target profile," "new acquisition," "similar energy signature" – spoke of a cold, clinical detachment, a process so devoid of human empathy that it was almost alien. It wasn't about revenge, or passion, or even simple greed. It was about a systematic operation, like a farmer culling a herd, or a scientist analyzing a specimen. And she, Alice, had been a specimen under the microscope, her reactions, her vulnerabilities, meticulously cataloged. The fear she had experienced, the violation of her personal space and her sanity, had been data collection.

The sheer audacity of it all was staggering. To orchestrate such a sophisticated campaign of psychological warfare, to deploy agents with such unnerving precision, all while operating from the shadows, beyond the reach of any conventional authority. It was a ghost in the machine, a phantom limb of a larger organism. The intruder's calm, almost robotic demeanor now made a terrifying kind of sense. He wasn't a man driven by rage; he was a tool, wielded by an unseen hand. And the knowledge of this tool, and the hand that controlled it, was a dangerous burden.

Alice felt a tremor run through her. This wasn't just about survival anymore. This was about understanding the nature of the threat, a threat that had proven it could infiltrate, manipulate, and destroy. The thought of the new target, the next "acquisition" mentioned in those chilling whispers, sent a fresh wave of nausea through her. A couple, perhaps, seeking a new beginning, their hopes and dreams a fragile tapestry waiting to be ripped apart. They were the perfect prey, their optimism a blindfold, their desire for a peaceful life a vulnerability that this network exploited with ruthless precision.

What was she supposed to do? The question echoed in the hollow space of her mind. Reporting this... to whom? The police? They would listen with polite skepticism, their eyes perhaps conveying a subtle pity, a suggestion that her ordeal had fractured her mind. Her story, pieced together from fragmented whispers and the lingering scent of fear, would sound like the fevered ramblings of a traumatized woman. "I overheard a conversation on a motel television... about acquiring new targets... with similar energy signatures..." It was a narrative designed for disbelief, a tale plucked from the pages of a pulp thriller, not a report to be taken seriously by law enforcement.

And even if, by some miracle, they did believe her, what then? This network, this organization, operated on a level that seemed to transcend traditional boundaries. They were not bound by jurisdiction, by observable evidence. They were a whisper in the digital ether, a shadow in the periphery. How could you combat an enemy you couldn't see, an enemy whose existence was defined by its elusiveness? The very act of trying to expose them felt like walking into a trap, a deliberate move that would only solidify her status as a threat, and perhaps, the next victim.

The intruder had been a harbinger, a single, terrifying manifestation of their power. But these whispers... they were the sound of the machinery itself, a glimpse behind the curtain, revealing the cold, calculating engine that drove their operations. The knowledge was a double-edged sword. It made her acutely aware of the pervasive danger, the invisible threads that connected seemingly isolated incidents into a terrifying pattern. But it also placed her in a precarious position. She knew too much. She had seen the blueprint. In the eyes of this network, she was no longer just a victim; she was a liability.

Alice hugged herself, a shiver coursing through her despite the room's warmth. The fear was no longer a sharp, immediate terror, but a dull, pervasive ache, a constant thrum of anxiety that had settled deep within her bones. It was the fear of the unknown, amplified by the terrifying certainty of what was possible. Her own experience had been a brutal lesson in the efficacy of their methods. They knew how to unravel a person, how to exploit their deepest insecurities, how to turn their own minds against them. And now, she knew that they were capable of replicating this process, of systematically targeting others, of continuing this cycle of destruction.

She thought of Duke, his gentle snores a comforting counterpoint to the chaos in her mind. He was an anchor, a tangible presence in a world that felt increasingly unreal. But even his presence couldn't alleviate the crushing weight of this knowledge. He was a protector, but he couldn't protect her from a threat that was intangible, a threat that operated on a different plane. He couldn't decipher coded whispers, couldn't understand the nuanced language of psychological warfare. This burden was hers, and hers alone.

The urge to run, to vanish again, was potent. To disappear into the anonymity of a crowded city, to shed her identity like a snake sheds its skin, hoping to outrun the tendrils of this unseen network. But where could she go? They had found her before, their reach seemingly limitless. And the thought of leaving others vulnerable, of knowing that this cycle would continue unabated, felt like a betrayal, a capitulation to the very forces she abhorred.

Perhaps, just perhaps, the very fact that she had overheard them was a sign. A crack in their armor. A momentary lapse in their omnipresent surveillance. If they could be overheard, then they were not infallible. If their plans could be glimpsed, then perhaps they could be disrupted. The idea was a fragile spark of defiance in the overwhelming darkness, a whisper of hope that she desperately clung to. But how could she leverage this overheard information? How could she translate a few cryptic phrases into a tangible defense?

She found herself staring at the tattered remains of the Gideon Bible on the bedside table, its pages dog-eared and worn. It offered no solace, no divine intervention. This was a battle fought in the shadows, with weapons of the mind, not of faith. The network operated in the gray areas, exploiting the cracks in the system, the blind spots of human perception. They were masters of the unseen, and their greatest weapon was not brute force, but the erosion of trust, the cultivation of doubt, the systematic dismantling of a person's sense of reality.

Alice rose and began to pace the small room, her movements restless. The intruder's meticulousness, his almost surgical precision, had been disturbing. But now, understanding it as part of a larger protocol, it was terrifying. It meant that every action, every psychological jab, had a purpose, a predetermined outcome. They weren't improvising; they were executing a script. And she, unwittingly, had stumbled upon the next scene.

The question of motive gnawed at her. Was it purely financial? Was this network a shadowy entity dealing in human distress, a contractor for some unknown entity? Or was there something more insidious at play? A desire to control, to manipulate for the sake of manipulation? The sheer lack of observable emotion in their whispered conversation suggested a profound detachment, a cold pragmatism that was more frightening than any overt display of malice. They were like a virus, replicating and spreading, their existence defined by their ability to infect and disrupt.

She paused at the door, her hand hovering over the doorknob. Stepping outside meant re-entering the world, a world that now felt teeming with unseen dangers. The pickup truck, a fleeting image from the parking lot, flashed in her mind. Had it been theirs? Had its occupants been the ones speaking, their hushed tones amplified by the motel's weak acoustics? The thought sent a shiver down her spine. They were out there, somewhere, their focus shifted, their next move already in motion.

Alice knew, with a certainty that chilled her to the bone, that she could not simply let this go. The knowledge she possessed, however terrifying, had transformed her. She was no longer just the victim of a personal nightmare; she was a witness to a crime that was actively unfolding. The cycle had not ended with her; it had merely shifted its gears, preparing to grind another life into dust. The weight of that knowledge was almost unbearable, a crushing responsibility that threatened to suffocate her. But in that suffocating weight, a flicker of resolve began to ignite. She had been broken, manipulated, and terrified, but she had survived. And now, armed with the terrifying clarity of their methods, she had to find a way to fight back, not just for herself, but for the unknown couple, for all the future "acquisitions" waiting in the crosshairs of this relentless, invisible enemy. The cycle would continue, yes, but perhaps, just perhaps, she could find a way to introduce a new variable, a wrench in their meticulously designed machinery.

Duke's presence was a warm, breathing weight against Alice's side, a constant, reassuring pressure that belied the turmoil churning within her. His soft snores, a low rumble that had once been a mere lullaby, now served as a comforting metronome against the frantic, irregular beat of her own heart. He was a physical anchor in the swirling chaos of her mind, a tangible manifestation of a world that still held genuine connection, a stark contrast to the insidious, abstract threat that had revealed itself. His unwavering loyalty, a silent testament to their shared history, now felt less like a passive comfort and more like an active sentinel. His large, gentle eyes, usually soft with affection, now held a subtle, perpetual vigilance. They would drift, scanning the periphery of their motel room, flicking towards the window, the door, even the shadows dancing on the ceiling. It was a subtle shift, almost imperceptible to an outsider, but Alice, attuned to every nuance of his being, felt it acutely. He seemed to sense it too, the lingering, corrosive residue of the intrusion, the psychic stain left behind by the whispers of "acquisition" and "energy signature."

He hadn't directly witnessed the terror, hadn't heard the chilling pronouncements that had irrevocably shattered Alice's sense of safety. His world had remained one of the familiar, the mundane, the comforting rhythm of their journey. Yet, he responded to Alice's heightened anxiety, the tremors that ran through her when she recounted even the vaguest details, the sleepless nights punctuated by her sharp intakes of breath. He was a creature of instinct, and his instinct was telling him that something was deeply, fundamentally wrong. This innate sense of danger manifested not in barks or growls, but in a quiet, unwavering watchfulness. He would position himself strategically, often between Alice and the door, or with his back against the wall, a silent, furry bulwark. His tail, usually an expressive barometer of his mood, now lay mostly still, an occasional, hesitant thump against the worn carpet the only sign of his underlying affection. His vigilance wasn't born of aggression, but of a profound, protective instinct that had always been there, dormant beneath layers of domestic contentment. Now, that instinct had been awakened, amplified by the palpable fear radiating from his human companion.

Alice found herself watching him, finding a strange solace in his very stillness, in the predictable rise and fall of his chest. His presence was a tangible reminder that not everything in her world had been corrupted, that genuine bonds still held true. He was a testament to the enduring strength of their relationship, a bond that had weathered storms far less terrifying than this. He was the constant in her rapidly unraveling reality, the thread that refused to snap. His silent vigil was more than just a dog's presence; it was a promise. A silent vow, understood without words, that he would remain by her side, a steadfast guardian against whatever shadows lurked beyond the thin walls of their temporary sanctuary. He was the living embodiment of loyalty, a force of nature in his own right, and in his unwavering devotion, Alice found a fragile ember of hope.

The silence of the motel room, once a welcome respite, now felt heavy, laden with unspoken fears. Alice would catch herself staring at Duke, her gaze lingering on the gentle curve of his spine, the almost imperceptible twitch of his ear. These were the details that grounded her, the ordinary observations that tethered her to a reality that felt increasingly fragile. She remembered the intruder, his chilling calm, the almost surgical precision with which he had moved. Duke had been asleep then, a deep, innocent slumber that had shielded him from the terror. Now, he was awake, his senses on high alert, his instincts honed by Alice's own fear.

She would sometimes whisper to him, the words tumbling out in a hushed rush, her voice laced with a raw vulnerability that she couldn't afford to express to anyone else. She spoke of the whispers, of the chilling implications of the words she'd overheard, of the unseen network that preyed on unsuspecting lives. Duke would listen, his head cocked, his deep brown eyes fixed on her face, as if comprehending the very essence of her distress. He would offer a soft whine, a low rumble of empathy, and then nudge her hand with his wet nose, a gesture of comfort that spoke volumes. It was a language they had developed over years, a silent communication that transcended spoken words.

He seemed to understand the weight of her fear, the suffocating burden of her knowledge. He didn't flinch when she described the chilling efficiency of the intruder, the detached, clinical tone of the voices she'd overheard. Instead, he would press closer, his body a solid, reassuring mass against her leg, as if to absorb some of her terror. His very physicality was a balm, a solid counterpoint to the disembodied threat that haunted her. He was a force of nature, a primal embodiment of loyalty, and in his presence, Alice felt a flicker of her own strength return.

He was more than just a pet; he was a guardian, a protector. His presence had always been a comfort, a steady presence in her life. But now, it was something more. It was a shield, a tangible barrier against the unseen. He was her silent vigil, her constant companion in this new, terrifying reality. His watchful eyes, the subtle tensing of his muscles when a car door slammed outside, the way he would position himself between her and the door – these were all signs of his unwavering devotion. He was her furry sentinel, guarding her against an enemy she could not see, an enemy that operated in the shadows.

Alice would often find herself stroking his fur, the rhythmic motion a form of self-soothing. The warmth of his body, the steady beat of his heart against her hand, were anchors in the storm. He was a reminder of the life she had fought to protect, the life that this insidious network sought to unravel. He was a symbol of resilience, of the enduring power of love and loyalty in the face of overwhelming darkness. He was her Duke, and in his silent vigil, Alice found a sliver of the courage she needed to face the unknown. His unwavering presence was a silent promise of protection, a steadfast beacon in the encroaching gloom. He was her protector, her confidant, her furry shadow, and in his unwavering loyalty, Alice found the strength to continue.

He was her early warning system, her furry barometer of unease. Even before Alice consciously registered a shift in the atmosphere, a subtle change in the ambient sounds, Duke's ears would perk, his body would stiffen, and a low growl would begin to vibrate in his chest. It wasn't an aggressive sound, but a warning, a primal alert that something was amiss. He would fix his gaze on a point in the distance, a patch of darkness outside the motel window, or the shadowy corner of the room, his hackles rising almost imperceptibly. Alice learned to trust these cues implicitly. When Duke tensed, she became hyper-aware, her own senses sharpening, searching for the source of his unease. It was a silent partnership, a dance of heightened awareness forged in the crucible of shared fear.

His protective instincts extended beyond mere vigilance. If Alice was particularly agitated, pacing the small room with restless energy, he would gently nudge her hand, a silent plea for her to calm down. If she seemed lost in thought, her eyes distant and unfocused, he would rest his head on her lap, his warm weight a grounding force, drawing her back to the present, to the tangible reality of their shared space. He seemed to understand, on some primal level, that her mental state was as vulnerable as her physical safety. He was a living, breathing form of emotional support, his every action designed to reassure and protect.

The thought of leaving him behind, even for a moment, was unbearable. He was more than just a pet; he was family, a vital part of her survival. The idea of him being alone, vulnerable, while she was out there investigating, was a prospect that chilled her to the bone. He was her constant, her unwavering ally, and she couldn't imagine facing this threat without him by her side. His presence was a comfort, yes, but it was also a strategic advantage. His heightened senses, his natural instincts, were tools that could help them navigate the treacherous landscape ahead.

Alice would often find herself running her fingers through his thick fur, a mindless, soothing ritual. The simple act of petting him, of feeling the warmth of his body and the steady rhythm of his breathing, helped to dissipate the fog of anxiety that threatened to engulf her. He was a tangible reminder of what she was fighting for – not just her own survival, but the preservation of the bonds that made life worth living. He was a symbol of innocence, of unconditional love, and in his presence, Alice found a renewed sense of purpose.

He was her silent vigil, her furry guardian angel, and in his unwavering loyalty, Alice found the strength to face the darkness. His presence was a constant, a reassuring constant in a world that had become terrifyingly unpredictable. He was her anchor, her protector, and her friend, and she knew, with a certainty that settled deep within her soul, that they would face whatever came next, together. His silent vigil was a promise, a testament to the enduring power of their bond, and in that promise, Alice found a fragile, yet potent, hope. He was more than just a dog; he was a lifeline, and in his watchful eyes, Alice saw the reflection of her own resolve. He was her shield, her confidant, and her unwavering companion, a constant reminder that even in the deepest darkness, there was still light to be found. His silent vigil was not just a passive presence; it was an active force, a constant reinforcement of their shared will to survive.

The gnawing realization had settled in Alice's gut like a cold stone, a truth so stark and terrifying it threatened to suffocate her. The motel room, with its peeling wallpaper and the faint scent of stale disinfectant, had initially felt like a temporary reprieve, a clandestine port in a gathering storm. But the words, "acquisition," "energy signature," had clung to the air long after the intruder had vanished, leaving a psychic residue that no amount of air freshener or brisk walks could dispel. She had harbored a naive hope, a desperate wish that once they were on the move again, once they put enough miles between themselves and that encounter, things might somehow revert to normal. That the illusion of safety could be resurrected, however fragile.

But the intrusion had been more than just a physical violation; it had been an existential one. It had ripped a hole in the fabric of her reality, exposing the hidden currents of a world she had never suspected existed. Now, every rustle of leaves outside the window, every distant siren, sent a jolt of adrenaline through her. The open road, once a symbol of freedom and possibility, now felt like a vast, exposed stage, with unseen eyes watching her every move. The very air seemed to hum with a latent threat, a constant, low-grade thrum that vibrated beneath the surface of everyday life.

The notion of a 'safe haven' had always been a comforting, if abstract, ideal. A place where the past could be left behind, where the scars of trauma could finally begin to heal, and where a semblance of normalcy could be reclaimed. But that dream now felt like a cruel mirata. How could she find a haven in a world where the predators moved unseen, where the very essence of a person could be targeted and exploited? The places that had once represented sanctuary – quiet towns, secluded cabins, even the anonymity of a bustling city – now seemed like potential traps, carefully orchestrated environments designed to lure and ensnare. Her mind replayed fragments of conversations, clinical and detached, about "targets" and "harvesting." The desire for a perfect, untouched life, the very thing she had striven for, now seemed to be the bait that drew them in.

She looked at Duke, his head resting on her lap, his breathing slow and steady. He was an anchor, a tangible piece of the life she desperately wanted to protect. But even his presence, usually a source of unshakeable comfort, was now tinged with a new layer of concern.

Was he safe? Could they be tracked through him? The questions, once unthinkable, now clawed at her consciousness. The innocence he represented, the unconditional love he offered, made him all the more vulnerable. He was a beacon of light in her increasingly shadowed world, and that very light could make them a more visible target.

The fight, she was beginning to understand, was not a discrete event with a clear beginning and end. It wasn't a battle to be won and then forgotten. It was a constant, insidious war waged in the shadows, a relentless campaign of erosion. The network, or whatever they were, didn't just snatch people; they seemed to dismantle them, to chip away at their essence, their very will to survive. They preyed on the cracks, the vulnerabilities that life inevitably carved into everyone. Her own past, the trauma she had so desperately tried to outrun, now felt less like a distant memory and more like a carefully curated map for her pursuers. They knew her weaknesses, her fears, the triggers that could send her spiraling. Her past, the very foundation of her identity, had become the blueprint for her potential destruction.

She remembered the casual cruelty in the intruder's voice, the chilling efficiency with which he had operated. There was no passion, no overt malice, just a cold, calculated purpose. It was this detachment that made him so terrifying. He was a cog in a much larger, far more sinister machine. And she, Alice, was a resource. A potential commodity. The desire for a life free from the constant specter of danger, a life of peace and stability, was precisely what made her susceptible. The yearning for that idyllic, untouched existence was the very thing that had drawn the attention of those who dealt in the corruption of such desires.

Alice found herself staring out the motel window, the neon sign of a distant gas station casting an eerie glow on the deserted highway. The world outside was a vast, indifferent expanse, and she felt utterly alone within it. The idea of finding a place where she could truly escape, where she could shed the weight of her experiences and simply exist without fear, felt like a fantasy from another lifetime. The shadows of her past had not receded; they had grown longer, stretching out to encompass her future. They were no longer just memories; they were active participants in her present, shaping her every decision, dictating the terms of her survival.

The illusion of escape was a potent, seductive lie. It whispered promises of safety in secluded cabins, of anonymous reinvention in distant cities, of a return to a life untouched by the horrors she had witnessed. But every time she dared to entertain such thoughts, the chilling pronouncements of the intruder echoed in her mind. "Energy signature," "acquisition." These weren't metaphors; they were descriptions of a process, a cold, clinical extraction of something vital. And if that energy could be detected, if that signature could be traced, then no physical distance could truly sever the connection. The network was a web, and she had been caught in its strands. To think that she could simply untangle herself and walk away was a dangerous delusion.

Her fight wasn't about reaching a destination anymore; it was about enduring the journey. It was about learning to navigate the treacherous landscape of a world that had revealed its hidden dangers. It was about becoming a ghost, a phantom, capable of slipping through the cracks, of leaving no discernible trace for those who sought to claim her. The desire for a perfect life, for a clean slate, had to be purged. It was a vulnerability, a weakness they would exploit. Instead, she had to embrace the imperfection, the scars, the very aspects of her past that she had tried to bury. For in those buried aspects, lay the resilience, the knowledge, the grit required to survive.

Duke stirred beside her, letting out a soft sigh. Alice reached down, her fingers tracing the familiar contours of his head. He was real. Their bond was real. And in that reality, amidst the encroaching shadows, lay the only hope she had. Not the hope of a pristine escape, but the fierce, desperate hope of simply continuing, of outmaneuvering, of surviving another day, another encounter. The world hadn't changed; she had. And that change, born of terror and the instinct for self-preservation, was the only tool she had left in this ongoing, invisible war. The illusion of escape had shattered, replaced by the grim, stark reality of perpetual vigilance. The cycle, she now understood with a chilling certainty, was not something to be broken, but something to be outlived.

The chipped ceramic mug felt unnaturally heavy in Alice's hands, its lukewarm coffee a bitter counterpoint to the gnawing unease that had become her constant companion. The motel room, a transient purgatory of faded floral wallpaper and the persistent hum of a faulty ice machine, was to be their last stop before whatever came next. Duke, his furry head nestled on the threadbare blanket, snored softly, a comforting anchor in the churning sea of her anxiety. But even his innocent slumber couldn't quite quell the storm brewing within her. The encounter in the previous motel, the cold, precise words spoken by the intruder – "acquisition," "energy signature" – had etched themselves into her consciousness, a permanent scar on the landscape of her perceived reality. The illusion of safety, a fragile edifice she'd desperately tried to reconstruct, had been irrevocably shattered.

The open road, once a symbol of freedom, now felt like an exposed nerve, each mile a further testament to her vulnerability. The intruder hadn't just physically entered her space; he'd breached the very core of her existence, revealing a world where individuals were not just people, but potential resources, their very essence a commodity to be harvested. The idea of a "safe haven" had dissolved into a cruel mirage. Where could one truly be safe when the predators operated with such chilling detachment, their motives inscrutable, their methods precise? Every shadow seemed to lengthen, every unexpected sound – the distant wail of a siren, the rustle of wind through the sparse desert scrub outside – sent a tremor of fear through her. Her past traumas, the very things she had fought so hard to outrun, now felt like an open invitation, a roadmap for her unseen pursuers. They knew her weaknesses, her triggers, the carefully guarded vulnerabilities that defined her.

The fight, she was beginning to understand, wasn't a battle with a definitive end. It was a relentless, insidious war waged in the hidden spaces of existence, a campaign of psychological and perhaps even metaphysical erosion. They didn't just seek to control or conquer; they sought to dismantle, to chip away at the very will to survive, to exploit the inherent fragilities that life inevitably carved into every soul. Her own history, the pain and loss she carried, had become a tool for her own potential destruction. The intruder's voice, devoid of emotion, had been more terrifying than any outburst of rage. It spoke of a system, a network, where individuals were merely data points, their "energy signatures" cataloged and exploited.

Alice closed her eyes, trying to push back the rising tide of panic. She focused on Duke's steady breathing, on the familiar weight of him against her leg. He was her reason. He was the tangible embodiment of the life she yearned to protect, the one untouched by the encroaching darkness. But even his presence, once a source of unshakeable solace, was now tinged with a new layer of dread. Was he safe? Could they track them through him? These questions, once unthinkable, now gnawed at her, the innocence he represented making him all the more vulnerable, a bright beacon in her increasingly shadowed world.

The desire for a pristine, untroubled life, the very thing she had strived for, now seemed to be the bait that drew them in. The yearning for that idyllic existence, a quiet existence free from the specter of danger, was precisely what made her susceptible. It was the very aspiration that had attracted the attention of those who dealt in the corruption of such pure desires. She had been naive to think that putting distance between herself and the previous encounter would be enough. The network, she now understood with a chilling certainty, was not bound by physical limitations. It was a web, and she had been ensnared. To believe she could simply untangle herself and walk away was a dangerous delusion.

She traced the rim of the coffee mug, the rough ceramic a grounding sensation. The world outside was a vast, indifferent expanse, and she felt profoundly, terrifyingly alone. The notion of finding a place where she could truly escape, where she could shed the weight of her experiences and simply

*be* without the constant hum of threat, felt like a relic from another lifetime. The shadows of her past hadn't receded; they had lengthened, stretching out to engulf her future. They were no longer mere memories; they were active participants, shaping her every decision, dictating the terms of her survival.

The fight, she realized, wasn't about reaching a destination anymore. It was about enduring the journey. It was about learning to navigate the treacherous landscape of a world that had revealed its hidden, sinister undercurrents. It was about becoming a ghost, a phantom, capable of slipping through the cracks, of leaving no discernible trace for those who sought to claim her. The desire for a perfect life, for a clean slate, had to be purged. It was a vulnerability, a weakness they would exploit. Instead, she had to embrace the imperfection, the scars, the very aspects of her past that she had tried to bury. For in those buried aspects, lay the resilience, the knowledge, the sheer grit required to survive.

She looked at Duke, his breathing a soft rhythm in the oppressive silence. He stirred, letting out a small sigh, and Alice's hand instinctively moved to stroke his fur. He was real. Their bond was real. And in that undeniable reality, amidst the encroaching shadows, lay the only hope she possessed. Not the hope of a pristine escape, but the fierce, desperate hope of simply continuing, of outmaneuvering, of surviving another day, another encounter. The world hadn't changed; she had. And that change, born of terror and the primal instinct for self-preservation, was the only tool she had left in this ongoing, invisible war. The illusion of escape had shattered, replaced by the grim, stark reality of perpetual vigilance. The cycle, she now understood with a chilling certainty, was not something to be broken, but something to be outlived.

With a sigh that felt heavy with unspoken burdens, Alice stood and began to pack their meager belongings. The fluorescent lights of the motel cast long, distorted shadows that seemed to writhe and stretch with a life of their own. Each creak of the suitcase, each rustle of clothing, sounded amplified in the stillness, raising the hairs on her arms. She avoided looking too closely at the window, at the bleak expanse of asphalt and scrubland beyond. The open road beckoned, a path into the unknown, and for the first time, the uncertainty felt less like a terrifying void and more like a deliberate act of evasion.

She checked the rearview mirror one last time, a habitual gesture honed by weeks of constant vigilance. The motel sign, a garish beacon of transient lodging, flickered erratically, its neon glow bleeding into the deepening twilight. Duke was settled in the back, his eyes heavy with sleep, a picture of canine innocence. Alice's hands tightened on the steering wheel as she pulled out of the parking lot, the gravel crunching loudly beneath the tires. The highway stretched out before her, a ribbon of asphalt disappearing into the bruised purple of the evening sky.

She drove in silence for a long while, the only sounds the hum of the engine and the low thrum of the tires on the road. Her mind replayed fragments of the intruder's chillingly detached pronouncements, the clinical language of "acquisition" and "energy signature" echoing like a phantom limb. It was this dispassionate efficiency that unnerved her the most. It wasn't born of anger or malice, but of a chillingly objective process, a systematic exploitation of something intangible yet vital. She was a resource, a data point in their vast, unseen network.

As she crested a small rise, the headlights of her car cutting a swathe through the encroaching darkness, a flicker of movement caught her eye. It was distant, almost imperceptible against the vast, unlit landscape. At first, she dismissed it as a trick of the light, a play of shadows cast by the mesquite and scrub. But then it resolved itself, a solitary figure standing by the side of the road, silhouetted against the faint glow of the distant horizon. There was no reason for anyone to be standing there, in the middle of nowhere, at this hour. No town, no farmhouse, no sign of life for miles.

Her breath hitched. The figure didn't move, didn't wave, didn't react to the approaching headlights. It simply stood there, a sentinel, a silent observer. Alice's heart began to pound against her ribs, a frantic drumbeat of primal fear. Was it him? Or someone like him? Someone from the network, still watching, still waiting? The distance was too great to tell, the light too poor. But the unnerving stillness of the figure, the unwavering gaze that seemed to bore into her, sent a shiver down her spine that had nothing to do with the desert chill.

She instinctively slowed the car, her knuckles white on the steering wheel. Every instinct screamed at her to accelerate, to put as much distance between herself and that unsettling presence as possible. But a morbid curiosity, a desperate need to confirm her deepest fears, held her captive. Or perhaps it was a grim acceptance, a dawning realization that no matter how far she ran, the shadows would always find a way to follow.

The figure remained motionless as her car drew nearer, a stark, unsettling figure against the desolate backdrop. Alice kept her gaze fixed on the road ahead, her eyes darting to the side every few seconds, trying to glean some detail, some confirmation of her worst fears. Was it the same build? The same posture? The chillingly detached demeanor she'd witnessed before?

Just as her headlights began to illuminate the immediate vicinity of the figure, a sudden gust of wind swept across the open land, kicking up a swirling cloud of dust and debris. When the dust settled, the figure was gone. Vanished as if it had never been there. Alice slammed on the brakes, the tires skidding slightly on the loose gravel. She scanned the roadside, her eyes darting back and forth, her breath coming in ragged gasps. Nothing. Just the empty highway, the whispering wind, and the deepening darkness.

Had she imagined it? Was it a hallucination, born of exhaustion and paranoia? Or was it a deliberate misdirection, a tactic to sow further unease? The ambiguity was almost worse than a clear confirmation. It left her with a gnawing uncertainty, a sense of being perpetually watched, perpetually hunted, even when there was no tangible threat in sight.

She sat there for a long moment, the engine idling, the silence of the desert pressing in on her. Duke whined softly in the back, sensing her distress. Alice took a deep, shaky breath, trying to regain some semblance of control. The figure was gone. For now. But the image of that solitary, watching presence was seared into her mind, a stark reminder that her journey was far from over. The cycle, as she had come to understand, continued. It wasn't a linear path with a clear beginning and end, but a perpetual state of vigilance, a constant dance with the shadows. She put the car back in gear, her gaze sweeping across the rearview mirror, her senses heightened, her resolve hardening. The road ahead was uncertain, but one thing was clear: she would keep moving. She would endure. And she would, in her own way, survive. The highway stretched before her, an endless possibility, an endless threat, and she drove on, a shadow in the distance herself, forever looking over her shoulder.

# Back Matter

**Acquisition**: In the context of the narrative, this term refers to the act of obtaining or capturing an individual, not for monetary gain in the traditional sense, but for the exploitation of their "energy signature" or other intrinsic qualities.

**Energy Signature**: A fictional concept representing the unique, intangible essence or vital force of an individual, which can be detected, tracked, and potentially exploited by certain entities or individuals.

**Network**: A clandestine, far-reaching organization or system that operates beyond conventional societal structures, characterized by its ability to track, identify, and "acquire" individuals based on their energy signatures.

**Transient Purgatory**: A metaphorical description of a temporary, unsettling, and often uncomfortable state of being, such as a cheap motel room, that feels like a holding place between one stage of life and another, fraught with unease.

www.ingramcontent.com/pod-product-compliance
Lightning Source LLC
LaVergne TN
LVHW091302240326
834671LV00011B/371